CAPTAIN PICARD HEARD A WARNING HISS . . .

. . . and then the door in front of him flew open.

Picard's arms flew outward and caught the doorway on each side, keeping him from being cast out into space. The pressure from behind was terrific, and the roar of air competed with the now-deafening hum of energy throbbing through the station.

His arms were growing tired: He began to hyperventilate intentionally, to oxygenate his blood as much as possible and ensure maximum survival time in the vacuum of space.

Picard's efforts were cut short when something slammed into his right side. He felt himself flying through the airlock toward the open door.

He saw the station convulse around him, shaking as another surge of energy shot through the superstructure, and Picard realized the vacuum of space was the least of his troubles. Then a blast of whiteness took him. . . .

Look for STAR TREK Fiction from Pocket Books

Star Trek: The Original Series

Star Trek: The Next Generation

Star Trek: Deep Space Nine

STAR TREK
THE NEXT GENERATION®

REQUIEM

MICHAEL JAN FRIEDMAN
AND KEVIN RYAN

POCKET BOOKS
New York   London   Toronto   Sydney   Tokyo   Singapore

An *Original* Publication of POCKET BOOKS

POCKET BOOKS, a division of Simon & Schuster Inc.
1230 Avenue of the Americas, New York, NY 10020

This book is published by Pocket Books, a division of Simon & Schuster Inc., under exclusive license from Paramount Pictures.

ISBN: 0-671-79567-8

First Pocket Books printing October 1994

10 9 8 7 6 5 4 3 2 1

Printed in the U.S.A.

For Isaac and Jack
          —M.J.F.

For Paullina, Natasha and Misha
                    —K.R.

REQUIEM

Prologue

Stardate: 16175.4
Earth Calendar Date: 2345
(Twenty-five Years Ago)

THE LIFT DOORS OPENED and Captain Picard entered the bridge. Crusher, he noted, was already at his post.

"Good morning, Captain," Crusher offered cheerfully.

"Good morning, Jack," Picard replied, watching as the lieutenant commander on watch quickly vacated the center seat.

Picard took his place in the captain's chair. Vigo was next on the bridge, placing his tall, blue-skinned form at the weapons console. Picard's exec, Gilaad Ben Zoma, came a moment later, and the others quickly followed.

Crusher had already prepared the morning report, and his handsome human features were typically animated.

"Very little activity, sir," he said evenly. "A minor course correction at 0600 to avoid an asteroid—

1

location noted and logged. We've compensated and will arrive on time at Alpha Pensura."

"Excellent," Picard replied. "Run a level-one diagnostic on sensors. We'll need them at peak—"

"Captain," his communications officer interrupted. "A priority message from a ship in Beta Quadrant. No identity codes, just the priority channel."

"Answer hail," Picard said. "Put them on the screen." Picard stood and turned his attention to the forward viewer. "This is Captain Jean-Luc Picard of the *U.S.S. Stargazer.* How may we be of assistance?"

Picard had never spoken directly to a Gorn, so he started ever so slightly when the alien face appeared on the screen. As the Gorn considered him, Picard had only a moment to take in the reptilian features: the coarse green skin, the multifaceted, almost insectoid eyes, and the prominent teeth.

"Captain," the Gorn said—the computer rendering the voice against a background of hisses and the sounds of guttural breathing. "We wish to speak with you in person. Bring your ship to the coordinates we are transmitting now."

Picard kept his tone and expression even. "Of course, we welcome—"

But the image of the Gorn snapped off the screen.

Jack Crusher was the first to speak. "Captain, *what* was that?"

Picard turned to face his science officer. "I suspect it was a beginning, Mr. Crusher . . . a beginning."

Picard watched intently as the tape neared its end. The starship commander—the tape's protagonist—was obviously exhausted, and favoring his left leg. The captain instantly recognized the signs—and knew the commander was near the end of his endurance.

The story never lost its appeal for Jean-Luc, and for perhaps the hundredth time in his adult life, he watched as the moment of inspiration hit the starship commander. Watched as the nearly beaten man collected his materials: simple chemicals, stones, and a bamboo tube. Watched as the commander faced his enemy, aimed his crude homemade cannon, and then prepared to take his impossible chance.

As enthralled as ever, Picard looked on as the commander lit the fuse . . . and then nothing. The tape ended where it always did, a split second before the fight was won or lost, a split second before the death or survival of the starship commander and his crew would be decided forever.

The architects of that long-ago conflict, the mysterious and powerful Metrons, had pitted the two commanders against each other and set the stakes. They had chosen that moment to end their transmission. Starfleet had subsequently sealed the records of the incident, and the commander's solution had remained a mystery.

Picard, of course, had faced the identical situation more than once. Captain James T. Kirk's encounter with the captain of the Gorn ship on a stark and desolate world had become legend . . . and simulations of that encounter were a common test of cadets at Starfleet Academy.

By Picard's recollection, he'd been "killed" six times by the Gorn. The first time, he had been caught by surprise and died after a brief hand-to-hand battle with the immensely strong reptilian humanoid. On another occasion, he'd tried Kirk's trick with the cannon, earning himself painful burns on his hands and four weeks with an eye patch.

In Picard's last four encounters with the Gorn, he'd died trying to negotiate with the alien captain.

Somewhere in between, Picard knew, was Kirk's solution. Somehow, the captain of that early *Enterprise* had altered the game. The rules that the Metrons had set down were simple: the two captains would face each other in single combat, for their lives and the survival of their ships. The game had, in fact, only one rule . . . survive. That much, it was clear, Kirk had done.

Yet, apparently, the Gorn ship had been spared as well. Kirk had found a way to win much more than his own life and the lives of his crew. *Somehow.* It was an intriguing problem.

Picard's thoughts were interrupted by the arrival of his officers, led by his exec, Ben Zoma—the first officer's dark gaze already fixed on the captain, indicating his concerns about their situation.

Ben Zoma was followed by the very tall, imposing Dr. Greyhorse and then by the equally imposing blue-skinned figure of Lieutenant Vigo.

Science Officer Jack Crusher was the last to enter and the first to speak. "We've run a number of computer checks, sir, and the message was indeed from the Gorn. It originated from the dead center of Gorn space, and the rendezvous coordinates will place us a short distance from the conjectured position of the Gorn homeworld."

Picard felt the excitement rise in his face. *The possibilities.*

"It would seem," he said, "the Gorn are very serious in their overture—which means we could become the first Federation citizens to see their world."

Weapons Officer Vigo frowned. "They are certainly serious, but not necessarily friendly. After all, we don't know what they want."

Most of the others nodded in agreement, Picard among them. "True, Mr. Vigo, but we can guess. Mr. Crusher?"

Jack Crusher stood and walked toward the conference-room viewscreen, where Captain Kirk was facing the Gorn in a still image. With his characteristic half smile, Crusher began, "Captain James T. Kirk's encounter with the Gorn nearly seventy-five years ago is well documented, up to a point. In what is commonly known as the Cestus Three massacre and officially known as the Cestus Three incident, the Gorn attacked an innocent Federation outpost.

"The *U.S.S. Enterprise* NCC-1701 then engaged the Gorn, but the fighting was stopped by a powerful alien race called the Metrons, who arranged for Captain Kirk to face the Gorn captain in single combat. Of course, we don't know what Kirk's solution was, but we do know that he saved his ship. We also know he came to an arrangement that spared the Gorn ship as well.

"At that time the Gorn had technology and weaponry roughly equivalent to Starfleet's—phasers, comparable warp drive, and so on—and the Gorn ship was a fair match for the *Enterprise* of the day. But I'm not telling you anything that you didn't learn in the Academy."

Crusher gave an uncharacteristic frown. "And three-quarters of a century later, most of what we know or can deduce about the Gorn is still based on these records from the *Enterprise*. After that encounter, the Federation ceded Cestus Three to the Gorn, recognizing that it resided in Gorn space. Then the Federation and the Gorn negotiated a border via subspace communications. Since that time, the Gorn have declined repeated efforts to establish formal diplomatic or trade relations. What contact we've had has been through neutral free traders who tend to operate on the fringes of Federation space."

First Officer Ben Zoma gave the Gorn on the viewscreen a cool appraisal. "They have offered a meeting, and I don't want to ignore the historic implications here, but I recommend caution. They could be hiding something."

Vigo nodded his agreement. "They could be preparing for another encounter, something that will give them an advantage over us."

Dr. Greyhorse shifted his large body in his chair and raised his deep, resonant voice. "Could they be afraid?"

Crusher shrugged. "Maybe they're merely keeping to themselves. We simply don't have enough information to make an informed guess." Crusher returned Picard's steady gaze. "I'm sorry, sir."

Picard waved off the apology. "What do we know about the Gorn themselves, Jack?"

Crusher took a moment to gather his thoughts. "They are obviously reptilian, closely resembling Earth crocodilians and lizards. They're what we used to call cold-blooded. Lacking a mammal's internal thermostat and the need to maintain a constant temperature, their bodies require less fuel and are almost certainly able to survive in harsh climates with little available food and water. And of course, they have a high degree of intelligence."

"And they're highly aggressive," Vigo volunteered. "After all, their first contact with the Federation was the attack on Cestus Three."

"True," Crusher allowed. He manipulated the viewscreen controls, and an image of a Gorn appeared. "Following a reptilian model, it stands to reason that the Gorn are very territorial. They also appear to move slowly for a sentient species, and slower reptiles tend to have an immediate fight response. They did claim that the attack on Cestus Three was a defensive measure, which is why, ultimately, the base was ceded to the Gorn."

Picard gestured for Crusher to sit. "Excellent insights, which we will have to bear in mind."

"Unfortunate that we don't know more," Ben Zoma sighed.

"Certainly," Picard replied. "But I doubt we will ever have all the information we need or would like. For now, we can think the best of the Gorn initiative and hope that they will not disappoint us." Picard anticipated Vigo's response. "Though we shall proceed with caution and take every possible precaution to ensure our own safety—so that we are able to report our findings back to Starfleet."

Picard leveled his eyes at Ben Zoma. "Prepare a landing party that includes representatives of all of the sciences, and a full security team. We may very well be witnessing history here, gentlemen. These days will both test and define us. For now, all we can do is keep our best foot forward when we meet our hosts."

Seventeen hours later, Picard was on the bridge when the *Stargazer* reached the Gorn's coordinates.

"Coming into visual range, sir," the ensign at communications announced.

The captain was out of his chair before he gave his order. "On screen, full magnification." The oblong shape of the Gorn ship appeared on the forward viewer.

Picard's next comment was addressed to the bridge crew at large. "We are privileged to be the first Starfleet crew to see a Gorn starship. No other vessel has come this close."

"Full sensor scan, sir?" Crusher asked without taking his eyes off the screen.

"Absolutely not, Mr. Crusher. They might find a full scan invasive. Passive sensors only."

Quiet ruled the bridge for the next few moments as the crew watched the growing image of the Gorn ship. It had two nacelles, which Picard recognized as typical of most warp-capable spacefaring races. The Gorn's nacelles were forward-swept on the underside of the vessel—the most graceful feature of a ship that was fairly stark, with hard angles.

We are the first, Picard thought, with the mixture of pride and gratitude that had characterized so much of his Starfleet career. The first to see this ship. And we will be the first to know these beings.

Ben Zoma was the first to break the silence. "She won't win any prizes for beauty."

"For that matter, neither will we," Jack chimed in.

Picard smiled and let the comment pass.

"The Gorn are raising shields, sir," Crusher said, his voice carrying the concern that Picard felt as well.

"Shields, Captain?" Vigo asked from the weapons console.

"No," Picard said without hesitation. "We will take no provocative action."

"Their phaser banks are on-line, sir," Crusher added. And then before Picard could respond: "They're discharging."

Two greenish beams leapt out from the underside of the Gorn ship. From the angle of the beams, Picard could tell that they would strike the main hull. An instant later, he felt a subtle vibration through the deck of his ship. Strange, he mused. By rights, a full-power shot should have shaken them much harder, even if the Gorn hadn't upgraded their weapons at all in the seventy-five years since their last encounter with the Federation.

"Mr. Vigo, shields up. Mr. Crusher, calculate the power of that shot, double it and feed the data to the weapons console. Mr. Vigo, fire now."

The phasers leapt from the *Enterprise* and caught the Gorn ship aft, striking the vessel's shields and creating a brilliant display.

"Return fire?" Picard asked.

"None, sir," Vigo replied.

"Damage?"

"None, sir," Jack Crusher replied. "Their shot was a very low power discharge, and ours was easily deflected by their shields."

"We are being hailed, sir," the communications officer announced.

"On screen," Picard ordered.

As near as Picard could tell, the same Gorn as before snapped onto the screen.

The lizard-being spoke first. "Captain Picard, your challenge has been well met. Now we wish to meet with *you.*"

The Gorn seemed to be waiting for a response. The translator didn't relate any tension in his voice, nothing to indicate that their two ships had just exchanged fire.

Picard took a step closer to the screen. "You honor us with this opportunity to know your people. I would like to prepare a team and meet with you as soon as possible."

The Gorn's face was nearly unreadable. "No, we would like to meet with you alone."

Picard felt the tension on the bridge go back up a notch. He kept his voice measured. "It is our custom to meet unfamiliar races with a small number of individuals trained in different disciplines. It helps us to better communicate our diversity, and to better understand a new people."

The Gorn's face remained impassive, but its voice went up a notch in volume. "For the purposes of this meeting, others will be unnecessary. You may transport to our ship in exactly one of your hours. We will take you to a place for the meeting. Stand by to receive coordinates."

"Acknowledged," Picard said, as the viewscreen went blank.

Ben Zoma was at his captain's side in a moment. His voice was an insistent whisper, his dark brows meeting over the bridge of his nose.

"Captain, I hope you are not considering going over alone."

Picard sighed inwardly as he stepped toward the turbolift. Ben Zoma followed him.

"Number One, I understand your concern, but it seems that the Gorn have left us with little choice."

Stepping inside the lift, Ben Zoma continued without a pause. "Sir, I can't sanction this sort of action. Besides the obvious danger to yourself, having you in the hands of the Gorn places the entire Federation at risk. We don't know their intentions are peaceful—"

Picard dismissed the concern with a wave of his hand.

"Sir," Ben Zoma went on, "there is precedent here. In our first encounter with the Gorn, they launched a sneak attack on one of our outposts."

"Starfleet Command ruled that they acted in self-defense," the captain countered.

The color rose in Ben Zoma's cheeks, and Picard could hear the arguments forming in his exec's mind, even before he voiced them. "And maybe they did, sir, and maybe their motives are pure here. All I'm saying is that we need to be sure before we allow anyone as important as a starship commander to meet with them alone."

Picard had already considered everything Ben Zoma had said. There was a risk, but the potential benefits were enormous. The Gorn could have destroyed the *Stargazer* when her shields were down if hostility was their sole intent. No, he wouldn't let concerns over his personal safety destroy this opportunity. When he spoke, his voice was firm.

"Commander, I intend to comply with the Gorn's

request. I feel we must seize this opportunity. I will not be responsible for allowing another seventy-five years to pass before we make contact with these people again."

Picard saw Ben Zoma forming his final pitch. "Captain—"

"Gilaad," Picard interrupted, "I will take every possible precaution to ensure my own safety. That will have to be enough."

The turbolift doors opened to his deck. "For the moment," he continued, "I will be making preparations in my quarters. You have the conn."

As Picard stepped into the corridor, he made a silent vow that he would not allow his next exec to mollycoddle him as Gilaad Ben Zoma did.

Jack Crusher waited for a moment until he heard the captain's invitation. "Come," Picard said, and Crusher entered his commander's sparsely decorated quarters. One of the few ornaments was an artist's rendering of the *Stargazer,* with her awkward four-nacelle design. *No, she'll never win any beauty prizes,* Jack thought. The only other notable decoration was a large volume of the collected works of Shakespeare that the captain displayed on his desk.

"Status?" Picard asked, from behind that same desk.

"We've left warp and we're following the Gorn escort ship to the fourth planet of the Vontalimar system, sir."

"Is it the Gorn homeworld?"

Crusher shook his head. "I don't think so. Only a few million life-form readings in just two population centers. My guess is that we're headed toward one of their colony worlds."

"Any additional messages?"

"Not since we encountered the escort ship and they made their . . . request." Jack thought over the speech he'd planned to make again and then abandoned his prepared statement. "I don't like it, sir."

The captain raised an eyebrow in interest.

"The Gorn are an unknown quantity," Crusher explained. "For the record, I don't approve of you meeting with them on your own. They've given us no agenda for the meeting, not even a list of demands—except that they would like to speak to you alone, in person. I suggest that we treat this meeting like a first contact, which is not far from the truth, with a full security and cultural contact team."

In a single, economical movement, Picard was out of his seat and standing to face his friend. "The Gorn representatives have asked to speak to me by myself, Jack. They were very clear on that issue. I suspect that if we don't meet the only request that they have made of us, we will be risking any potential rewards the meeting might bring."

The captain's tone was resolute, though his eyes registered concern over Jack's reservations. Crusher felt compelled to play his last card, though he suspected he knew what the outcome would be. "Sir, we don't know that there will be any rewards at all."

Picard favored his officer with one of his rare, wide grins. "But we do, Jack. We've already seen something that no Starfleet vessel has seen in over seventy-five years—a Gorn starship. And this time, we haven't tried to destroy each other. I'd say we've already done remarkably well for ourselves. Beyond that, we don't have any idea what possibilities a face-to-face meeting might bring. Truly, anything can happen."

"That's what scares me," Crusher said—but couldn't help punctuating it with a grin. The captain's enthusiasm was infectious. Nevertheless, Jack tried to keep his expression neutral. "I'd like to encourage you to take as few risks as possible out there, sir. And don't hesitate to push the panic button. We'll be there as soon as we can."

Picard patted the younger man on the back as he walked him to the door. "I will keep that in mind."

Jack left the captain's quarters no less concerned over Picard's safety, but for the first time excited about the prospects of the meeting. He entered the turbolift with two thoughts. First, he had just been "handled" by his captain—and handled well. Second, he'd never had a chance in the galaxy of changing Jean-Luc Picard's mind.

When the turbolift doors opened, Captain Picard was pleased to see that his senior officers had assembled to see him off. Ben Zoma, in particular, looked remarkably relaxed. No doubt he had accepted the logic of Picard's decision.

"Captain, we'd like to wish you luck. Our thoughts go with you," the exec said.

He's almost cheerful, thought Picard. Maybe Jack has spoken to him. The captain kept the surprise out of his voice. "Thank you, Number One." Then he swept a grateful glance over the rest of his crew. "And all of you as well."

Picard stepped up to the transporter pad and turned around to face his officers, giving a faint nod to the transporter chief. "Energize."

Crusher was moving before the order left the captain's lips. As Picard heard the hum of the first few moments of the transporter cycle, he watched as his friend rushed to the pad, stopped directly in front of him, and attached a phaser to the captain's hip.

The last thing Picard saw before the transporter took him was Crusher's smile.

I'll have to reprimand him when I return to the ship, Picard thought. Ben Zoma as well, no doubt.

Then the Gorn ship solidified around him. Unlike the harsh lines of the hull, inside the ship was all rounded edges and smooth, burnished metal surfaces, some silver and some dull gold. Forms of aluminum and copper, Picard guessed.

The Gorn themselves looked very impressive up close. There were three of them. The largest stood a full two heads taller than the captain, and Picard recognized him as the one who had communicated with the *Stargazer* over the viewscreen. His reptilian features were blunt and on a larger scale than his smaller companions. He was also the same greenish color as the Gorn captain who had battled Kirk, while the others had large stretches of reds and browns mixed into their "skin."

They were all dressed the same, in subtle variations of a one-piece metallic tunic.

Looking at the Gorn, Picard didn't feel any of the revulsion he had expected. Instead, he felt nothing but anticipation. Another benefit of the Academy simulations, he supposed.

The leader hissed and sputtered to one of his companions in their native language. One of the smaller Gorn reached for his belt and what looked like a sidearm. Picard was suddenly very aware of the phaser at his own side, and reaffirmed his resolve to have a serious talk with Jack Crusher.

The smaller lizard-being was now holding a cylinder that was perhaps the width of Picard's thumb and about fifteen centimeters long. The Gorn stepped up to Picard and handed the device to him.

Picard took hold of the cylinder, relieved that it wasn't a weapon. The device immediately translated the Gorn's next words.

"Captain," the Gorn said. "Welcome to our ship."

Ben Zoma finally stopped pacing and forced himself to sit in the command chair. "Mr. Crusher . . . status?"

Jack Crusher looked up from his monitor at the science station. "Gorn shields are up at full strength. I'm also getting a reading on the captain."

"Does he still have the phaser?" Ben Zoma knew that Picard wouldn't be happy about their little "gift" when he returned, but the first officer was prepared for his wrath—as long as the captain did return.

"Yes, sir," replied Crusher. "I'm getting a clear lock on the iridium patch. As long as he has the phaser, we'll be able to trace him anywhere in the sector."

Ben Zoma fell silent, only to be interrupted by the lieutenant at communications. "We're being hailed, sir. It's the captain. I have visual."

"On screen, Lieutenant."

Picard appeared on the viewscreen, and Ben Zoma could immediately feel the mood on the bridge lighten. Their captain was safe.

"Captain," the first officer said.

"Number One. My hosts have asked me to accompany them on a short voyage, and I have agreed."

"May I suggest the *Stargazer* as an escort, sir?"

Picard actually smiled. "Not this time, Gilaad."

Ben Zoma looked carefully at his captain. The man didn't seem to be acting under duress, but his first officer needed to be sure. " 'The air bites shrewdly; it is very cold,' " Ben Zoma said, making the statement a question.

Picard answered without hesitation. " 'It is a nipping and an eager air.' "—That was the proper coded response they'd agreed on, and the captain even punctuated his *Hamlet* with a subtle grin. All was indeed well.

"When can we expect you back, sir?" the first officer asked.

"My hosts inform me that I will be returned in no more than thirty-six hours."

Ben Zoma nodded. "We will be waiting, sir."

"Excellent, Number One. Picard out."

"Maintaining a lock on the phaser, sir," Crusher said. "The captain still has it with him. We can track him anywhere."

"Well, that's something," Ben Zoma muttered. *Picard seems certain that everything's in order. I should have had nothing to worry about.*

Still, he shifted uncomfortably in the command chair. Gilaad Ben Zoma couldn't figure exactly why, but something about this mission still made him damned nervous.

Several hours later, Picard found himself staring at the walls of the small quarters he had been assigned by the largest Gorn—in the human's estimate, the captain of the ship.

From the beginning, the captain had noticed what at first seemed like extreme formality in the lizard-being's speech and movements.

It was as if the Gorn were trying very hard to mimic human protocol. Picard grunted. Perhaps it should have encouraged him that his host was trying to make him comfortable. But for reasons he couldn't explain, the Gorn's effort to do everything "right" simply made him uneasy.

His musings were interrupted by a low-pitched buzzing that gradually filled the room. He was half out of bed when the Gorn captain and two other officers he recognized unceremoniously entered his quarters.

His host gave the human an exaggerated nod and said, "Captain Picard, we have reached our destination. Please accompany us."

Picard was on his feet an instant later, following the Gorn through the ship. They quickly reached the vessel's transporter chamber. Picard noted that the device didn't have individual pads but a contiguous floor panel. Following the others, he took a random spot on the panel.

His instinct was to turn around to face the transporter operator, or rather operators, since it seemed to take three to operate the transporter. But Picard quickly saw that the Gorn captain and the others didn't turn around. Instead they merely continued to face the room's far wall.

The small difference in transporter protocol reminded the human that he was dealing with an alien race about which he knew virtually nothing. Up until now, they had tried to communicate with him on more or less human terms. But soon, Picard suspected, he would be meeting them on theirs.

The transporter took them—and an instant later, a large chamber coalesced around them. A high, stone wall, framed by the same metal forms he had seen on the ship.

As his companions turned around, Picard was quick to follow suit. They were now all facing a contingent of half a dozen Gorn. The largest of them, who was shorter but stockier than the Gorn captain, was wearing a translator as well.

"Captain Picard, welcome to our world. I am leader here. You may call me Leader Keeyah." The stocky one gave Picard the approximation of a human bow, which seemed about as natural for him as a tutu on a sumo wrestler.

"Leader Keeyah," the human replied, "it is a great honor for me personally—and as a representative of the Federation—to be invited to your world. It is my hope that our meeting is the first of many, and the beginning of an exchange that will enrich both our peoples."

Leader Keeyah considered Picard for a moment in silence and then said: "Please come with me."

The entire group walked from the large, open

chamber to a long corridor, with doors on either side, until they reached the end of the corridor and passed through an archway.

The human found himself in a small chamber with a table in one corner. Leader Keeyah and the Gorn captain conferred with each other for a few moments. Then Keeyah faced Picard squarely.

Raising his hand, the Gorn leader held out a small electronic device, which the human quickly grasped. Then Keeyah spoke—deliberately, forcefully and with no room for misinterpretation.

"Captain Picard," he said, "the first meeting between our two races was a mistake, born of confusion on both our parts. I am giving you a message to take back to your fellows, so that our future communication will be accurate."

Picard nodded. "Of course. We have found accurate communication to be the cornerstone of good relations with other beings."

The Gorn eyed him. "In this case, Captain, the communication is very simple. Your expansion in the galaxy represents the greatest threat my people have ever faced. We are formally declaring a state of war between our races. We will return you to your ship; you will deliver this message without delay. There can be no misunderstanding, nor will you be able to accuse us of failing to make our challenge openly."

The Gorn remained completely calm, keeping the same even tone he had used previously in polite speech, and for a moment Picard questioned if he had heard correctly. That moment of peace was horrifyingly short, however—and then all doubt was gone.

War, he thought, stunned. As all of the implications of the word sank in, Picard felt his stomach turn.

He would be a messenger of bloody conflict; his fine ship and crew would be the harbingers of destruction. His face flushed with that biting fear.

"You may go," Keeyah said. A Gorn took Picard by the arm and led him out toward the door.

The human shook off the Gorn, angrily. He would . . . he would . . .

Not!

Picard turned on his heel and faced Leader Keeyah. For a moment he didn't have the slightest idea what he would say. Then it came.

"No."

"This is not a request, Captain." The Gorn's whole demeanor changed. Gone was the pretense of courtesy. He drew himself to his full height and then lifted his head further, exposing his throat.

Picard didn't know anything about Gorn body language, but he was quite sure that it wasn't a polite gesture.

Around him, Picard sensed the other Gorn in the room tensing, waiting expectantly. For him to leave? Or . . .

Then suddenly he was moving, propelled not by a plan, or a thought, but by a feeling.

"I . . ."

The captain took three quick strides.

". . . said . . ."

Face-to-face with Keeyah, Picard clenched his fists and turned his head, shouting his words up the half meter distance to the Gorn's face.

21

"*NO!*"

And his right fist drove upward as well, aiming not for the face, or head, but the still-exposed throat.

The Gorn snapped his head down in defense, muffling the blow, the scales around his mouth turning down in what Picard assumed was surprise. Still propelled by the feeling that he knew was his only chance, the captain took advantage of Keeyah's momentary disorientation. He placed his left foot behind the Gorn's and shoved the larger creature—hard, with both hands. Keeyah crashed down to the floor, falling flat on his back.

In surprise, Picard noted that the fist he had used to hit the Gorn still carried the electronic message device, which had given the blow extra weight. The human felt the continuing rush of adrenaline and the warm flush on his face. If his instincts were right, and luck was with him, the Gorn would spare his life. But if he were wrong and Leader Keeyah got up to fight, the alien could kill him with a single blow.

The Gorn rose slowly and looked directly at Picard, this time with his head turned down. It was either to protect his throat from further attack, or—as the captain hoped—as some sort of a gesture of respect.

The blow came an instant later. The fact that Picard was ready for it did nothing to dull its impact. Keeyah simply swatted the human on the shoulder with one hand and sent him sprawling backward, landing hard on his other shoulder. Rolling into the fall, Picard dropped the Gorn device and drew his phaser as he got to his feet, taking a split second to check the setting before he fired it.

The blue beam of the phaser's heavy stun setting lit

the room and struck Keeyah directly in the chest. For a moment, the alien simply stopped all movement and then fell unceremoniously on his back.

As Keeyah lay motionless, Picard realized that the eyes of every Gorn in the room were on him. *Will I have to fight them all?* the human wondered, though they seemed to be remaining still. Then the one on the floor began to stir. Quickly and steadily, he rose to his feet, apparently already shaking off the effects of the stun.

Keeyah eyed Picard and slowly moved closer to him, until they were face-to-face. Tensed for another attack, the captain wondered if he would have time to fire before the next blow came. *I thought they were supposed to move slowly,* he thought.

When the lizard-being didn't strike him, Picard had a moment's hope that there might still be a way to salvage the situation.

"You challenge me," the Gorn said through the translator, "you challenge all." He gestured to the others in the room—but the captain thought that the alien was referring to an even larger group.

"You made the challenge," Picard answered. Had he instinctually interpreted the Gorn's earlier gestures correctly? It seemed so. "I have met it and defeated you."

"Yes," Leader Keeyah answered without hesitation.

"I now make my own challenge. I challenge you to a negotiation," the captain went on.

"A *negotiation,* human?" The alien made a series of hisses and guttural sounds that the translator couldn't interpret. The Gorn considered him carefully for a moment.

And in that instant Picard knew that nothing was decided, nothing was inevitable.

As the moment passed, Keeyah seemed to have come to a conclusion. He said, "Let us *discuss* it."

The Gorn gestured for Picard and the others to move to the table at the other side of the room. The captain made an effort to take slow and steady breaths. Feeling himself relax by degrees, he made a mental note to thank Jack Crusher for the phaser.

Chapter One

Stardate: 47821.2
Earth Calendar Date: 2370

CAPTAIN PICARD STOPPED outside the door and tapped his communicator. "Number One, I'm outside, may I join you?"

"Certainly, sir," came the response.

Taking another step, Picard waited for the holodeck door to open. A moment later, he was looking out at a rocky ledge. His first officer was sitting at the brink of it, looking down into the bone-dry valley below. The place was hot, the air thin. And somehow, it looked familiar.

Of course, thought Picard, realizing the reason for its familiarity. I'm not the *only* one who has been studying history.

"Research, Number One?"

"More like a review, Captain," replied Riker. As the captain entered the scenario, the younger man turned his attention to what was going on farther along the ledge. From the intense look on Riker's face, it was

25

obvious that he was deep in concentration. Then, abruptly, he shook his head.

"Freeze program," he said, getting up to stretch his legs. Joining him, Picard saw what his first officer had been studying.

A Starfleet officer was leaning over the cliff. Bare-chested, the man was in the middle of waving his tunic to something down below.

The captain peered down over the side of the cliff. At least 150 meters below, a Gorn stood looking up at the bare-chested officer.

Abruptly, Picard realized that something was wrong with this scene: Captain Kirk had never baited the Gorn in quite this way, at least not in the official Starfleet records. Then it came to him that the uniform the frozen officer was waving was not Kirk's command gold—but Starfleet Academy's maroon. And on closer examination, Picard saw that the mysterious officer was clearly William Riker as a first-year cadet.

He grunted. "That first encounter with the Gorn was still a simulation in your Academy days, Number One?"

"It still is, as far as I know, sir." Riker shook his head. "This was not one of my finer moments. I was trying to lead the Gorn to a crude trip wire."

"Did the trap work?"

The first officer grinned. "Perfectly. Of course, it didn't stop him for a moment."

Picard smiled in return. "I had my share of troubles with this simulation as well." He took a moment to scan the holodeck scene. The captain had been reviewing the official records on the monitor in his quarters, though he decided now that it might be worthwhile to run the sequence in the holodeck after all. He would almost certainly have time before they reached Gorn space.

"Number One," he said, "would you accompany me to my ready room? I would like to begin preparations for the summit meeting while we have plenty of time. I prefer not to leave anything to chance."

"Of course, sir." Riker turned back to the scene for a moment. "Computer, end program."

Without a sound, the planetscape around them vanished, leaving the two men standing in the empty holodeck.

Picard led the way into the corridor. "I've been doing some review of my own, Will. Captain Kirk's encounter has always fascinated me."

Riker sighed. "I always had trouble with the Metrons' editing. If they'd let us watch just a few more minutes, it would have saved us all a lot of trouble at the Academy."

The captain shrugged. "Perhaps . . . though we did see a great deal. Kirk's situation came down to a choice and a set of consequences. Anything could happen—he could live, or die. His ship and crew would be won or lost. The moment we see is uncertain, yet full of possibilities—including the one possibility that Captain Kirk saw but we do not."

Riker eyed his commanding officer. "And we never will know what that possibility was. The Metrons stopped sending the signal, and Starfleet sealed the records. We don't know what he *did.*"

"True," Picard conceded. "However, we are privileged to see the moment when the choices came into focus. I suspect Captain Kirk merely seized the moment and did whatever he had to do. Or, perhaps, the only thing he *could* do."

The first officer looked rueful. "That kind of thinking didn't help me in the Gorn simulation at the Academy. My adversary killed me twice before I beat him."

Picard halted in mid-stride. "You *defeated* the Gorn on your third attempt?"

Riker nodded. "I was actually in the middle of trying to reproduce the primitive cannon Captain Kirk had prepared, when I realized what a pointless exercise it was. Besides the risk the cannon posed, the chances of hitting anything—let alone a moving target—were astronomical. Instead, I went through the motions with gunpowder but no projectiles. When the Gorn came close enough, I set off the cannon for effect. In all the smoke and haze, I clubbed him with a rock."

"You . . . won?" As the two men reached the turbolift door and entered, Picard shook his head in disbelief. "Bridge," he said.

"Won is a strong word," Riker amended. "I beat the Gorn captain all right. But as a result, the Gorn fought a simulated war on the Federation. By the time I finished counting the casualty figures, I had learned my lesson."

The captain turned to him. "And what was that, Number One?"

"I'm still not sure, sir. I'd say it was another example of the no-win scenario, but we know that there was at least one solution that didn't entail the destruction of a Starfleet vessel or the beginning of a war. That was Captain Kirk's solution."

Picard folded his arms across his chest. "On to business, Will. I want you to become almost as familiar with Gorn concerns as I am. It's not my intention to be the only one who can carry out this assignment."

Riker shifted uncomfortably, Picard noticed. "Something, Will?"

"May I be frank, sir?" Riker asked.

"Of course," Picard nodded.

"This summit is happening now solely on the basis of your meeting with the Gorn twenty-five years ago. It was the strength of your work and personality that kept us from going to war then."

Now it was the captain's turn to feel uncomfortable. "It wasn't quite like that, Number One. A great deal of the credit goes to the Gorn. They did most of the work in actually creating the agreement. I merely stumbled onto a method of communicating with them."

The turbolift opened and deposited the two men on the bridge. Picard moved toward his chair but didn't sit down. This would not take long.

"Mr. Data, report."

Commander Data took his eyes off his control panel at the ops station and turned his head to face his captain. "Sir, we have begun our detour around Metron space. At warp four, we will reach the coordinates provided by the Gorn in six-point-four days."

"Plenty of breathing room," Riker interjected.

The android gave a practiced nod. "Yes, sir." He looked directly at the captain. "Enough time that I would like to suggest investigating a very large mass— one which was not charted when the *Stargazer* explored this sector of space under your command."

At that, Picard decided to sit down after all. "Did we miss something, Data?"

"Quite possibly, sir. However, the mass is giving very low energy readings. In all likelihood, the *Stargazer*'s sensors would not have been sensitive enough to detect it except at very close range."

The captain noted that Riker had sat down beside him.

"Low power," the first officer said, making the statement a question. "I guess that means it can't be an asteroid. Anything else, Data?"

"It is symmetrical and appears to be artificial," the android reported. "We will need to move in closer for a more detailed analysis."

Picard weighed the question. On the one hand, they did have plenty of time before the summit. On the other, he didn't want to take any unnecessary risks that might delay their arrival. The meeting with the Gorn was too important.

In the end, it was Data's interest that persuaded him. *This is as close to excited as he gets,* the captain observed. For now, he would indulge his third officer.

"All right, Mr. Data, I will allow a short detour. Scan the object carefully for any possible threats. If there is any sign of danger at all, we will have to take a closer look on the way back."

Data's matter-of-fact report had not even come close to preparing Geordi La Forge for the sight that greeted him on the main viewscreen. He stood in front of the open turbolift from which he had just emerged.

"Wow" was all he could think to say.

Geordi quickly made his way to the Engineering console. "Tell me that the magnification circuits are on the blink."

"That is not the case," Data replied. "The computer imaging system is functioning normally. The object is actually as big as it looks."

Taking his seat, the chief engineer began punching up the android's scans on his console. "And how big is that?"

"Five kilometers in diameter," Data said in his customary emotionless tone.

"Wow," Geordi repeated. "That's some doughnut."

He noticed that Captain Picard, Commander Riker, and Counselor Troi were all staring raptly at the screen.

"An apt analogy, Mr. La Forge," the captain interjected. "Any explanation for the shape?"

Geordi took in the thick, circular shape of the alien station. It had more or less regular external markings that resembled windows, small protruding structures he couldn't even guess the significance of, and what looked like airlocks or docking bays.

A quick look at the information on his screen told Geordi what he needed to know. "Well, the engineering is pretty advanced. The power they're generating shouldn't be nearly enough to maintain a gravity field for an object that size—yet somehow, it does."

Commander Riker had approached Geordi and was looking over his shoulder at the incoming data. "It's too symmetrical to be an arbitrary design."

Data turned away from his console to face them. "It does not appear to be arbitrary at all, sir. In fact, the entire structure seems to have been designed as an immense coil of some sort."

Geordi continued to study the readouts at the console before him. Of course, he thought. *Look at all that verterium in the station.* That suggested a subspace field coil—not unlike the ones that drove the *Enterprise* through warp space.

"But why would anyone need a coil that large on a stationary platform?" Riker asked.

"You could generate a lot of power," the engineer responded. "But I'm not sure what you would do with it." He watched the data scroll across his screen. "Wait a minute, they've got a lot of matter-transport circuitry. Now, that makes sense; theoretically, a large enough subspace coil would allow for interstellar transport . . . or even time travel."

The others on the bridge started at that remark, but the captain remained still, studying the station with his face as composed as ever. Nonetheless, he's as excited as any of us, thought Geordi.

Picard turned to Data. "Commander, any sign of what happened to the beings who created this object?"

"No, sir," replied the android. "Though the station has enough internal volume to accommodate three hundred thousand humanoid inhabitants, there are no substantial deposits of organic matter, no remains of the inhabitants, no food stores."

"They just left," Geordi commented.

"Counselor?" Picard asked.

Troi shook her head. "I don't sense anyone. It feels as deserted as it looks."

"Apparently so," Data replied. "The computer dates the station at approximately twelve thousand years of age. And it seems to have been abandoned for several thousand of those years."

"A Metron artifact?" Picard suggested.

The android frowned ever so slightly. "We know virtually nothing of Metron technology, so we cannot make a comparison, sir. However, scans indicate that some of the technology is similar to known Iconian designs."

Geordi watched the captain's interest level go up a notch. Captain Picard was an accomplished amateur archeologist and the lost Iconian culture was one of his favorite fields of study.

"A great many interesting questions," Picard said simply.

Commander Riker looked up from Geordi's console and took the few steps necessary to return to his position at the captain's side.

"We do have time for a quick preliminary study," the first officer said, "before we need to leave for the Gorn summit."

For a moment, Geordi considered adding in his own two cents, but one look at the captain's face told him it wasn't necessary.

Twenty minutes later, Geordi was standing on a transporter platform with Commander Riker, as well as engineers Barclay, O'Connor, and Varley.

Geordi was certain the captain wished he could come along. Maybe, if it was safe, Picard would be able to make his visit later, after the Gorn summit.

What about Data? he wondered. He could have

sworn he heard excitement in the android's voice. But disappointment over staying behind? Geordi dismissed the idea.

In any case, Data belonged on the ship where he could quickly sift through the mounds of information as they came through the sensors. That would satisfy whatever programming he had that might pass for curiosity.

"Energize," Riker ordered the transporter chief. And Geordi's musings were cut short by the transporter.

The *Enterprise* disappeared around him.

And was replaced by nothing.

Complete and utter darkness. With a few slight exceptions, there were no infrared signatures, nothing in the visual spectrum, no radio waves—in fact, almost no EM rays of any kind. It was very rarely that Geordi came across any artificial construct that was this dead. Any ship or place functioning even marginally was usually awash with all sorts of radiation.

Here, most of the readings were coming from Commander Riker, the two security guards, Barclay, and his two fellow engineers.

Almost simultaneously, Riker and the security guards ignited their handlamps. Geordi followed suit as Barclay and O'Connor powered on the two portable light sources.

As the light sources gently bobbed on their antigravs, their diffuse illumination described a small, empty chamber.

Geordi saw that the room they were in was . . . comfortable. Though empty, the walls were decorated with subtle, rounded moldings and a few intricate designs that—according to his tricorder readings— served no purpose other than the obvious aesthetic one. Even without normal sight, and relying on his VISOR, the chief engineer was sure the others would find it—

"Now that's *beautiful,*" Riker said to the away team, pointing behind them.

Geordi turned to see what the commander was referring to and saw a large window on the far wall. The *Enterprise* was hanging in space outside.

A sense of detail and windows to boot, thought La Forge. Whoever built this place cared about the environment they lived in.

Suddenly, for a split second, he thought he saw a quick blip of energy run through the outer wall, near the floor. Just a blip on the edge of his vision and then it was gone. It was the kind of shadow image his VISOR occasionally picked up on the ship—a stray signal from some piece of equipment. In a place this big, that kind of thing was sure to happen.

Riker took a deep breath. "The air is a little stale, but not bad. And the place looks clean. I was expecting several thousand years' worth of dust."

Barclay spoke up immediately, "Perhaps the air-filtration system continued to function after the inhabitants left."

The first officer gazed directly at Barclay, and the lieutenant seemed to shrink. "You think so, Mr. Barclay?" asked Riker.

"Ah, yes, sir, it's a possibility, sir," Barclay replied.

Geordi could see heat rush to the lieutenant's face. Barclay was blushing, probably sorry he'd opened his mouth in the first place. Riker, whether he noticed or not, headed mercifully for the exit—an archway much like the one they'd entered by.

"I'd say it was a *good* possibility, Lieutenant," the first officer tossed back as he led the team out into the corridor. Barclay and his light source brought up the rear.

This corridor looked much like the place they had come from, smallish and comfortable. The ceiling was a couple of inches higher than Riker's head and wide enough for two people to walk side by side. The walls were again molded and gently curved into the distance. From the angle of the curve, Geordi guessed the corridor ran the entire outer edge of the station.

He took some tricorder readings. "I'm picking up chambers and windows as well as hatches and airlocks all along the outer wall of the station," he said. "This place is laid out very efficiently."

"Not the kind of thing you throw away," Riker commented. "Where could everybody have gone?"

"Commander," Geordi said, "if the station is really a large subspace field coil, it's possible that it could move the mass of the entire station. A major malfunction could have transported this place from light-years away."

The first officer was interested. "You're saying that the station may have left its masters behind?"

The engineer shrugged. "This early in the game, anything is possible."

Once again, Riker took the lead, heading down the corridor. "Let's see if we can pry some of those secrets out of her."

Geordi could see that Barclay was studying what

seemed to be a small access tunnel, possibly a meter and a half high and just wide enough for one person. "Anything interesting, Reg?"

"There's a lot of circuitry packed into here," the lieutenant replied.

La Forge nodded. "I'll give you a hand."

Riker was already heading for the next archway, barely visible in the distance. "I'm going to take a look around down there," he said.

By the time Geordi reached Barclay, the lieutenant was already crouched in front of the tunnel, shining his handlamp down its length.

"There's another chamber further on," Barclay said, crawling into the opening.

Taking a quick reading on his tricorder, Geordi confirmed that the tunnel was as innocuous as it seemed. He ducked his head inside tentatively. After a moment, he crawled after the lieutenant. "I'm right behind you, Reg."

Barclay was taking the short, dark trip in stride. "No fear of cramped, dark places?" Geordi called ahead.

"No, sir," came the other man's reply. "My cousins and I used to explore caves near our grandfather's house." His voice echoed along the tunnel.

"I didn't figure you for a spelunker, Reg." Geordi smiled at the image of a fearless Barclay making his way through dangerous caverns.

The lieutenant shrugged. "The dark never bothered me, sir. And I'm not claustrophobic. I thought it was kind of exciting, unknown and mysterious. My grandfather thought the caves were a good test of character." Barclay seemed to think carefully for a moment before he continued. "He always maintained that there were two kinds of people."

"Just two?" Geordi asked.

"Yes, sir," Barclay replied. "He said some people are made of steel and some are made of clay, some bend and some fall apart. Sooner or later, you find out what you are. And he thought caves were a good place to find out what you were made of."

For a moment, Geordi was taken aback. This was not the Reginald Barclay he knew, shy and unsteady. The lieutenant was opening up about his personal life for the first time since they had met.

"Did he ever tell you what *you* were, Reg?"

Barclay stopped for a moment and turned in the tunnel to look at Geordi directly. He seemed to be considering the question. "Yes, sir. He said I was an unsaturated hydrocarbon polymer resin."

"But that's . . . rubber?" Geordi replied, dumbfounded.

The other man nodded. "That's right."

"Your grandfather had a strange sense of humor," La Forge remarked.

"Yes," Barclay said, his face a mask. "Funny, but I don't miss it," he added with a nervous grin.

Well, well, Geordi thought. Old Barclay has a sense of humor. I didn't think he could surprise me anymore.

Suddenly, the lieutenant was up and out of the tunnel. Geordi followed closely, glad to give his knees a break. As Barclay swept the room with the handlamp, Geordi scanned it with his VISOR and took a quick reading with his tricorder.

This was definitely some type of control center. The room had no windows, but there was a great deal of circuitry running into the panel and monitor on the far wall. And the circuitry seemed remarkably intact, considering its age.

Geordi's observations were cut short when he heard a sound on his left. Seeing motion, he jumped—and then chided himself when he realized it was Commander Riker's familiar form standing in front of another access tunnel.

The exec nodded by way of a greeting as he dusted himself off. "Fancy meeting you here."

La Forge smiled. "For a second there, I thought you were the landlord."

Riker grinned. "No. But let's hope that if they *do* come home, and find us here, they're in a good mood."

Taking a few steps toward the entrance, Geordi leaned in to quietly address the first officer. "Sir, it seems safe in here, and we don't have time for much more than a quick look around. I was thinking that maybe the captain would appreciate a chance to see this firsthand. And if it *is* Iconian . . ."

Riker gave the suggestion a moment's sober consideration. "Let's ask him."

Not more than a second or two after the captain had materialized on the alien station, his communicator chirped.

"Picard here," he responded.

As he had expected, it was Riker. The captain and the first officer had transported to and from the ship and station simultaneously.

"Just wanted to make sure you arrived safely, sir. I'll be on the bridge if you need me."

"Thank you, Number One. Picard out."

"What do you think, Captain?"

Picard turned and saw it was Geordi who'd asked the question.

For a long moment, the captain did nothing but study his surroundings. The alien station was surprisingly . . . comfortable. The walls displayed soothing earth tones, though he didn't doubt they were made of sophisticated alloys and polymers.

Each bulkhead was made of rectangular panels whose edges were molded with a simple but elegant design. The ceilings stood a comfortable two and a half meters high, and the small chamber they occupied was so pleasing as to almost seem quaint.

Space stations were all too often coldly functional, or intimidatingly open and airless, or dark and forbidding as he had seen in Cardassian design. But the effect here was like no other station he had ever visited. It was almost like an old-fashioned front parlor.

"Cozy, huh?" Geordi asked.

"Yes, quite pleasant," Picard answered. "The builders seemed to be at least partly guided by aesthetics."

"Wait'll you see the control center," said the engineer. "Come with me, sir."

The captain did as La Forge requested, trailing the younger man out into the corridor, to what appeared to be an access tunnel. Hunkering down, Geordi crept inside, and Picard again followed suit.

The chamber on the other end was a flurry of

activity. Barclay, O'Connor, and Varley had set up all kinds of diagnostic equipment, in an effort to understand the station better. They all nodded respectfully as the captain entered.

"As you were," said Picard. He turned to a bulkhead full of differently shaped monitors and what looked like computer controls.

"Whoever constructed this place was pretty advanced," Geordi said. "Not only did they create a sophisticated set of instruments—and some of this stuff, I can't even guess at—but they really built it to last."

The captain noted the single operating monitor, which was displaying a starfield. "A portion of the equipment is still functional, I understand?"

Geordi ran his hands over the controls with what seemed like reverence to Picard. "Yes, but it shouldn't be. This monitor started functioning shortly after we arrived."

Watching closely, the captain saw the scene on the screen shift abruptly. "What's causing the changes?" he asked.

The engineer shook his head. "They're random, as nearly as I can tell. I can't make heads or tails of the controls, and I can't find any correlation between the controls and the monitor."

"Incredible," Picard observed, watching as the scene changed again.

"If we had more time," said Geordi, "I'd love to hook some of this stuff up to a portable generator."

The captain nodded. "With luck, we will have that time after the summit."

"I hope so, sir. For now, all I can do is continue the two-credit tour." With a wave for his commanding officer to follow, La Forge got down on his knees and led the way back out through the access tunnel. Once they were outside in the corridor again, he stood and dusted off the legs of his uniform. "You know," he commented, "it almost seems too good to be true. A fully functional station, completely empty, just waiting for us to poke around."

As they walked, Picard listened to the slight echo of their footsteps. The sound seemed to travel ahead of them down the gently curving corridor, which was lit by a succession of portable light sources.

"We're getting some interesting energy readings from the area closest to the core," Geordi noted, "but for now, we're just studying what we've found in this section of the outer edge."

Picard grunted. "I suspect our hosts will be an interesting people to get to know."

The engineer started to say something, then cut off his own response. He turned quickly to catch a glimpse of something behind the captain.

"Commander?" Picard asked.

La Forge frowned. "I thought I saw something for a moment, sir. A slight electromagnetic blip. And it wasn't the first time, either." He tapped his communicator. "Reg, were you running any scans just now?"

"Yes, sir," came Barclay's reply.

"Rerun your recordings from the last two minutes. Look for microsurges of power."

Silence for a moment, and then Barclay said, "Nothing. Sorry, sir. I'll, ah, keep my eyes open."

"Thanks, Reg. La Forge out."

Picard watched as his officer scanned the corridor with his VISOR. "Anything, Commander?"

"Nothing now, sir. But I was sure I saw *something.*"

"The station still has active power reserves?" the captain asked.

"Yes, though after all this time, it shouldn't be possible. At least, not according to any technology I understand . . ." Geordi let the statement hang in the air.

This time, even Picard saw it. A quick flash of energy between the panels on the outer wall. He noticed that the engineer was looking at the same spot.

"Bingo," said La Forge.

"Sir," came Barclay's voice from the commander's communicator. "I just recorded one of those surges."

Abruptly, Riker's voice sounded, too—this time, from Picard's communicator. "Captain, is anyone running experiments over there? We're reading some small power spikes."

"That was not us," Picard replied. "The station seems to have some active power stores."

"Geordi," asked the first officer, "do you see anything that looks like an operational security system?"

The engineer checked his tricorder again and looked around. "I don't think so," he replied. "But it's hard to say for sure."

Riker's voice was calm and even, but Picard could hear the slight edge of concern. "Captain, I recommend returning the away team to the *Enterprise.* We'll have plenty of time to sort this out after the summit."

"Agreed, Number One. Commander La Forge and I will collect the others and the equipment as soon as possible."

"We'll lock on transporters in the meantime—just in case. Riker out."

Picard gestured in the direction of the chamber in which he had originally materialized, which was also the direction of the control center. Geordi took the lead. Before the engineer had gone very far, he'd activated his communicator.

"All away-team personnel report to the beamdown site. Bring your equipment. We're going back to the ship."

Walking briskly along the corridor, the captain felt as well as saw another crackle of energy. This one seemed to run through both the floor and ceiling. Without asking La Forge, Picard knew that it was a substantial surge. There was a smell of burnt . . . *dust* . . . in the air.

Accelerating his pace, the captain noted how his previously pleasant surroundings suddenly seemed quite alien. His instincts were strongly suggesting that he get his people back to the *Enterprise*.

As Picard passed the tunnel that led to the control center, he bent to get an idea of how well the engineers were coming along. La Forge stopped, too.

"Need any help?" the younger man called.

Inside the tunnel, Varley and O'Connor were crawling out of the control center, pulling their equipment after them. Barclay wasn't far behind.

"No, sir," reported Varley. "We're fine. This'll just take another minute, Commander."

Suddenly, another surge channeled through the

station. With it came a resounding crash, and Picard watched as a heavy door slammed down between him and the three engineers.

"Damn!" exclaimed La Forge.

As the door hit the deck, the captain's hand was reaching for his communicator. "Commander Riker," Picard said.

"Riker here, Captain. We just read another surge. This one was off the scales for a moment. Are you in any danger?"

Picard exchanged looks with his chief engineer. "So far we're uninjured, but Geordi and I have been separated from the rest of the engineering team. Have the transporter beam all of us over now."

"Yes, sir," came Riker's crisp reply. "We'll have you . . . one moment sir." The captain could hear his exec speaking to Data in the background. "Sir," Riker continued, "we've got a problem maintaining a transporter lock. . . ."

Suddenly, another surge coursed through the station. For a moment the interior lights flashed on. Picard and Geordi were bathed in a harsh, white light as the visible burst of energy raced through the walls.

For a second or two, Riker's voice was replaced by static. Then it returned. ". . . suggests that the area you are in may be shielded. Can you all move to one of the outer chambers by a window?"

"I'll call you when we're there. Picard out." The captain saw that Geordi had his tricorder out and was already working on the door.

After a moment, the engineer shook his head. "The mechanism is simple," he remarked, eyeing the small control panel next to the door. "But there's no power.

If we hold the control and wait for another surge, we might . . ."

Picard waved the suggestion away. "Too long. We don't know when or if another surge will happen, or if there will be enough power when it does. What about phasers?"

Geordi drew his phaser at the same moment the captain did. "I suggest we stand back, sir."

They took a position a few steps back.

"Setting five, to start," ordered Picard, as he adjusted his weapon. Geordi did the same. Then the captain tapped his communicator. "Mr. Barclay, lead your team as far away from the door as possible. We're going to try to get you out with phasers."

"Yes, sir," came the reply. "We're clear, sir."

On Picard's nod, the two men fired simultaneously. The captain watched as the two red beams leapt from the phasers, struck the door . . . and *disappeared*.

Geordi's tricorder was immediately in his other hand. He scanned it quickly. "The wall just absorbed and dissipated the beams, Captain. We can try force ten, but I wouldn't go any higher in here."

A moment later, they tried again at the higher setting. Two brighter beams struck the door and also disappeared into its surface. This time, he and Geordi maintained their fire for several seconds. Finally, on Picard's signal, they ceased firing. Except for a brief glow of red that disappeared almost immediately, the door was undamaged.

The engineer frowned. "Somehow, the structure is dissipating the energy throughout the wall—actually, throughout this entire area. Even if we could get through, it would take a while."

"Are there any other exits out of that room?" Picard asked.

"There's another access tunnel," La Forge replied, "on the far side of the control room. It cuts into the corridor maybe a hundred meters farther down— though there may be a door blocking off that way, too."

The captain frowned. "Couldn't they tell that from inside?"

Tapping his communicator, the engineer said: "Reg, the access tunnel at the far end of the room . . . is it still open?"

A pause. "Yes, sir," came the response. "It seems to be."

Geordi nodded. "Good. Then exit that way. We'll meet you in the corridor outside."

At that moment, Picard heard the brief hum that he now associated with the onset of an energy spike. A moment later, the surge came, and with it the rush of interior illumination. The captain watched as lights snapped on and off again down the long corridor.

"Come on," he told his companion.

Together, he and La Forge covered the hundred or so meters in a matter of seconds. Reaching the aperture of the second access tunnel, Picard looked inside and saw that the way was clear. He could discern the shadowy shapes of the three engineers as they made their way into it from the control room.

However, this tunnel was a good deal longer than the other one, and darker as well. It would take Barclay and the others several more minutes to negotiate.

Peering in over the captain's shoulder, Geordi

muttered a curse. "This is going to take longer than I'd hoped," he observed.

Nonetheless, in a matter of moments, the engineers were slithering through the tunnel, their handlamps flashing back and forth as they moved. Before long, Picard could make out the taut, frightened face of engineer Martina O'Connor peeking out at him. Spying the captain up ahead, she managed to move a little faster.

Picard would have met her partway, considering all the equipment she was dragging behind her. However, there wasn't room in the tunnel for both of them. And a couple of seconds later, she was emerging into the corridor anyway.

Ensign Varley was next. He passed out his load of technical devices, then squirmed out to the mouth of the tunnel. The captain had just enough time to recognize his young, earnest features when another surge came, this time without the precursor hum.

Varley had barely dragged half his body out when the hatch above him began sliding down. Noting the flash of motion, La Forge reacted quickly, diving for the small control panel next to the access tunnel—hoping to prevent what had happened at the other opening.

He was quick enough to raise the hatch before the power went out—but not to prevent it from briefly meeting with the floor, despite the fact that Ensign Varley's midsection was directly under it.

Picard looked on in horror. The young man hadn't even had time to scream as the door efficiently cut him in half. Varley's face registered just a brief, ghastly flicker of surprise before the light went out of his eyes.

"My God," the captain breathed. Geordi and O'Connor couldn't even do that.

Picard pushed away his frustration and rising grief for the young man. Barclay was still in there. And his away team was still in danger.

And then a cry filled the chamber. Loud, piercing, nearly hysterical.

"Mr. Barclay," Picard shouted over the man's wail. "You have to come through. Now." The effect was immediate. Barclay stopped screaming. But the captain, who had stooped to look into the tunnel, saw that the engineer wasn't moving. He was just looking at Varley's bisected body in mute terror.

Recognizing that the corpse wouldn't give Barclay enough room to get through, the captain reached in and, as quickly and gently as he could, dragged Varley's remains out of the tunnel. Geordi was right behind him, helping.

In a calm, even tone, the captain addressed Barclay. "Lieutenant, exit this tunnel now." But the man had assumed a sitting position against the tunnel wall and was inching backward. "Stop," Picard ordered. The engineer stopped. "Move out now," the captain continued.

"But sir . . . the hatch . . ." a motionless Barclay said in a frightened near-whisper. Seeing where the lieutenant was pointing, Picard looked up and realized that the hatch, with its bloody bottom edge, was directly above him.

In an instant, the captain reviewed his options and

took the quickest course. Crawling inside the tunnel, he reached for Barclay, grabbed the engineer by the arm, and pulled. Nearly limp, Barclay moved easily and Picard had them both out in a few minutes.

Pulling him to his feet, the captain addressed the engineer directly. "Are you all right, Lieutenant?"

Picard noted that the question registered immediately. Barclay nodded, and then said, "Yes, sir."

With that, the captain slapped his communicator. "Number One, emergency transport *now.*"

The response was not encouraging. "Captain, we're still getting interference . . . almost continuous, low-level power readings from the station that are creating a corresponding low-level subspace field. We can't risk transport."

Picard realized that the room's illumination had come on. The light was low, but fairly steady.

"Captain," Riker continued, "I can have a shuttle there in four minutes. Sensors indicate a large chamber that looks like an airlock one thousand meters from your position."

Geordi already had his tricorder out. "I know where it is, sir."

"We'll meet your shuttle, Number One. Picard out."

The captain turned to the others. "Mr. Barclay, can you travel?"

The engineer was obviously still shaken, but mustered a nod. "Yes, sir. I'm fine, sir."

"Mr. La Forge," Picard said, "we'll follow you."

Geordi led them down the hallway at a trot. Picard had time to wonder how they would get into the airlock, open it to the outside, and get into the shuttle. Then they reached the entrance to the airlock. The archway was open, and the captain could see that the outer door on the other side of the chamber was closed.

The interior lights were getting stronger. With luck, they would be able to work the airlock. The captain hoped it was still operating, and that it had the kind of forcefield that would allow the shuttle to enter and exit—but not void the atmosphere and the away team into space. Of course, at the moment, they had no choice but to try.

"Let's get inside," he barked. "Commander La Forge, give yourself a crash course in the alien airlock system." The engineer nodded and entered the airlock. O'Connor followed, and Barclay brought up the rear. Picard made his move just as another surge coursed through the station. This time, the captain could actually feel the walls shake. Suddenly, the floor moved out from under him and he was thrown backward.

Picard landed on his back—hard—and realized that the fall had probably saved his life. He saw the heavy door to the airlock slam shut with a resounding clang, right in the spot he'd occupied only a moment ago.

He was on his feet quickly. From the window in the door to the airlock, the captain could instantly see why the door had closed so suddenly. The semitransparent barrier that separated the interior of the airlock from open space had raised perhaps a foot from the deck.

Geordi and the others were on the ground struggling for handholds on the almost perfectly smooth surface of the airlock floor. Based on their slow movement toward the barrier, Picard was certain that there was no forcefield holding in the atmosphere.

And judging by the size of the opening, Picard knew the away team had less than ninety seconds to live.

"Picard to shuttlecraft, where are you?"

"Worf here, sir. We are less than two minutes from your position, Captain."

"We have an emergency, Mr. Worf. You'll have to do better than that."

Picard could hear Worf issue the order for full acceleration. He imagined the rescue crew being shaken as the inertial dampeners were pressed just past their limits.

"Lieutenant," he went on, "most of the away team is in an airlock which is now partially open to space. They do not have long."

"I've got a sensor lock, Captain," Worf announced —just as the shuttle swept into sight less than a hundred meters from the station.

Picard felt his teeth grating together. "Get as close as you can and lock on the shuttle's emergency transporters. You may be able to punch through the station's interference by lining up the transporter beam with the open door."

"Locking on transporters now," came the Klingon's clipped reply. "Where are you, sir?"

"I'm in a protected area, safe for now." The captain saw that Barclay and O'Connor were both less than two meters from the open airlock door with Geordi just behind them. They had seconds left now, and were all moving slowly, as if they were already suffering from the effects of the rapidly diminishing atmosphere.

Picard hit the controls to the door separating him from his people again, but it didn't budge. He recognized that the effort was futile—there was nothing he could do on the inside. Their fate was in Worf's hands now.

"Lieutenant, get them aboard that shuttle. That's an order!" the captain barked, enduring the frustration of watching the team's final struggle.

"Yes, sir," the Klingon replied evenly. And then the security chief made good on his word. Picard saw the shimmering of the transporter effect—and a moment later, the team disappeared.

"Mr. Worf?" the captain asked hopefully.

"They are aboard, and apparently sound, sir," said the security chief. The captain let out a long breath.

"Excellent work, Lieutenant. Excellent work." Picard saw the lights in the station flicker again, tentatively, and then attain a steady, if low, illumination.

"Captain, we are having difficulty locking transporters on to you. The structure of the station seems to be interfering with the transporter beam. If you can open the inner door to the airlock, we should be able to beam you aboard before—"

Picard cut him off. "I am afraid not, Mr. Worf. The controls are frozen, even though the station seems to have minimal power."

Suddenly, the captain's comm badge activated. "Sir, Riker here. Maybe the *Enterprise* would have more luck. If we come in closer, our transporters may be able to get through the interference."

"All right, Number One," Picard replied. "But proceed with caution. And take the *Enterprise* out of the area if there is any sign of danger. The station seems to be behaving erratically, at best. That goes for you too, Mr. Worf."

"Yes, sir," came their simultaneous replies.

Waiting, the captain saw that the level of illumination in the station was rising steadily. And the humming had resumed along with the occasional flash of power along lines in the ceiling, floor, and walls.

In the distance, Picard could see the *Enterprise* approaching on a direct line to the airlock. As the humming rose, louder than any time previously, he felt a growing sense of . . . unease. This rise in power seemed different than the other, previous surges, which were short in buildup and duration.

This increase seemed to be slower in coming, and the telltale hum deeper, more resounding.

Fortunately, the *Enterprise* was only a few thousand meters away. Picard decided that he would be glad to have this whole business resolved.

"Captain," Riker said. "Power readings are very high . . ." The voice disappeared into static: ". . . interference curve . . ." was the only other phrase he could make out clearly. The humming was thunderous now, as flashes of power ran through the panels of the station.

Something is going to happen, Picard thought with certainty.

"Commander Riker, remove the *Enterprise* to a safe distance now. Mr. Worf, do the same." The captain spoke into his communicator but could hear no discernible reply.

Watching out the small window, he could see the *Enterprise* and the shuttle clearly, and neither seemed to be moving. But the airlock's large, outer barrier was once again in motion. It rose quickly, and suddenly the airlock was completely open to space. It made little difference, Picard thought. The atmosphere was probably already gone.

He had only a flash of warning in the form of a momentary hiss—and then the door in front of him flew open as well.

The captain's arms flew outward and caught the doorway on each side, keeping him from being cast into space. But the pressure from behind was terrific, and the roar of air competed with the now deafening hum of the energy throbbing through the station.

As Picard felt his arms yielding to the outrush of the station's atmosphere, he hoped that the *Enterprise* would be able to lock on transporters quickly. He wouldn't last long in open space.

Briefly, he considered trying to pull himself into the corridor and escape into the interior of the station, but his arms were nearly exhausted. He was barely able to fight the flow of air as it was.

The captain guessed that he had less than a minute before he lost his battle and submitted to the inevitable. He began to hyperventilate intentionally, knowing that he would need to oxygenate his blood as much as possible to ensure maximum survival time in the vacuum of space.

But his efforts were cut short when something slammed into his right arm and shoulder. He registered the blow as a fleeting pressure, and then he felt himself flying through the airlock toward the open door.

In the same instant, he saw the station convulse around him, shaking as another surge of white energy shot through the superstructure. But this surge didn't dissipate. Instead it seemed to continue and grow. In that last instant, Picard was certain that the vacuum of space was the least of his troubles—and then a blast of whiteness took him.

Chapter Two

As a matter of reflex, Commander Riker turned his head and shut his eyes at the brilliant flash on the main viewscreen. A moment later, he remembered that the effort was unnecessary—the optical system automatically filtered out dangerously bright light.

Willing his eyes to stay open, Riker saw the nearest portion of the doughnut-shaped space station enveloped in a long pulse of blue-white light. It was as if the initial flash of energy was frozen in place for long seconds.

"Riker to shuttlecraft. Come in, Mr. Worf."

No response.

"Riker to Picard."

"No response to hails, sir," Data reported.

Damn, the first officer thought. "Sensors, Mr. Data? Can you get a fix on the shuttle?"

The android shook his head almost imperceptibly.

"No, sir, too much interference from the power surge."

Riker watched the station, its nearest segment awash in light, and felt completely and utterly useless to his captain and crewmates on the away team—who, for all he knew . . .

And then there was a momentary flicker in the cloud of light that hung around the station. After a moment, Riker was sure, the light was dimming.

"Power levels dropping," announced Data.

The first officer could see that for himself. The nimbus of light and energy quickly dulled to a haze and then disappeared, leaving the affected part of the station with small points of light emanating from the windows.

"Station power at nominal levels," Data said.

"Any sign of the away team?" Riker asked anxiously.

The android manipulated the controls at the ops station for a moment. "Yes. I have located the shuttle, and I am receiving life-form readings from within." The exec heard Troi let out a breath of relief beside him.

"However," Data went on, "shuttle communications and propulsion are out."

Riker got up. "Throw a tractor beam around the shuttle. I'll meet it in bay three." Making his way to the turbolift, he noticed that Deanna was right behind him. They didn't speak a word as they entered the compartment, but they didn't need to. The counselor wore her concern on her sleeve, and the first officer knew he was no harder to read than she was.

The ride seemed interminably long, though Riker

knew it was really only seconds. Then the doors opened and he practically sprinted to the landing area, just as the shuttle was being brought through the forcefield that separated the shuttle bay from the vacuum of space.

A quick glance told him what he needed to know. The shuttle was completely dark inside and out. That meant power had been knocked out completely. Still if they hadn't been hurt by the blast, the away team would be fine; even without life-support, a shuttle would be safe for at least an hour.

The craft touched down with the help of the bay tractor beams. The moment it touched the deck, Riker nodded to the two waiting technicians. The men fixed a capacitor to the shuttle next to the door and hit the switch.

The door slid open and Worf was outside almost instantly, face-to-face with the first officer.

"We were unable to retrieve the captain," the Klingon snapped. Riker could see the frustration in his scowl.

Geordi came out next, no less frustrated. "He was caught behind a bulkhead door in the station, sir. The shuttle's emergency transporters got to us, but couldn't reach *him.*"

"Commander," Worf interjected. "Request permission to take another shuttle immediately to effect rescue. If we act quickly, we may be able to avoid the next power surge."

Riker hit his communicator. "Data, do sensors show the captain on board the station?"

There was a brief pause as they awaited the android's reply.

"Negative," Data answered at last.

Riker cursed inwardly. "Any life signs at all?"

"Negative," the android replied again.

Looking at Worf, the first officer didn't need to guess how the security chief felt, because he felt the same way himself. *Damned useless.*

The swish of the opening door broke Geordi's concentration. He looked up from his work to see Counselor Troi entering with Lieutenant Barclay in tow. They approached the engineering console where Geordi and Data were working.

To the engineering chief's surprise, Barclay spoke first. "Sir, I'd like to help with the analysis."

Geordi was taken aback. He hadn't expected the counselor to put Barclay back on duty so quickly, if at all. The man had had his ups and downs on the *Enterprise,* and when he panicked on board the alien station, Geordi felt all of the old doubts about Barclay's future in Starfleet rearing up again.

Over the past couple of years, Geordi had watched as Barclay overcame what had once seemed like crippling self-doubt. And to his surprise, he had come to like the tall, thin engineer.

However, that didn't mean Barclay was cut out for starship duty. As much as Geordi didn't like to admit it, there was a very good chance that the young officer wouldn't recover from the day's events—at least not enough to remain in the Fleet.

But one look at the counselor told the chief engineer that she approved of the idea. Otherwise, she would have approached Geordi in private later.

Without further thought, he said, "Sure, Reg. We could use a fresh pair of eyes."

Turning to the main engineering console, he pointed to the data streaming across the terminal. "We're trying to build a computer model of what happened on the station, using records from the *Enterprise* and shuttlecraft sensors as well as the limited tricorder readings we took on board. Commander Data can bring you up to speed."

Geordi then turned his attention to Deanna. "Counselor, if you have a moment?" he asked.

Troi nodded, and the engineer led her into his office. Inside, he didn't waste a second.

"Counselor," he asked, "do you really think Barclay is ready for duty? I assume he told you what happened on the station."

"Yes," she replied. "He said he panicked when Mr. Varley was killed, and failed to respond to orders. He feels responsible. . . ."

"Look," La Forge interjected. "I don't have time to hold his hand right now. I've lost one of my staff and the captain is missing. I can't take any chances on Barclay falling apart."

The counselor kept her voice conversational. "Geordi, you've said more than once that Barclay often has good insights."

"Yes, but—"

"And," Troi added, "I'm not suggesting that you subject him to any pressure or make him part of another away mission. I'm merely hoping that you will make use of Barclay as a resource, just as you would have if today hadn't happened. It may help the investigation. And it would *certainly* help Lieutenant Barclay."

Geordi felt a response rising up in his throat, but he knew there was no sense behind it—only frustration. "Okay," the engineer said finally, "you're right." Nodding, he secured control of his emotions. "Right now," he admitted, "I can use all the help I can get."

Riker drummed his fingers on the conference-room table. Damn it, he hated waiting around at a time like this.

He tapped his communicator. "Lieutenant Burke, this is Commander Riker. Any change on the station?"

"No, sir. No change in power levels." And then the answer to the question the first officer hadn't asked. "And no life signs."

Damn.

Moments later, Geordi, Data, and Barclay filed into the room, with Beverly Crusher, Deanna, and Worf right behind them. They were right on time—early, actually. Riker nodded his approval. Until they knew the captain's status for certain, they would have to assume that every minute counted.

He turned immediately to Geordi. "What have you come up with?"

The chief engineer got up and walked over to the monitor at the front of the room. "Computer, replay station simulation one."

Immediately, the station appeared on the screen. It was already bright with light from the inside, as flashes of energy pulsed through a portion of the exterior structure.

"This," Geordi continued, "is the station's status at the moment when the away team reached the airlock —and the captain was locked out. And here is the shuttle's approach." He pointed out the small ship's trajectory. "This is also about where ship's sensors lost the landing party completely."

The engineer went on as the screen focused on the slightly raised airlock door. "Worf was able to get us out through the opening airlock, but there was still too much interference to even get a reading on the captain. A moment later, the shuttle's sensors got a flash of life signs when the inner door to the airlock opened."

Riker leaned forward. "If that's the case, then Captain Picard should've been thrown into space."

"True," Geordi allowed, touching the screen's controls and turning it blank. "And that's what the shuttle's sensors seem to indicate was happening. But the interference went up exponentially here, and the shuttle lost its shaky sensor contact. It seems, though, that the captain was not ejected into space. Instead, he simply . . . disappeared."

The first officer didn't hesitate to ask the next question, even though he dreaded the answer. "Is there any chance that the captain was . . . disintegrated by the energy fluctuation?"

Geordi shook his head slowly. "It's possible, but . . . I don't think so. All known methods of disintegration leave certain particle traces and electromagnetic signatures. The signatures we found here were entirely different. The closest analogy we can make is a super-high-energy transporter field with a strong subspace component."

"A transporter?" Riker asked.

The engineer nodded. "That would be consistent with some of our early analyses of the station's technology. A lot of it seems dedicated to sophisticated and very powerful transporter circuits."

Worf was scowling. "But sensors would have indicated if the captain had transported to any other site on the station."

"That's just it," Geordi said. "We think he transported *off* the station—*far* off the station."

Riker found himself vacillating between outright disbelief and budding hope. "But . . . there's nowhere to go. The nearest planet is light-years away."

The engineer shrugged. "The station had built up enough energy to transport the captain's mass much farther than that. There's something else, too." He paused a moment. "There was a subspace component to that energy. Which makes it possible that the captain was transported through *time* as well."

Riker heard Beverly gasp. "Is that *possible?*" he asked.

Geordi grunted. "*We* couldn't do it. But then again, we couldn't have built that station either."

"All right," the exec conceded. "But why, after thousands of years, did the station activate *now?*"

Geordi took his seat. "I think our transporter beams interacted with the station's systems and activated them somehow."

Riker nodded. "Then if we're operating on the assumption that all of this is possible . . . where is the captain? And can we use their equipment to bring him back?"

The engineer sighed. "Difficult to say. Even if we

could get it going, we wouldn't know where to look."
He turned and addressed the computer. "Computer,
run Picard parameters one."

A three-dimensional star chart appeared with a
glowing dot in the middle, surrounded by a large,
shaded circle, inside of which were a huge number of
stars.

Geordi continued. "By analyzing the power curve
and compensating for the captain's mass, we can
make a pretty good guess about the range of the alien
transporter. It's about one and one half sectors and
sometime in the last three hundred years. Of course,
the closer the final *spatial* destination is to the station,
the further through *time* the captain would have been
transported—and vice versa."

Riker considered the star chart. "Is there any
chance the captain could have been transported into
the future?"

The engineer shook his head. "No. Not according to
our analysis of the subspace transporter circuits. If he
was transported through time at all, it would have
been into the past."

"So we've got a search on our hands?" Riker asked.

"A pretty big one, sir," Geordi replied.

The first officer nodded. "Mr. La Forge, if the
Enterprise executes the search, can you get the alien
transporter going well enough to retrieve the captain
from the past—if that's where he is?"

Geordi thought for a moment in silence. "Given a
little time, I think I could figure it out."

"Would going back to the station be safe?" Riker
asked.

The engineer hesitated again. "Assuming we went

over by shuttle instead of by transporter, I think we could avoid setting off the equipment. Power is building up again on the station, but it's happening very slowly. We'd have plenty of time to get off if there was any trouble."

Riker bit the inside of his mouth. "All right. Prepare a team and the equipment you'll need. Just make sure you take every possible safety precaution."

He turned to Data. "How many star systems are in the search area?"

"One hundred and seventy-four, sir," said the android. "Of course, we should be able to eliminate most of those as uninhabitable. But before we continue, I should point out that given the size of even a single sector, the chances that the captain was transported to a planet, let alone a habitable one, are . . ." Data hesitated for a moment as he performed his calculations. "Very remote indeed."

Riker's hopes fell.

"Hold on, Data," Geordi said. "Don't forget the aliens who built the station had life support requirements similar to ours. They probably had safety devices to prevent the transport signal from depositing a living being anywhere but on a habitable world."

But the android wasn't satisfied with that response. "We have already observed that many of the station's systems, including some of its safety routines, were not functioning. We have no reason to believe—"

The first officer cut him short. "Mr. Data," he said. "It is my firm belief that Captain Picard is on a class M world somewhere in this sector. Any other situation would be unacceptable. We will search every possible system until we find him. Understood?"

"Yes, sir," the android replied evenly.

Riker cleared his throat. "Then the only remaining question is how quickly we can execute the search. Mr. Data?"

"I will have to actually plot the search pattern to be certain," the android told him. "But I would estimate at least ten days to two weeks."

"And we've got less than one week," Geordi muttered.

The first officer stood up, ending the meeting. "Then we had better get lucky and find him before it's up."

Leaving the meeting, Geordi was already making a list in his head: portable generators, portable computer, diagnostic kit, subspace transmitter, and general food and supplies for as much as a few weeks.

He entered the turbolift with Beverly, Troi, and Barclay. No one said a word, which gave Geordi a chance to work out the logistics of his mission.

The makeup of the team . . . that was a problem. It wouldn't pay to take very many of his people with him. They'd just be tripping over each other. Besides, he wanted to minimize the number of people he exposed to risk.

Earlier, he had held a brief staff meeting to tell the crew about Varley's death. His people were professionals, but the chief engineer knew the news had taken its toll on his staff. Undoubtedly, they were nervous. Well, he certainly could understand that.

The idea of spending an extended period back on the station gave *him* the creeps, too.

He'd have to ask for volunteers. He wouldn't order anyone to sign up.

"Sir?"

Geordi snapped out of his reverie and saw that he and Barclay were alone in the turbolift. Geordi had a vague memory of watching Beverly and Troi get off a moment ago.

"Yes, Reg?"

"I'd like to volunteer, sir," Barclay said, looking his superior square in the eye. "For the team that will be boarding the station, I mean."

"Volunteer?" Geordi repeated uncomprehendingly.

"Yes, sir. The captain lost several seconds getting me out of the access tunnel. And he only missed the airlock door by a second or two. If I hadn't—"

The engineering chief shook his head. "Reg, you can't do that to yourself. What happened to Captain Picard was nobody's fault."

"Maybe," Barclay answered. But Geordi could see that the man didn't believe him for a second. "Still, I would like to help if I can."

The commander gave a mental sigh. "To be perfectly frank, Reg, I don't know if I can take the chance. It may get rough out there."

"I know that," said Barclay, "And I'm ready, sir. I'd really like to help . . . and I'd like to show you . . . well, I'd like to show you what I'm made of, sir."

Geordi watched Barclay's expression turn deadly serious, and saw something he'd never seen before in the man: *resolve.*

That made two times that Lieutenant Barclay had surprised him today.

"Commander Riker," came Worf's voice from behind the first officer. "Priority-one message from Starfleet Command, for Captain Picard."

"I'll take it in the captain's ready room," Riker responded, already on his feet.

It took the commander only a few long strides to reach the ready room door and then the captain's desk. Once before, when Picard had disappeared, Riker had been extremely uncomfortable at that desk. Since then, he'd adjusted to command in the captain's place—though he still hated the circumstances.

Sitting down, the exec touched the control and the Federation seal popped onto the small viewscreen. A moment later, Admiral Kowalski's stern, weathered features replaced the seal. In less than an instant, the admiral recognized Riker. His scowl deepened.

"Where is your captain, Commander?"

"Missing, sir. I'm preparing my report now."

Kowalski frowned. "We've got a tense situation over here, Commander. Give me the highlights."

Riker quickly reviewed the discovery of the alien station, Picard's disappearance, and their plan for a rescue. The admiral listened carefully, with no change in expression.

"I assume," Kowalski said, "that Captain Picard briefed you on his plans for the summit."

"No, sir. There wasn't time."

"Damn," the admiral exclaimed.

Riker leaned forward. "Sir, I think we still have a

good chance of finding the captain and continuing the mission as planned. We still have six days—"

"Yes," Kowalski interrupted. "But no more. The Federation regards the summit as critical. To date, we have had little contact with the Gorn. The fact is, we really don't know what's going on there, but we have been getting reports of internal tension within their homeworld's governing body. If that tension reaches a crisis point, it could mean a number of things for the Federation—and none of them good. At best, we will have lost the hope of progress Picard's breakthrough gave us twenty-five years ago. And at worst . . . well, I don't intend to see the worst happen."

Riker saw from the look on Kowalski's face that the admiral was not exaggerating. The situation and possible consequences worried him greatly. "What can I do, sir?"

"You can get me Picard," Kowalski replied. "He's the closest thing we have to an expert on the Gorn. I want both him and the *Enterprise* at the Gorn homeworld in five days—at the outside."

Riker grunted. Now it was *five* days. "We could use some help in our search, sir. Are there any Starfleet vessels close enough to assist?"

Kowalski shook his head. "Not so much as a scout ship, commander. I'm afraid you're on your own." For a moment, the admiral allowed his expression to soften. "I'm sorry about your captain, Commander. But in the event you are not able to recover him, you are to proceed as per the new schedule—and complete the mission. Is that understood?"

The first officer nodded. "Yes, sir."

"I'll expect your full report on Captain Picard's disappearance in fifteen minutes. Kowalski out."

The admiral's face was replaced by the Federation symbol, which Riker shut off a moment later. As soon as the report was finished, he would have to call Geordi and Data to apprise them of the new developments. They were no longer just looking for a needle in a haystack, they were doing it with the barn burning down around them.

Chapter Three

A BUZZ *filled Picard's ears. He felt himself moving, and he soon recognized his motion as the familiar sensation of flying. Not the indiscernible hum of spaceflight, but the rocking progress of atmospheric flight. Suddenly he felt his craft buck, twist, and then resume its irregular but more or less steady course.*

A moment later, the captain was able to open his eyes. Outside the small cockpit was a strangely familiar haze of white. Picard knew he was inside heavy cloud cover. A sputter that broke the monotony of the buzz drew his attention forward—and he saw the craft's propeller rattle and come to a halting stop.

What followed happened quickly. As the captain felt the craft's sudden descent, he grabbed the joystick and rolled the vessel until it was upside down. Popping open the canopy, he felt a rush of wind on his face. As he removed his restraints, Picard pushed outward and let gravity take him. Free of the ship, he felt himself falling.

He reached out with his failing memory. There was something he still needed to do, something to pull . . . a cord. He clutched his stomach and found it, then yanked with all of his strength. . . .

A moment later, the captain felt the first stirrings of consciousness, as the dream left him and began to slowly fade. Odd, he thought. He hadn't had that dream since he was a cadet, though when he was very young it had haunted him. In the dream, he was a World War II fighter pilot from a story he had read —and he was bailing out of his Royal Air Force aircraft over the English Channel.

The dream always ended there. But in the story, the pilot woke up in a British hospital. After a short time, the pilot realized that the hospital was a fake, as were the nurses and doctors he had met. The pilot put together the clues, the minor discrepancies, and realized that the hospital and staff were a ruse perpetrated by the Germans to induce him to give up military secrets.

As a boy, Picard had had the dream a number of times—usually when he was confronted with any unfamiliar situation, such as a new school. In those days, he had assumed the dream was a reminder from his subconscious not to take new situations at face value—good advice that had been borne out by his experience in Starfleet. But the dream always left him uneasy, as if some of the surprises he faced might not be pleasant.

As the fog lifted slowly over his brain, the dream

faded even more from his consciousness. But the feeling remained: something was wrong.

Memory flooded back—the alien station, losing Ensign Varley, the airlock.

Forcing his eyes open, the captain tried to scan the room, but his vision was blurred. Even so, he could tell that he was not on the *Enterprise.* The ceilings were too low, and the walls were made of welded plates. And the sounds . . . they were not the sounds of his ship.

The first step, he knew, was to take better stock of his surroundings. Concentrating, he tried to pull himself into a sitting position. When his body responded sluggishly, he leaned back and threw himself forward, trying to use momentum to force himself up.

The pain was remarkable. It was centered in his head and his right shoulder, but seemed to radiate through most of his body. Picard immediately lay back down and waited for it to pass. After what seemed like a few minutes but was probably only a few seconds, the pain retreated to a point in his forehead and another point in his right shoulder.

Taking careful stock of himself, he determined that aside from his head and shoulder, the rest of him was in reasonably good condition. He moved his left hand and found that it could move freely. Using it, he traced the surface he was lying on and found it was a thin mattress on a hard platform. Similar to the beds in Beverly's sickbay but not identical.

It was that difference that made up the captain's mind. If he was in the hands of a friendly party, that party certainly wouldn't mind if he tried to leave to sort out what was going on. If, however, he was in the hands of a hostile force, his best chance lay in getting away quickly, while his captors assumed—not incorrectly, he mused—that he would be incapacitated.

For Picard, the memory of his time as a Cardassian prisoner was too fresh for him to take the risk of remaining still if he was in the hands of an enemy. If he erred here today, it would be on the side of caution.

The captain determined that his right arm was not only injured, it was immobilized in some sort of a sling. Using his left arm to support himself, he slowly rolled onto his left side and pushed himself up. With only that arm, he forced himself into a half-sitting position.

Next came his legs, which he moved to the side of the bed. Working them over the side, he let gravity take them, using the resistance of his muscles only to control their descent. As a result, he found himself in a full sitting position—though his legs were still not touching the ground.

The price was a gradual increase in the pain, but in a moment that had subsided. When his head was once again clear, Picard could see that the floor was perhaps a foot beneath his feet.

Bracing himself against the pain he was sure would follow, the captain slithered off the bed. His feet found purchase immediately, and he kept his left hand on the bed to steady himself. Aside from a brief period of queasiness, Picard was gratified to note that he felt no ill effects from the effort. Perhaps he was in better condition than he had first thought.

Scanning the room again, the captain noted that his

vision was improving, but the dim light prevented him from making out much detail. He could see that there were half a dozen empty biobeds like the one he had just occupied, as well as some additional equipment that he didn't immediately recognize.

He also saw that the room seemed to have only one door. Keeping his good hand on the biobed, he took his first step toward that door. Another step and he was out of reach of the bed. He kept moving forward in slow careful steps, until he reached the door—which he could now see was red.

Before he could step through, however, he heard voices. He couldn't be sure if they were speaking English, but he could tell that they were close and coming closer. For a moment he considered retreat, but knew this was probably his one chance at escape.

Picard stepped into the doorway and watched as the door slid open. Light poured in and partially obscured the two figures entering the room. Seeing one of the figures reaching out, the captain pressed forward, but recognized his mistake immediately: he didn't have the strength or the balance for the task. Hitting the newcomers, he crumpled to the floor.

A moment later, he was looking into a face. Forcing his eyes to focus, Picard could see that the face was human. A closer look told him the face was friendly. In fact—he suddenly realized—it was quite lovely.

He heard one word: "hypo." Then a brief hiss.

And then nothing.

Riker leaned forward from his place in the captain's chair. "Mr. Data?" he ventured.

The android, who was manning the ops station, turned his head.

"Sir, as you requested, I have mapped out a search pattern for the captain, with an eye toward maximizing our efficiency. Given the size of the search area and allowing for a single-orbit search pattern of each world, total time for the mission is nine days fourteen hours."

"That's still about four days more than we have," Riker observed.

"Yes, sir," Data concurred.

The first officer noted that the bridge's turbolift doors had opened. With his peripheral vision, he could see Geordi enter.

The android continued. "We face additional problems as well. If the captain is currently alive and if he is still in possession of a functioning communicator, then he will be easy to locate. However, we will have to allow for the possibility that he is lost in the past. In that case, finding signs of his appearance on a given world will be extremely difficult, especially considering that the *Enterprise* will be relying on a single orbital scan."

Riker shrank inside. Data was only saying what the first officer had known all along: that the mission they were embarking on was nearly impossible. Probably completely impossible, when you factored in the time-travel factor and the time constraints. He had secretly been hoping the android would come up with some magic solution to the problem.

"You're right, Data. But I'm depending on the captain's ingenuity. He should recognize that the

Enterprise will be searching for him. I'm counting on him to have left a sign, something that will be relatively easy to find."

"I think I may have found a way to take the guesswork out of the search, sir," Geordi announced, suddenly turning away from his engineering console.

Riker listened to the other man's solution, and found his spirits rising again. It was simple, it would work and, in fact, seemed as close to foolproof as they would get on this mission.

"Brilliant," he said simply. "Thank you, Mr. La Forge."

Geordi just nodded. The *Enterprise*'s chief engineer might have just saved the mission and the captain's life, but Riker could see that his mind was already on other matters.

"Are you ready to go right away?" he asked.

Geordi nodded. "Yes, sir. I'm just here to collect Data."

The android got up immediately and joined his fellow officer.

"Where's the rest of your team?" Riker asked.

"In shuttle bay one, checking our equipment. I'm keeping the party small—just myself, Data, O'Connor, and Barclay."

"Lieutenant Barclay?" Usually, he made an effort not to question an away team leader's choice of personnel, but this time his surprise betrayed him.

"Yes, sir," said the chief engineer. "I think he'll be an asset while we're sorting out the alien systems."

Riker didn't grill Geordi any further. Even though the first officer had heard the reports about the incident on the alien station and Barclay's performance, La Forge was the one who had been there. If the *Enterprise*'s top engineer thought Reg Barclay was fit for this away duty, then Riker was satisfied. But still, Barclay . . .

"Geordi, Data . . . I wish you luck," the first officer said.

"You too, sir," Geordi replied.

Riker nodded. "Report in via subspace at one-hour intervals and don't take any unnecessary risks. If you see any signs of trouble, any signs at all, don't wait— get off the station."

Once again, the engineer nodded his assent. Together, he and Data turned and entered the turbolift.

Perhaps two minutes later, Riker watched the shuttle's departure on the viewscreen. Once the craft was safely aboard the alien station, he would give the order for the *Enterprise* to warp out of orbit and begin the search. But first, he had one more duty to perform.

"Ensign Ro, in the ready room, please," he intoned.

Ro looked up from her forward position at conn.

Moments later, from behind the captain's desk, Riker watched Ro look at him expectantly, almost impatiently.

The commander paused, drew out the moment, and then began, "I'm assigning you to be acting first officer, Ensign—effective immediately."

"Sir?" Ro replied incredulously.

Riker didn't respond to that. He decided to wait until she had said what was on her mind. Of course, he didn't have to wait long. The ensign quickly composed herself.

"I don't understand, sir. There are more senior officers on board."

Suppressing a grin, Riker responded coolly. "Ensign, am I to understand that as your first duty as first officer, you are questioning my judgment in assigning you the job?"

"No, sir," Ro countered. "Your judgment is impeccable. But I am . . . curious about your logic."

Riker nodded. "Of course. You're correct when you say that there are more senior officers on board, but few with more command experience during crisis periods. And, frankly, I need Lieutenant Worf at the sensor console during the delicate maneuvers we will be performing."

The big man leaned forward. "For the next week or more, I'll be walking a very fine line, balancing my commitment to the search for Captain Picard against the importance of the Gorn summit—and the captain's own importance to that summit. I need someone who will not be afraid to speak up immediately if I'm stepping over that line. I'll also need creative thinking and additional options during the search and during the summit—if we are forced to go without the captain. For now, that will be your job."

Ro kept her face impassive, but Riker knew he had annoyed her by intentionally surprising her with the assignment. He couldn't deny that he had enjoyed catching her momentarily off guard, but his reasoning was much more practical—right now, he needed her on her toes.

"Permission to make preliminary recommendations now, sir," the ensign asked.

"Granted."

Ro's face took on a serious cast that was almost a scowl. "I recommend that we immediately abandon the search for Captain Picard and proceed to the Gorn summit. Frankly, the odds against finding the captain alive, in the time allotted to us, are astronomical. Our time and resources would be better spent formulating a contingency plan for the negotiations." She paused. "Your loyalty to the captain is admirable, sir. But in this case, the summit must be the overriding concern. We cannot afford to let it fail."

Riker's response was clipped and forceful. "I'm assessing the risk differently, Ensign. Our chances of success with the Gorn are considerably higher with Captain Picard, because of his experience, and because he is a known and respected quantity among them. In addition, I have a hunch that we will be able to find him. A hunch is a command tool, and playing it is a command prerogative."

He knew that in her place, he would be raising the same questions. But he also knew that he had already decided on his immediate course of action.

Ro maintained her composure, though Riker could see that it was taking some effort. "I recognize the value of intuition in command situations," she said. "But even a course of action based on a hunch must have a reasonable chance of success. I see no such chance here."

"I see it differently, Ensign," Riker said, letting a note of finality creep into his voice. It was time to get back to the search, and—

"You've never lost anyone, have you?" Ro asked.

Riker glared.

"Wait a second," she said, eyeing him closely. "You have, haven't you? Who was it? A parent, a sibling?"

"None of your damn business," he replied.

"You're right," she conceded. "But it doesn't matter. Because losing one person doesn't tell you what it's like to lose everyone. Do you know what that means, to lose everyone? We Bajorans almost lost our whole world. And you know what that teaches you? It teaches you that some losses are inevitable. You've got to accept them and move on. Because if you can't save everything, you can at least save something."

"Please, Ensign," Riker said sarcastically, "*Don't* hold back."

"Frankly, sir, I don't think I can afford to. The stakes of the summit are too high." Ro paused for a moment, in which she seemed to be consciously reining herself in. When she spoke again, her voice had softened.

"Sir, when I was sixteen, I was part of a perimeter guard at a hidden weapons factory. In my squad was a fifteen-year-old boy who began following me around. He was small for his age, slow in drills, and scared most of the time. But he kept up his end. Because he was persistent and because in the end I had no choice, we became friends. One night, our squad was hit and we scattered. I saw him go down.

"Instead of leading the defense, I wasted precious seconds going back for him. Well, I got there in time to watch him die—and then returned to my squad just in time to catch the last few moments of a massacre. I went back for one person, and because of that we lost an entire squad. Bajorans learn young to cut their losses. I did."

It was Riker's turn to be caught off guard. He had served with Ro for almost two years, and she had never spoken about her past to him. Certainly, she had never revealed anything so personal. He was tempted to respond, but decided not to make the situation any more difficult for her.

And in any case, his mind was made up for now.

"Thank you for your counsel, Ensign. While we continue the search, I will be counting on you to research the Gorn as thoroughly as you can—check rumors, tall stories, anything you can find—and formulate a contingency plan for the negotiations. Dismissed." Then he shot her a look that made it clear the discussion was closed.

Ensign Ro acknowledged his command with a nod, turned, and left. When the door shut, Riker watched it carefully. It would only be a moment.

The chime came right on schedule. "Come," Riker intoned, watching the door. Deanna walked into the room, wearing the blue uniform that she now wore during duty hours. Too bad, he thought. He liked the green dress better.

"Counselor," he nodded.

"A challenge?" Troi said without preamble.

"No more than what I expected."

"How do you feel about it, though?"

Riker shrugged. "It's her job now to raise questions about important command decisions. And to recommend options," he said evenly.

"And how do you feel about the questions she has raised?" Troi probed.

"You mean how do I feel about my decision to search for the captain?" Deanna responded with a nod, and Riker thought about it, carefully. In many ways everything that Ro had said was absolutely true. The logical thing to do would be to abandon the search and commit all of his resources to the summit. To do anything else would be bucking pretty strong odds. And all he had was a hunch that he was doing the right thing.

The exec looked inside himself for that pit of certainty that had been so easy to find several hours ago. He could still find it, he was pleased to learn.

Looking up at Troi, he knew that the counselor had finished the job that Ro had started. For now, he was sure.

When Picard opened his eyes again, the room came into focus with surprising speed and clarity. He had expected the pain that he still remembered vividly from his last conscious moment, but now he felt fit and lucid.

The captain kept his head still as he looked up at the ceiling and scanned the room with his eyes. He immediately recognized the modular, prefabricated construction. He had seen it before on older bases and some Starfleet sponsored colonies of different sorts.

Then a face obscured his vision. It was human, a female. Judging by the faint lines around the vibrant, green eyes and the mouth, and the short, dark hair peppered with gray, Picard guessed that she was about his age, and—he noted almost as an afterthought— she was quite attractive. She looked him over with a professional eye that he had seen Beverly use before. A doctor, then.

Her features softened a bit as she spoke. "You're human, you know."

For a moment, the captain could think of no response. "Am I?"

She nodded. "Yes, I have scanned you and everything checks out. You're human, all right."

"To be perfectly honest, Doctor," Picard ventured, "I'm surprised there was any doubt."

"Not doubt as much as speculation," she said, her eyes twinkling. "You see, we don't get many unannounced visitors here." She ran a small scanner of a type the captain didn't recognize over him. Then, after studying a readout above his head, she returned her attention to him.

"Would you mind telling me where 'here' is?" Picard asked.

"You are in my infirmary," the doctor said evenly.

"And where is that?"

For a moment, she looked at him askance. "Are you suggesting that you don't know what planet you are on?"

The captain shook his head. "I am suggesting nothing. I am saying it plainly. Where am I?"

To Picard's surprise, she smiled broadly. "You really expect me to believe you came all the way out here and don't know where 'here' is?"

"Yes," he said. "Please, indulge me. I can tell you with certainty that I did not come here willingly."

She regained her professional demeanor. "All right, I'll assume for the sake of argument that you are telling the truth."

"That's very gracious of you," the captain replied.

"Not at all," she told him. "It will simply make our conversation easier on both of us if I assume what you tell me is the truth. That frees you from having to be convincing and it frees me from having to be on my guard. Besides, if you're lying, it'll come out soon enough. For now, I prefer to see the best in you. You have what my father used to call a kind face."

He grunted. "In that case, would you please tell me where I am?"

She thought for a bit, then shook her head. "Sorry. That sounds like the commodore's area. You'll have to wait for the commodore to discuss it with you."

"Really?"

"Really," she confirmed. "In the meantime, would you care to tell me where you're from?"

Picard sighed. "I don't suppose I could get off easily and claim amnesia?"

The doctor harrumphed. "Not likely. Do you intend to try?"

"That depends on whether or not you would believe it."

She smiled a second time. "Again, not likely."

The captain nodded and took stock of himself. His right arm was in a sling and a quick examination with his left hand confirmed that he had a bandage on his head.

"A few abrasions, one medium concussion, and a dislocated shoulder," the doctor offered. "No permanent damage. Because of the concussion, I have resisted giving you painkillers. I had to partially reattach some ligaments and tendons in your shoulder, but they'll be fine. The residual swelling and soft-tissue damage will correct itself in a few weeks."

"Weeks?" asked Picard. Beverly would have had him as good as new in a few *days*.

The woman shrugged. "Sorry if that's inconvenient, but I think it's the best you'll do. I could refer you to another doctor, I suppose—but there isn't one for two dozen light-years."

"No, I'm sorry. I meant no offense," said the captain. "I appreciate your efforts on my behalf."

"Not at all," she told him. "You should have pretty good movement in the arm in about a week. Though for now, I'll bet it smarts."

Smarts? thought Picard. He felt a growing sense of unease. There was something wrong here. "When can I speak to the commodore?"

"He'll be by shortly. He's out checking the—" The doctor caught herself. "You know, he tells me I'm a lousy security risk. I suspect he's right. Anyway, he'll be back shortly, Mr. . . . ?"

She was looking at him expectantly. The captain hesitated for a moment, as something told him to withhold the truth. "Hill," he supplied. "Dixon Hill."

"Well, Mr. Hill, I'm Julia Santos. It's a pleasure to meet you—even under the circumstances."

"The pleasure is mine," Picard said, forcing a smile. He would feel better when he could speak to someone in charge, someone who would be able to answer his questions. He had a growing sense that this place was not the safe harbor it appeared to be.

The loud crash was enough to make Geordi jump. From his crouched position, that meant lifting his head, which in turn connected solidly with the control panel he was working under. Ignoring the pain, he scrambled out from under the thing and was out the door with Data on his heels. At the far end of the hallway, he found Barclay and O'Connor working on another open control panel—this one beside the now-closed door to the airlock.

Inside, the shuttle they had taken here was safe and sound. Geordi breathed a sigh of relief.

Barclay looked sheepish. "Sorry, sir. My fault. I tripped the mechanism."

Data had his tricorder out and was scanning. "No sign of a recent or impending power surge," the android said after a moment. "Station power functioning continuously at minimal levels."

Geordi took a moment to feel the back of his head, which had begun to throb dully where it had hit the panel. Finding the tender spot, he was certain that he would have a good-sized bump there within the hour.

"That's okay, Reg. We're all just a little jumpy," he said.

Peering inside the open control panel, the engineer could see the places where Barclay and O'Connor had spliced into the alien circuitry. "How's this going?" he asked.

"Fine, sir," the thin man replied. "We'll have this on-line in a few minutes."

Geordi nodded his approval. Actually, Barclay had done remarkably well since their return to the station. The lieutenant's assignment had been to install safety devices on each of the exits, beginning with the airlock door, and he had been successful almost immediately in isolating the circuits that operated the opening and closing mechanisms in it. Then, using small portable generators and switches they had brought from the *Enterprise,* Barclay and O'Connor had created a closed power loop for each door, so that it could now be opened and closed only by the large button controls they had installed—red for down and green for up. These were a great improvement over the still indecipherable alien controls.

After the safety system on the doors was in place, Barclay and O'Connor would set up the portable forcefield generators at the airlock door and at two points about a hundred meters apart in the corridor. These forcefields would operate on independent power and preserve the atmosphere in case a door opened to the outside somewhere nearby and the station began to decompress. The forcefields would give them a working area that included the airlock, the control room, and the various access tunnels that they would need.

Of course, they were assuming that the control room would be able to operate the transport functions in this part of the station. But it was a fair bet, based on their scans of the equipment during the brief functioning moment it took to transport Captain Picard.

Unfortunately, Geordi couldn't be sure until he knew more about how the alien technology operated. So far, he and Data hadn't had much luck figuring out the subspace physics involved in the time/space transport circuits. In fact, Barclay had obtained more tangible results working with the doors.

"Good work, Reg. Would you please make this as fast as possible? We could use some help."

"Yes, sir," came Barclay's steady reply.

Geordi and Data headed back to the control room.

"I have noticed that Lieutenant Barclay's performance has been exemplary," the android remarked. "He seems to have overcome the fear that immobilized him during the crisis."

Geordi nodded. "Back then he was responding to an immediate threatening set of circumstances—tangible danger from the door. Now he doesn't have that kind of intense pressure. The question is, will Barclay be able to perform in a danger situation when a few seconds mean the difference between life and death?"

Data appeared to mull it over for a moment. "It seems ironic," he said finally, "that the fear response, which is intended to protect humans from danger, can immobilize them just when quick and decisive action is required."

The engineer had never thought of fear in those terms. But, of course, his friend was right. "Call it a design flaw, Data—and be glad it's not one you share."

The android nodded. Geordi noted that Data was more apt than he used to be to simply accept the inconsistencies of human existence without probing too deeply.

The bottom line, the engineer knew, was that some emotional responses just *were*. Some people—like Captain Picard, for instance—were rocks under pressure. Some fell apart, or froze as Barclay had. How would the lieutenant respond if faced with a similar situation? Especially if things got rough and his life—or maybe even all of their lives—depended on quick action? It was hard to say.

Of course, Barclay had made a real effort to face his fear when they arrived, by volunteering to retrieve Ensign Varley's body from the control room and place it in the shuttle's temporary stasis chamber. That had surprised Geordi, who had been prepared to do it himself. But when the crunch came, there was no way to know if Barclay would play his hand well or fold.

The chief engineer brushed the subject aside. He had to get to the alien transport system on-line. So far, they hadn't been successful in getting the monitor in the control room working again. In fact, they hadn't been able to even isolate the power and imaging circuits. Maybe when Barclay and O'Connor were through with the doors, they would have better luck working all together.

The doctor entered, followed by a man in a gold tunic. Picard placed his age at about sixty. He had neatly trimmed, silver-gray hair and firm if weather-beaten features. He wore his command on his face and in his posture.

The captain was certain that this was the commodore. And judging by the man's serious, almost sour expression, he was also certain that this was not a social visit.

Picard made those determinations in perhaps two seconds, but his most important observation took him some additional time to comprehend. The gold tunic, the starburst crest on the commodore's chest: the captain was looking at a Starfleet uniform of a type that had not been worn in about a hundred years.

The implications of that were staggering, and could mean only one of two things: either he had been sent back in time by the alien technology as Geordi had suggested was possible, or this place and these people were an elaborate setup.

But the idea of a setup was already beginning to lose credence as he considered it. There would be little point in anyone going to the trouble of setting up such a scenario, when it would so quickly put him on his guard.

No, Picard was now nearly certain that he was as much as one hundred years in the past, on a Starfleet base. Of course, this was the more chilling of the two possibilities. The dangers of upsetting the time stream were grave. Besides ethical and Prime Directive concerns, he was in very real danger of altering history just by being there. Even a small misstep could have incalculable repercussions.

As the commodore studied him, the captain realized that he had only one path open to him. He would have to make certain that, at all costs, he avoided doing anything that could upset the flow of history. At this point, his most fundamental duty was to involve himself as little as possible with these people—until he could find a way to get back to his own time.

Then it struck Picard that the damage could have already been done. His communicator was not on his medical smock. If the commodore had it, even a cursory examination would reveal advanced circuitry that would not exist for the better part of a century.

The commodore was watching him closely with either concern or suspicion, or both, on his face. Had the captain betrayed his surprise when he saw the Starfleet uniform?

"Welcome, Mr. Hill," the man said in an even tone. "I'm Commodore Travers of Starfleet."

"Dixon Hill," Picard replied. "And I thank you for your hospitality and medical care."

Travers harrumphed. "We were pleased to offer it, especially considering how lucky you were that we found you at all."

The captain could see the man making an effort to be personable. He was doing exactly what Picard himself would have done, trying to establish a rapport with the subject—while still watching him very closely.

"The ridge where you were found," Travers continued, "is given to frequent landslides. Up until now, we have made a real effort to avoid it. But fortunately for you, we had a team installing seismic monitoring equipment in the area yesterday."

"Yes, indeed," the captain replied. "Very fortunate."

"And something of a surprise for us," the commodore went on. "We haven't had many ships come out this way, and I doubt our scans would have missed you if you preceded the establishment of the colony on this planet."

While Travers spoke, Santos was watching him carefully, as if she were waiting for him to upset her patient. Picard realized that, though it wasn't formal yet, he was being interrogated. He'd need to frame his answers carefully.

"Actually, I arrived recently," he said. "I suspect, not much before you found me."

"Frankly, I find that hard to believe," the commodore said, an edge creeping into his voice. "We have had no ships out this way in over six months." Whatever this man's talents, Picard decided, diplomacy was not one of them. The captain could see that the minimal civility he was receiving came at some cost to Travers.

"Then allow me to tell you my story," Picard replied. He would have to defuse the situation rather quickly, before the commodore made the encounter a confrontation. "I am the master of a small commercial transport called the *Stargazer*—a fast ship with which we did a fair business transporting rare metals, until we were set upon by Orion pirates. The *Stargazer* is, or was, almost completely unarmed; we had always depended on speed to avoid trouble. But the Orions used cloaking technology to get close, and it was all over in moments."

"Your crew?" Travers asked.

"Dead."

The commodore nodded. "But they left you alive?"

"This Orion commander was superstitious about killing the master of a ship. He approached this planet under cloak and then beamed me down."

"Into a geologically unstable and dangerous area," the commodore interjected.

"Yes," the captain maintained. "I think the Orion's

superstition only prevented him from killing me directly."

"Interesting," commented Travers. "My sympathy for the loss of your ship and crew." A pause. "I will have to file a report to Starfleet about the new threat represented by Orions with cloaking technology." However, the commodore's features did not soften. Clearly, he was still skeptical.

"I can attest to that threat," added Picard.

Travers cleared his throat. The captain could see that the interrogation was nearly over, for now. "One minor detail, Mr. Hill. We couldn't find a match for your retinal scan in our data banks. Are you from Earth?"

"Yes," Picard answered. "Though I have not been back for some time."

The commodore frowned. "I'm sure that Starfleet will have more complete records. I'll order a search when I file my report." He made a show of checking the chronometer on the wall. "I'm afraid I must be going, though I'm sure we'll have time to talk again soon." He turned to depart, but stopped partway and eyed the captain again. "By the way, Dr. Santos tells me you have a bionic cardiac replacement."

Travers let the statement hang in the air. He watched Picard closely. Clearly, this was a matter of some importance to him.

"The result of a youthful indiscretion," the captain replied.

The commodore's eyes narrowed a notch. "What I find curious is that it matches no known model my people have ever seen. The power cell is, well . . .

extraordinary. And the device seems to be engineered on the molecular level to mimic your cell structure, presumably to prevent rejection."

Picard shrugged. "I bought the device from a Murani trader. Frankly, I don't know how it works."

Travers cleared his throat. "Well then, I hope you won't mind if Dr. Santos runs a few more scans on it. My engineering staff is fascinated by the technology."

"Of course," the captain said, wondering if he had already damaged history. The power cell and molecular construction techniques used in it would not be invented for many years still.

"Excellent," responded the commodore.

Picard held up a hand. "One question before you go, sir. What planet am I on?"

Travers seemed a little taken aback by the question, but he answered it nonetheless. "Cestus Three, of course."

The captain's breath caught in his throat. *Cestus III?* Suddenly everything made perfect sense. Both Santos and Travers had seemed familiar to him. Now he knew why. They had been mentioned in the history tapes on the Cestus III massacre. Picard fought to keep his voice steady while he asked his final question.

"And what is the stardate?"

The commodore looked at him. "Three-oh-four-one-point-six," he said. "Anything else?"

The captain shook his head. "No. Thank you."

Travers frowned. "In that case, good day, Mister Hill. Doctor Santos, could we have a word outside?"

Picard watched them go, while running the numbers in his head. The calculation took him only a split second, and confirmed his worst fears. In less than four days, the Gorn would attack the colony on Cestus III, killing Commodore Travers, Dr. Santos, and every man, woman, and child in the colony—save for one individual. The captain couldn't remember the name of the survivor, but he was absolutely certain it was *not* Dixon Hill.

Chapter Four

FOR PICARD, there was no question of what he needed to do. Escape was his only option. The events on Cestus III would have to unfold without him.

In fact, history would be served best if he kept his contact with the colonists to a minimum. The end was only three days away now and—though it was unfortunate that a colony full of fine people like Dr. Santos would meet such a tragic fate—that fate was nevertheless inevitable.

The only question that remained for him was *how* to proceed. In three days, the Gorn would arrive, and Picard needed to be far enough away to completely escape their notice.

The captain knew the colony would be ceded to the Gorn after Captain Kirk's first encounter with the reptilian beings. But that agreement would be negotiated by subspace radio without a face-to-face meeting.

And, as far as Picard was aware, no Federation personnel would return to Cestus III up until his own time. In fact, shared use of facilities was one of the items on his agenda for the upcoming Gorn summit.

Upcoming, the captain thought. It seemed to him to be only a few days away. In fact, he still felt the nagging need to make his preparations for the meeting —though he had a century, not days, to prepare.

Picard retained hope that he would somehow still be able to fulfill his mission. There was a good possibility that Commander Riker would deduce what had happened to him by examining the alien station and the ship's sensor readings. But would Riker be able to trace his captain's transport through time and space? Or would his Number One simply assume that Picard was dead?

Of course, it was possible that the station had been destroyed in the surge that sent the captain here. But if the station *had* survived, his crew might find a way to use the technology to retrieve him. To prepare for that possibility, Picard would need to find a way to leave a signal that could be found by Starfleet in the future. At the very least, he knew, he had a duty to record what had happened to him and make a final report. But how?

The questions were almost endless. In the midst of them, the captain realized that the only certainty was the fate of the colony. Unless he left the area quickly, his would be the same fate. He needed to begin collecting supplies and planning his escape.

He was almost certainly up to the task from a physical standpoint. After a full night of sleep, he felt refreshed. The pain in his head was gone, and though his immobilized right arm would be a handicap, it would not be a critical one.

Throwing his feet over the side, Picard got out of bed. The infirmary was perhaps seven meters across, with a total of five beds. At the front of the room stood the supply cabinet that Dr. Santos had indicated that morning, when she told him that they had cleaned his clothes—and that they would be returned to him when he was released from her care.

The cabinet was unlocked and full of dressings, bandages, slings, and other innocuous pieces of medical equipment—nothing that would be of much immediate value to him. However, there was a duffel bag on the upper shelf, which he opened to find his uniform neatly folded inside.

Taking the duffel bag with him, the captain ventured into Dr. Santos's adjoining office. The space appeared to be empty—but to be certain, he called to the doctor in a low voice. When he received no response, he made his way behind her desk and tried the door there. It opened with a push, and Picard could see a small room lined with Santos's more important medical supplies.

Moving quickly, he scanned the place for what he might need. Looking past the drugs and medicines, he located a row of neatly stacked tricorders. Taking one from the back, he moved on to the field medical kit—both pieces of equipment would be extremely useful. There was nothing else he could use at the moment, but he made a mental note to remember the open door.

Returning to Santos's office, Picard carefully closed the closet. Next, he relied on a hunch and began opening the drawers in the doctor's desk. He went through each of them quickly, making an effort not to disturb the contents. Finally, in the back of the bottom drawer, he found what he was looking for.

Pulling out the small type-I phaser, the captain studied the outmoded device—which until then he had only seen in the Fleet museum. The range, accuracy, and battery power would not be nearly as great as the equipment he was used to, but it would suffice for now. With any luck, he wouldn't need to use it at all.

Picard then closed the drawer, making a note of the lax security procedures. The lack of precautions was not out of the ordinary in a small, closed community, where everything was based on trust. That thought caused him a pang of guilt. Not only was he stealing from the colonists, he was doing so in a Starfleet facility—and from a doctor who had been extremely kind to him.

The logical arguments to support what he was doing came quickly to him, but he brushed them aside. The issue was not what was logical or practical, it was a matter of right and wrong. And at the moment, despite duty and compelling necessity, Picard knew that what he was doing violated his personal code of conduct. For that moment, he felt as if he was bringing something dark and sinister to the small secluded colony.

Quickly putting the equipment into the duffel bag, the captain placed it back on the shelf in the supply cabinet near his bed. Then he sat at the desk set aside for patients and turned on the reader. The screen lit up with prompts, but he ignored them and sat in silence.

His wait was not long. In a few minutes, Dr. Santos entered, smiling warmly at the sight of him sitting at the desk.

"You're out of bed," she observed.

"Yes. How soon can we discuss my release?" he asked.

Santos feigned a frown. "I'll assume you're asking only because you're anxious for activity—and not out of a desire to escape your harsh treatment here."

Picard allowed himself a smile. "You've been very gracious, and my care has been excellent, but I'm anxious to do something."

The doctor seemed genuinely pleased. "In that case, consider yourself released. Your shoulder doesn't need any more attention, just a chance to heal naturally. Give me a moment and I will arrange for temporary quarters for you—although I don't know how long *temporary* will be." She looked vaguely apologetic. "It's sometimes weeks between supply ships. And it may be longer than that before you find one going your way. The fact is, you may be with us for a little while."

Picard nodded. "In that case, I will have to try to make myself useful."

Santos shrugged. "If you have any technical skills, I know our chief engineer would love to get his hands on you. And if you stay for a couple of weeks, you'll be here when our sensor array goes on-line. It's actually an exciting time for us." She turned and headed for her office. "Just give me a minute."

The captain found that the smile remained on his face. The doctor had an enthusiasm that was undeniably infectious. But his smile faded a moment later when he realized how short her future would be.

Santos returned a moment later. From the serious cast of her eyes, Picard could tell immediately that something was wrong.

"Commodore Travers has assigned you guest quarters," she announced, not without a hint of cynicism. "He has also assigned you an . . . escort. Lieutenant Harold will be here shortly."

The captain could see what was troubling her. The same thing troubled him, though for different reasons—a Starfleet escort would complicate his own plans immeasurably. In the end he said, "The commodore is merely being cautious," keeping his tone noncommittal.

"He's a good commander, but a suspicious man," Santos remarked. Evidently, she hadn't foreseen this turn of events, and she was embarrassed by it.

Picard grunted. "I quite understand. I'm a commander myself, remember. And I have found that there are two ways to face the unknown. One is to embrace it, the other is to proceed with caution. In the past, perhaps, I have lacked caution, which is one of the reasons I'm here—so clearly, caution has its place.

"Besides," he went on, "I have given him a great deal to be suspicious about. And since I have nothing to hide, I certainly don't mind being kept under surveillance." It troubled him to lie so casually, but duty gave him no option.

As it happened, the lie was effective. Santos cheered a bit. "I'm sure it won't be for long," she offered.

At that moment, a young man in a gold lieutenant's uniform entered. He was in his mid-to-late twenties, with dark hair and a serious, earnest expression. It was his escort, Lieutenant Harold. Picard was certain of it.

Santos turned to address the lieutenant, keeping her tone light and informal. "Lieutenant Matthew Harold, may I present Merchant Captain Dixon Hill." The newcomer smiled reflexively and offered his hand. Midway, however, he reconsidered—no doubt troubled by the friendly informality the doctor had initiated with her almost social introduction. To his credit, Harold only hesitated for a moment, and then followed through with his hand.

"Captain," the younger man said, nodding.

"Lieutenant," Picard responded. "But please, my name is Dixon Hill. I'm afraid that with the loss of my ship, the rank has lost most of its meaning for me."

Harold nodded again. "I'm here to escort you to your quarters, which are next to mine. If you need anything or have any questions, I'll be happy to help you."

"Thank you," responded the captain. "I will want to discuss securing passage on the next supply ship. In the meantime, perhaps we could discuss the possibility of getting me assigned to one of your technical departments."

Harold seemed taken aback by the captain's friendliness, as much as by the suggestion of an assignment. No doubt, he had expected Picard to act more suspiciously—more like a prisoner.

The captain would need to establish trust with his escort, to gain the kind of freedom of movement his escape plan would require. Santos had unknowingly helped by setting a casual tone. Picard would now have to do his best to follow through.

"And if you don't mind, Lieutenant, I will accompany you both," Santos interjected.

Harold merely nodded, masking any further surprise at the unexpectedly warm atmosphere he'd found in the infirmary.

Then Santos turned to Picard. "Would you like to put your clothing back on? It's in good condition, and you might feel more at home. It's right in the closet here."

"No, thank you," Picard said quickly. If the doctor opened his duffel, his chances of escape would disappear in an instant. "You see, it's my uniform from my ship. At the moment, the associations aren't pleasant."

Santos appeared to accept the explanation. "Sorry," she told him. "Give me a moment, all right?" Abruptly, she disappeared into her office and came out with a pair of simple, blue coveralls, the kind that technicians still wore in the twenty-fourth century. Then she reached into the supply cabinet and pulled down the captain's duffel bag. For a moment Picard caught his breath, wondering if she would notice the extra weight. Fortunately, she didn't, and merely placed the duffel and the clothes on his bed.

"Doctor . . . did you recover a small gold insignia when you found me?" the captain asked.

Santos considered it. "No, I didn't. Was it important?"

He shook his head. "Not really. Just a sentimental attachment."

"You must have lost it in the rock slide," she decided. "I'd like to tell you that we can look for it, but the area isn't safe."

"Quite all right," Picard responded.

Well, that answered the question of what had happened to his communicator. It was fortunate. The device would have raised questions that he wouldn't have been able to answer without severely compromising the Prime Directive—if not history itself.

Dr. Santos and Lieutenant Harold left, granting him his privacy. Changing out of the infirmary pajamas, the captain took extra care to jostle his right arm as little as possible as he removed the sling and put on the coveralls. When he emerged into the infirmary's outer offices, he found Santos and Harold locked in low conversation.

"Ready," Picard said. The lieutenant offered to carry the duffel bag, but the captain politely declined. Once outside, he was enthralled by the sight of the outpost.

He had studied the raid on Cestus III years before —during his encounter with the Gorn on the *Stargazer*—so he was familiar with the layout. The compound was basically a semicircle of interconnected, low structures that from a distance looked like a curved wall. But Picard knew that the visible structures were merely the entrances to larger, subterranean buildings. Most of the compound's living and working space was underground—an effort to avoid the desert heat on the planet's surface.

The infirmary was roughly at the apex of the

semicircle. On his left were the residences and dining area. To his right was the life-support section, above which were large globes that Picard identified as sensor relays. Behind and beyond the semicircle, the captain recognized, was the massive sensor array, laid out across hundreds of yards of flat plains. Nearby would be the warp generator that ran the array.

Inside the semicircle stood two medium-sized buildings, which Picard knew were the administrative offices and the armory. In between them and farther ahead was the fusion generator that the colony depended on for power. Past the generator, in the distance, the captain could see low mountains.

Picard had expected all of this. Yet somehow, it looked wrong. For a moment, he couldn't place what it was, then it came to him: the colony was alive. The buildings were intact, recently created structures. And they were full of people. Technicians, scientists, and people in civilian clothing working, walking, or just talking to one another.

The few images the captain had seen of Cestus III were taken from Kirk's *Enterprise*'s logs. They showed a devastated compound, scorched with black scars, full of craters and rubble. Much of the basic structure and layout of the colony was visible in these pictures, but barely.

He was not prepared for casual activity, nor for the clean, slightly fragrant smell in the air. Picard's study of the outpost had centered on its death; he had not been prepared to confront the fact of its life.

"Sir?" Harold asked gently.

The captain snapped out of his reverie. "I'm sorry, I was staring. It's just that I have not been on a planet in some time," he replied. At least partially true, he thought.

They made the short walk to the residence area in silence.

"You're in residence eleven-H," Harold said. "I'll be in eleven-J. If you'll follow me—"

"That will be all, Lieutenant," Santos interrupted.

"Excuse me, Doctor?" Harold asked.

She smiled, but with a certain underlying forcefulness. "I will take charge of Mr. Hill from here."

The lieutenant stiffened. "I'm sorry, Doctor, but Commodore Travers ordered me to escort the . . . to escort Mr. Hill to his quarters and to see that—"

"He was made comfortable," Santos interjected again. "You've certainly seen that he arrived. And if you don't mind, I will take care of the rest. Mr. Hill has been cooped up in the infirmary for two days. If he's agreeable, I would like to offer him a tour of our humble outpost. I'm sure the commodore would approve, and I'm prepared to take full responsibility for Mr. Hill."

Harold listened carefully as the doctor spoke. When she finished, he simply sighed. Clearly, he knew when he was beaten—and when he was outranked. "All right, Doctor. You can reach me by communicator if you need anything."

As Harold smiled graciously in defeat, the recognition that had been nagging at Picard rushed to the surface. Staring at the lieutenant, he added some radiation burns to the likeness, hardened the expression, and then gave the face a frightened cast. When he was finished building the picture in his mind, Picard knew whom he was looking at: Lieutenant

Matthew Harold, the sole survivor of the Gorn massacre on Cestus III.

Except that instead of the haunted visage he remembered from pictures of the survivor, the captain was looking at an animated young face. The remainder of Picard's memory re-formed itself instantly. He remembered the logs from the *Enterprise,* the nearly hysterical face of Lieutenant Harold as he insisted that "there had to be a reason" for the horror he had witnessed.

Lost in thought, Picard jumped slightly when Santos spoke to him. "Your crew . . . you must have been close to them," she said gently. The captain turned to her, confused for a moment. Of course, she was referring to the loss of his merchant crew. "You must miss them," she added.

"Yes," Picard said. It was true enough.

"Would you like to have the tour another time?" she asked.

"Not at all," the captain said. "I'm looking forward to it."

"Approaching Aexix system, sir," Worf announced.

"How many class-M worlds?" Riker asked.

"Sensors indicate that the second planet and one of the moons of the fifth planet are class-M."

"Acknowledged, Mr. Worf." The first officer turned to Ro, who was sitting in the seat he customarily occupied. Riker gave a slight nod and the ensign was immediately on her feet.

"Mr. Halloran," she called to man at conn. "Come out of warp as close to the second planet as possible— and execute a low orbit at one-eighth impulse power.

When Lieutenant Worf reports that scans are complete, use one orbit to accelerate to one-quarter impulse and head for the moon of the fifth planet."

Next, Ro turned to the woman at ops. "Mr. Chang, collect data from Lieutenant Worf's and Ensign Halloran's stations and calculate time necessary to execute scans and maneuvers."

Chang went to work immediately. Less than a minute later, she turned around with a look of tired satisfaction on her face. "One hour and thirty-seven minutes, sir."

Under any other circumstances, Riker knew, less than two hours for the scans they needed would have been extraordinary. But in the last two days, that kind of performance had become routine—allowing them to cover eight systems directly and eliminate two dozen others with long-range scans. It was a fine effort, but it had used up nearly half of the time they had left, and had allowed them to cover perhaps one-fifth of the search area.

The cost was fairly high as well. The constant jumps in and out of warp, in addition to the difficult impulse maneuvers, were taking their toll on the engineering section at a time when both Geordi and Data were off the ship.

And the crew was showing signs of strain. Both Halloran and Chang had worked much more than a full shift. Riker would have to relieve them as soon as this system was scanned.

Having people at ops and conn who weren't fresh was inviting trouble. A slight miscalculation or a slow response could be disastrous during a high-speed impulse maneuver in a planet's gravity well.

And they weren't the only ones he needed fresh. Riker knew that he, Ensign Ro, and Lieutenant Worf had all been pushing themselves too hard as well. For Riker, the evidence was in the sandpaper texture that his eyelids had taken on. And though they didn't show it, he knew that Ro and Worf were feeling the strain, too. Riker would have to order four-hour rest periods for each of them in turn. The Klingon first, since he had been on duty the longest.

"Scan is negative," Worf reported sourly.

Riker could hear Ro's almost inaudible curse. It seemed to him that the ensign had taken on the search as a personal challenge and its failure so far as a personal affront—despite disagreeing with the search in principle. Riker was pleased but not surprised. It was, in fact, exactly what he had hoped would happen.

Ro walked over to Halloran at conn, standing over the ensign as he manipulated the controls, placing a hand briefly on his shoulder in a gesture of support. The acting captain was surprised to see the level of skill she used in handling the crew, pushing people without badgering them. He had expected her dedication—but *this* surprised him.

"Execute acceleration maneuver and follow course to the fifth planet," Ro said.

Several minutes later, Riker watched the planet fall away on the viewscreen. Then it was back to waiting, a state that more and more seemed to define this mission. Long periods of tense anticipation followed by short bursts of activity.

This time, however, the waiting was shorter than Riker had expected.

"Priority message from Starfleet," Worf bellowed.

Damn, the first officer thought. He had been dreading this. Whatever Command had to say, he was sure it wouldn't be good.

Already on his feet, he noted that Deanna and Ro were standing as well. He turned to them. "Ensign, Counselor, let's see what they have to say."

Moments later, Riker sat in the captain's ready room. He flipped on the monitor. Admiral Kowalski's face appeared instantly; the man's expression confirmed Riker's fears.

"Commander, we have what we consider a catastrophic situation on the Gorn homeworld," the admiral said without preamble.

"What is it, sir?" Riker asked.

"There's been an overt challenge made to the Gorn ruling body by a fringe group hostile to the idea of stronger ties to the Federation. Now, I can't pretend to understand all of the ins and outs of Gorn politics. In fact, we don't have the slightest idea of how their political machine works.

"However, all of the reports we're getting from our Gorn contacts say the same thing: if the challenge is successful, this could mean the total dissolution of the peace process. And the outbreak of hostilities with the Federation."

The admiral sighed, and for a moment seemed to age years in front of Riker. "It is critical that the *Enterprise* be at the summit on time. You have three days and no more. And if the situation deteriorates further, I will order you to suspend your search and proceed *immediately* to the summit. Is that clear?"

"Yes, sir," Riker said evenly. Abruptly, the admiral's face was replaced by the Federation symbol that signaled the end of the communication.

The first officer once again looked for that pit of certainty in his stomach that told him continuing the search was the right thing to do.

This time, he waited for some time before it came.

Picard and the doctor walked for a short time in silence. Then Santos led him nearly to the end of the residence side of the semicircle that defined the outpost compound.

"These are the kitchen and dining facilities, as you can see," she said.

The dining hall was clearly marked on the outside wall of the low building, just as the residential area had been. It was, the captain noted, the most heavily trafficked area in the outpost.

He also noticed that just beyond the dining area, there was the slightly raised structure he recognized as a phaser bank. From his study, he knew that there was an identical unit on the other end of the compound's semicircle. He also knew that the phaser banks would be destroyed by the first salvo of the impending attack. Santos didn't explain, or even mention the unit, and Picard assumed that she was under orders not to discuss outpost defenses.

"If you're hungry, we could stop in for something," she suggested. Picard was surprised to find he was indeed hungry. He nodded.

Santos led him to the entrance of the low concrete structure. Ahead of them was a young ensign walking with an equally young woman—probably his wife. A small girl, no doubt their daughter, walked between them, holding her parents' hands—alternately giggling and being swung by her parents.

Picard had known intellectually that children had perished—or would perish—in the attack. But again, it inexplicably surprised him to actually see a child.

"It must be difficult," he said, flinching inwardly, "for a youngster to grow up here."

Santos nodded. "It is, sometimes. But then, we're all hardy souls. And on Cestus Three, at least, we're getting somewhere. There are colonies that *never* achieve their goals—and a few that don't even come *close.*"

The captain turned to her. In his time, no colony was ever set up that didn't have a reasonable chance of reaching its objectives.

"Then why do they do it?" he asked. "Why do they make the sacrifice, if there's no reward in sight to give their work meaning?"

The doctor grunted. "Because there's no such thing as a meaningless sacrifice, Mr. Hill. Because any positive act, no matter how hopeless or insignificant, is ultimately worthwhile."

Picard found himself smiling. "Philosophy," he noted.

"One of my vices," she replied.

Leading the way down a couple of ramps, Santos guided him into an open, fairly spacious dining hall. The tables were laid out symmetrically in the center, with smaller-sized alcoves on the outer walls. The construction was rather stark, layers of concrete supporting the gray metal walls—but the right angles and shadows that defined the architecture appealed to the captain.

The hall didn't look molded or sculpted. Instead, it looked as if it had been built by human hands. Hands that had dared to establish a foothold on an isolated planet, far from the center of the Federation.

The doctor proceeded to the serving area, where human personnel worked behind the counter. Santos ordered sliced chicken and a rice dish and Picard followed suit. Then he followed her to one of the sparsely populated alcoves.

"It's near the end of lunch," the doctor told him. "Most people have gotten back to their assignments."

As he sat down, the captain noticed that the few remaining eyes in the area were on him. No doubt visitors were rare in this closed community.

"They'll get used to you quickly," Santos assured him, divining his thoughts. "In two weeks the sensor array goes on line. But until then, you're the biggest news we've had in months."

Picard took a bite of his meal and found it surprisingly good. "Excellent," he said. "I'm impressed. I assumed an outpost barely a year old would still be dependent on reconstituted food."

Santos smiled. "This is nothing compared to what you'll find at the commodore's table. He thinks it's impossible to make a permanent home when you're living on rations."

"An enlightened point of view," the captain replied. In fact, Travers was years ahead of his time. It wouldn't be until replicator technology made food preparation simple that families would be regularly deployed on starships—and Picard doubted that that was a coincidence. "My father would have approved. He wouldn't allow replicated—I mean *reconstituted* —food in the house."

They passed the rest of the meal pleasantly. The captain managed the food with his left hand without too much difficulty. Throughout, he took careful note of his surroundings. There was no security at all as nearly as he could tell. Not even locking doors, which, of course, would be unnecessary in this community. Apparently, the kitchen staff went home after the evening meal, which—he learned—was from five to seven-thirty. After that, Santos explained, the kitchen was open to whichever colonists cared to help themselves.

Once again, the atmosphere of trust that seemed to govern the outpost would work in Picard's favor. A pang rose up inside him at the thought of taking advantage of that trust, but he brushed it aside; he would have time for self-recrimination later. For now, he needed to concentrate on his escape.

Undoubtedly, the kitchen would be able to supply the essentials he would need for survival outside of the compound. Water and food were his biggest concerns. And the captain was certain there would be some reserves of food concentrates in the storage areas, regardless of the commodore's personal preferences.

Of course, his Starfleet survival training would allow him to sustain himself for a time without supplies. However, if he carried one or two days' rations with him, he would be able to move more quickly without stopping—which would allow him to put as much distance as possible between himself and the outpost before the attack came.

Picard already had the tricorder and medical scanners, which would enable him to track any pursuers. Yes . . . if he could secure some supplies after dinner, he could possibly even make his escape tonight.

He and Santos kept their lunch brief. The doctor was eager to continue the tour, showing an enthusiasm that the captain found charming. Outside again, she was animated and energetic, clearly happy to be showing off her home.

"This is the residence area, which you've already seen. In the lower levels, you'll also find the outpost stores. If you need blankets, or clothes, or entertainment tapes, Lieutenant Harold or I can show you where to find them."

Following the semicircle to its midpoint, they passed the life-support section and then came to two large globes supported on bases that were perhaps four meters high. "And these are our—" Santos began.

"Sensor relays," Picard finished. "I'm familiar with the technology. I just never expected to see any this . . . closely."

The doctor indicated a spot farther along the semicircle. "There's the sensor analysis section. And farther down is the sciences area. You can see them up close tomorrow if you like. For now, I have just a few more things to show you before I have to reprimand myself for overexerting my patient."

Santos gestured to two large buildings, situated more or less along an imaginary line that connected the two endpoints of the semicircle. "See those?" she asked. "One houses the administrative offices and the other is additional storage."

Picard remembered that the "additional storage" structure was in fact the armory, though he understood why the doctor wouldn't mention that. She described a third, lower building as "some engineering facility," but he knew it was the fusion reactor that powered the station's routine functions.

Then Santos pointed out the low-lying mountains, seen in the distance past the three buildings. "That is where you were found, about five hundred meters into those hills. Unfortunately, they're unstable and prone to landslides, which is how you were hurt."

The same hills, Picard mused, in which the Gorn had positioned themselves right before the appearance of Captain Kirk and his landing party. The invaders had been—or rather, would be—forced to retreat when Kirk fired a plasma grenade into the area. The captain supposed his missing communicator would be destroyed in the blast.

It was just as well. The communicator would have been useful to him if there were someone to receive the signal—but of course, there wasn't. Picard might even have thought about trying to retrieve the device if there was any hope of using it as a marker for Commander Riker or a future Starfleet ship, but he knew it was useless. Though he always made it a point to keep his communicator fully energized, there was no chance of the charge lasting one hundred years.

"And now," Santos resumed, "it's just a short walk to our sensor array. That's the main attraction around here."

For a moment, Picard considered declining. He

could use the time alone to make his final plans and perhaps collect what he needed from the kitchen. But he found it difficult to disappoint the doctor, to deny her the pleasure of sharing something she felt was important. Besides, he didn't want to arouse suspicion in his only ally on the outpost.

"So where's home for you, Mr. Hill?" Santos inquired, as they walked in between the sensor beacons and outside of the semicircle that defined the compound. "I mean, where were you from before you made *space* your home?"

"Is it that obvious?" the captain asked.

She nodded. "If you know what to look for. My father was a career merchant space traveler. He spent most of his life on freighters. Even when he was with you, it felt like he wasn't. I see some of the same things in you, Mr. Hill. Sometimes, it seems you're positively light-years away. However, unlike my father, you have the courtesy to at least respond to polite conversation."

He chuckled. "You know me well already, Doctor."

"Please call me Julia, Mr. Hill. Only the children and the newest batch of ensigns call me Doctor, and that's just because I haven't broken them in yet. And there's the commodore as well, I suppose—but he's in a class by himself."

"You don't like Commodore Travers," Picard observed.

She shrugged. "To be perfectly blunt, I don't. I think he's a good commander and I respect him for that, but I think he could be, well . . . kinder." Santos frowned when she said that.

The captain looked at her. "Doctor . . . please call

me Dixon." He felt absurd inviting the first-name informality when that name was not his own. But then, neither was "Mr. Hill," and that sounded even *more* absurd.

Santos's frown lifted. "In that case . . . Dixon . . . may I present the reason we're here?" They had arrived at the top of a small hill. She gestured to the sensor array just below them. It was incredible. Interlocking spheres of perhaps two meters in diameter made up a larger circle that was at least half a kilometer across.

The sight left Picard breathless. He had seen larger arrays in space, but somehow, looking at an object in space from a viewscreen took away the human scale.

Here, he was overwhelmed. And to think this had all been built by human hands . . .

"An eye to search the heavens," Santos remarked. "It's state-of-the-art. One of the biggest land-based arrays in the Federation, and certainly the most sophisticated. In fact, from here we'll be able to see farther out into uncharted space than anyone else in the known galaxy. We'll be paving the way for starships by peeking ahead at distant solar systems, and probably making long-range subspace contact with new races." The doctor smiled self-consciously, then continued. "Pardon my pride, but whatever is out there, we'll find it first."

"This is certainly an achievement worth taking pride in," the captain agreed. They both enjoyed the sight in silence for a moment. He could see, to the right of the array, the bunker that housed the matter-antimatter power source—essentially a stationary warp engine—that drove the entire mechanism. By twenty-fourth-century standards, the equipment was an antique, a relic. Yet for these people, it represented their highest aspirations—the pinnacle of human achievement. "Extraordinary."

"A few more shakedown tests and it goes on-line," Santos told him. "They're estimating just a couple of weeks."

Ironic, thought Picard. If the array was switched on sooner—its power boosted slightly—it would probably detect the Gorn civilization. In fact, he could this very moment make the suggestion to power up the array . . . invent a compelling enough reason that Travers would have to act on it immediately. Then, with defenses in place, the tragedy could be avoided. Santos and the other colonists wouldn't have to die.

Of course, the Prime Directive forbade it. And even putting the noninterference regulations aside, there were too many other reasons. If the massacre were averted, Captain Kirk could not have settled the dispute with the Gorn captain in single combat. Picard would not have had the basis for his first encounter with the Gorn, and the upcoming summit might never take place. Instead, the Gorn might have resorted to a full-scale attack on the Federation as a first contact. The possibility for devastation and loss of life was incalculable.

No. Clearly, the captain would have to let history play itself out as it must. Santos and the others would have to perish, so that peace could eventually come from their tragedy. Intellectually, Picard understood the situation perfectly. The question was . . . why did it feel so bloody wrong?

The doctor turned to him, delight illuminating her

face, somehow making her green eyes seem even greener. "We're explorers, Dixon. And in two weeks we begin a whole new phase of human exploration. Luckily for you, you'll be here to see it."

The excitement in her voice seemed to ask for some response, or at least an affirmation of what she was feeling. But Picard could not find his voice, so he simply nodded.

Santos misinterpreted his silence. "Come," she said. "Let me show you the control room. Chief Engineer Hronsky will be busy, but I think he would like to meet you, especially if you have any technical skills."

She led him down the incline to a short, rectangular building—the only structure that was unmarked, the captain noticed. It was probably because no one could mistake it for anything else but what it was.

Inside, they walked down a short flight of stairs to the main floor of sensor controls. Picard could see that the stairs extended down even farther—like the other buildings on the outpost, the bulk of the space was underground. The captain knew those lower floors held the matter-antimatter reactor that powered the sensor array.

The control center was a bustle of activity, with perhaps two dozen people working, in, under, and around various control panels—some of which were still being assembled.

No one seemed to pay them any attention as Dr. Santos led Picard through the maze of people and equipment. She stopped to ask a lieutenant where Hronsky was, and the young man shot the captain a quick, nervous glance before pointing to a two-meter-high catwalk at the back of the room.

Picard and the doctor made their way to the back of the room, where she started up the ladder to the catwalk, gesturing for the captain to follow. Up top, a husky man wearing a lieutenant commander's braids was giving instructions to two others. Santos approached the man and entered the conversation with a quick "Excuse me, Michael."

The lieutenant commander stopped the conversation with an uplifted hand. He favored the doctor with a harried smile beneath his dark, bushy brows.

"Yes, Julia?"

She indicated Picard. "Michael Hronsky, I would like you to meet our new guest, Captain Dixon Hill."

The man turned his attention to the captain. For a moment, Hronsky's face registered genuine surprise. "Captain Hill," he muttered.

"Michael, what's going on here? You and your men seem to be going full tilt," Santos noted.

Hronsky kept his eyes on Picard as he responded, "Uh, Julia . . . could I have a word with you in private?"

Before the doctor could respond, the man addressed Picard directly. "Captain Hill, I'm sorry, but I need to speak with the doctor alone. One of my men will escort you outside."

An ensign who was standing beside Hronsky gestured for the captain to return back down the ladder. On the ground, the same ensign led Picard back through the control room—and then waited with him in uncomfortable silence until Santos emerged.

Her face was blank, which the captain now recognized as a sign that she was upset. As she got closer, he saw the subtle frown lines at the corners of her mouth.

"I'm sorry, Dixon. Apparently, the engineering staff is very busy. Perhaps we could see this part of the outpost at a later date."

She didn't say anything else on the subject, but she didn't need to. Hronsky's expression had told Picard everything he needed to know. He regarded the newcomer as Lieutenant Harold had at first: as a possibly dangerous intruder. Undoubtedly, Commodore Travers had spoken to him already.

What's more, the captain couldn't muster any indignation at the suspicion he was facing. He *was* a bloody intruder, wasn't he? One who was as dangerous to the Federation as the Gorn strike force that was probably already amassing outside the system.

What troubled Picard was the near-feverish activity inside the sensor-array control room. He didn't think the engineering crew looked like a team working ahead toward a two-week deadline, and that raised a number of questions.

Picard and the doctor walked back to the residence area in silence. She showed him to his door, 11-H, and pointed out Lieutenant Harold's temporary quarters next door.

"If there's anything you need," said Santos, "you can ask your computer terminal, Dixon. Or call Lieutenant Harold. Or call *me.*"

The captain smiled. "Thank you. But I think, for now, I will just rest." Actually, with luck, he would be able to secure some supplies from the kitchen and then investigate the outpost stores on the lower level of the residence area. "Good-bye, Julia. Thank you for the tour."

All unintentionally, he had called her by her first name. The doctor seemed pleased by it.

"There's more tomorrow, if you feel up to it," she told him.

"I'm looking forward to it," Picard assured her. As she turned to leave, he entered his quarters and shut the door behind him. A quick scan told him the room was comfortable, relatively spacious . . . and *occupied*.

Lieutenant Harold jumped up. He'd been sitting at the small desk that held the computer terminal.

"Uh, Mr. Hill . . . sorry to intrude, but I wanted to talk to you."

"That's fine," Picard replied. "What can I do for you, Lieutenant?" He gestured for Harold to take a seat and then took one himself at the small all-purpose table near the desk.

The younger man frowned. "Well, sir, I wanted to ask you about merchant space service."

The captain looked at Harold askance. "Are you interested in a career change?"

"Well, not exactly," said the lieutenant. "I'm just curious about what it would be like." He looked uncomfortable, as if the mere idea of leaving Starfleet were traitorous.

"There isn't a lot of . . . excitement on this outpost, is there?" Picard asked.

Harold responded to the understanding tone and relaxed a bit. "Well, it's very interesting, from a scientific point of view. We'll be collecting a lot of data when the sensor array goes on-line. But I'm not much of a scientist. When I joined Starfleet, I was hoping to do some genuine exploring. Not that what we're doing here isn't important," he added hastily. "But I'm not sure it's for me."

The captain knew all too well what the lieutenant was feeling. "Have you tried to apply for starship service?"

Harold actually smiled. "About twice a month since I graduated." He shrugged. "But there aren't a lot of openings."

Of course, Picard thought. In this time, there were only twelve heavy-cruiser-class starships in service. Thus, there were less than five thousand of the coveted positions on board the vessels that were at the forefront of space exploration. In his own era, he knew, there was substantially more opportunity. But by then, the Federation had grown as well, so the competition was still heavy for positions on a starship.

If Starfleet Academy had denied his second application, Picard probably would have ended up on a merchant ship. If he had been posted for a few years on a starbase, with no hope of a position on a starship, he suspected he would have moved to commercial flight as well.

"I suspect that you might find serving on a freighter to be just as mundane," he said finally.

Harold grunted. "Excuse me, sir, but it's *space.*"

"True," the captain concurred. "But you're actually closer to the frontier where you are now."

"Mr. Hill," said the lieutenant, "I joined Starfleet to see what's out there. To make first contacts. To be a part of something. So far, I've served with only humans. In my entire Starfleet career, I have met two

Vulcans and one Tellarite. When I was a kid, I looked at the stars and decided I was going to meet the people who lived on them. If a job in the commercial sector is what I need to do, then that's what I will do."

Picard would have liked to assure Harold that staying in Starfleet was the answer, but he knew it wasn't true. An officer might very well spend his entire career on various outposts. Finally, the captain told him what he could about merchant service. He'd known more than one merchant commander in his time, so he was able to draw a fairly accurate picture.

In the end, Picard knew his advice probably wouldn't have much effect. Lieutenant Harold's life would be shaped and nearly ended by an attack that was a mere two days away. In fact, the captain had no way of knowing if his arrival had somehow subtly altered history so that, this time, Matthew Harold might not survive.

Unfortunately, even if history followed its course, Picard's study of the massacre hadn't told him what happened to the lieutenant later. Without knowing what the future held, Picard could only hope that Harold's first "first contact" would not destroy all of his youthful idealism.

Chapter Five

"OKAY, DATA, hit it," Geordi said from underneath the open circuit panel.

"Affirmative," came the android's response, from across the control room.

Sliding out from under the console, the chief engineer took his place next to Data, Barclay, and O'Connor, who were all huddled around the monitor —the same one that had been working before the power surge. Expecting another disappointment, Geordi was surprised to see static crackle across the screen. A moment later a shaky picture jumped, faded, and then finally planted itself firmly on the monitor. The image was of a star system that La Forge didn't recognize but was thrilled to see nonetheless.

"Excellent," he said, smiling broadly. "Excellent work, everyone."

This was the first piece of equipment that they had been able to get functioning with the station's own power. Using Barclay and O'Connor's diagnostic program, Data and Geordi had been able to trace the monitor's power circuits. The problem with those circuits was that like much of the station's circuitry, the power pathways had been built into the panels, walls, and bulkheads themselves.

As a result, tracing them was extremely difficult. The task was made tougher still by the fact that many of the circuits had been damaged by the power surge.

In the case of this one monitor, at least, they had been able to use jumpers to circumvent the damaged circuitry. With its power supply again intact, the screen was able to access the huge subspace sensor network that, like the circuitry, seemed to be built into the structure of the station. Of course, with so little juice available, neither the monitor nor the sensors should ever have functioned.

At another time, that mystery would have fascinated Geordi. Now it was simply an annoyance. If the alien technology refused to obey the laws of physics as he understood them, how would his team ever get the equipment working well enough to find and retrieve the captain?

As the rest of them watched, the android manipulated the controls on the forward panel. While he worked, the scene on the monitor shifted from one star system to another. Geordi came up behind him. "How are you doing that, Data?"

"I do not believe I *am* doing it," Data responded. "As before, there seems to be no correlation between the controls here and the images presented on the monitor. Certainly, there is no direct or quantifiable correlation."

The android ceased his manipulations and the monitor held an image for a moment—then shifted to another system. "It's random?" Barclay asked from the rear.

"Possibly," Data reported. "At any rate, it does not follow any pattern that I can discern."

"Could any of these have been the captain's destination?" O'Connor asked next.

"Possibly," Data said again, taking his tricorder and scanning with it. "There seem to be memory banks built into the system, but they are empty."

"Wiped clean by the power surge," Geordi remarked. "We'll have to count on Commander Riker to come up with some coordinates. But even so, that means we'll have to be able to retrieve the captain once the *Enterprise* determines his position. And we don't have the slightest idea of how this equipment works."

"Sir," Barclay said tentatively, "what if we gave up trying to understand the underlying principles here, and just concentrated on finding the operational parameters of the equipment?"

The lieutenant was right, of course. Geordi had spent hours trying to determine why things functioned here, and had come up empty-handed. The monitor was their first success, and it had only arrived when they stopped trying to figure out why it worked and concentrated on simply getting it powered up.

The chief engineer nodded. "Okay, so what do we know so far about the station's operational parameters?" He asked the question of the group at large.

Data spoke first. "We know that the entire station

functions as a subspace field coil. We also know that the station has a number of nodes, such as the one in this immediate area, that further focus the larger subspace field—apparently, for purposes of transport."

"And we can assume," O'Connor added, "that this equipment somehow controls this node."

"All right," Geordi said, "then our objective should be to trace the power circuits to each of the controls in the room. When we get them all functioning, we can figure out what they do."

It made sense. It was a plan of action and it gave them something to do, rather than buck up against theoretical problems that were—if not unsolvable— at least virtually impossible to figure out in a matter of days.

"Okay, let's get to work," the chief engineer told his team.

When the lights flickered a moment later, Geordi jumped. Directing his VISOR to the ceiling panels, he watched them brighten momentarily before returning to their customary low level of illumination.

Each of the four away-team members had his or her tricorder out and was scanning. Data was finished first.

"Definitely a power surge," he announced, just as Geordi's own tricorder confirmed the finding. "A much milder variety than the ones that occurred before the captain's disappearance."

"Did we do this by hooking up the power here?" Geordi asked.

"I do not think so," the android replied. "I suspect

that the initial disturbance created by our transporters may have rendered the power generators unstable."

"So we're looking at bigger and bigger surges until the station is enveloped again and . . ." The chief engineer let his voice trail off.

Data didn't respond, and for a moment the team was silent. Geordi had expected this danger, but had hoped it wouldn't come until after they had finished their work—or at least made some serious progress.

"How long?" he asked.

"It is difficult to say," the android responded. "I do not think it is safe to forecast a steady increase in these power surges. A random element seemed to be at work last time and will almost certainly be at work this time as well. However, given the relatively small magnitude of the surge, I would say several hours at least. Perhaps more, but we should be prepared to evacuate quickly."

Damn, Geordi thought. He touched his communicator, which was tapped into their portable subspace radio.

"La Forge to *Enterprise.*"

A moment later, he heard the crisp reply "Riker here."

"Commander, we have a problem," the engineer said evenly.

"Incoming communication from Lieutenant Commander La Forge," advised the Klingon.

"Patch it into my communicator," the first officer said, tapping his Starfleet insignia. "Riker here."

"Commander, we have a problem," Geordi told him.

Somehow Riker wasn't surprised. So far, this mission had been nothing *but* problems. After three days, the ship had surveyed twenty-two systems and eliminated thirty-eight others with long-range scans. More than one-third of the search was complete, but they had turned up no sign of the captain, and less than two days remained to them.

"What have you got, Geordi?" Riker asked.

"We've just experienced a small power surge on the station, sir. It was very slight, but it's now clear the station is unstable."

"Are you in any danger at the moment?" the first officer asked. He quickly did the calculations in his head. At top speed, the station was almost a day away.

"No, sir. Don't worry about us. Even if the worst happens, we should have enough warning to evacuate. We've rigged all the doors in the area and the airlock with independent power sources and controls. Before we have another surge like the one that caught the captain, we'll be well out of the way."

"Any estimate of how long that'll be?"

"Hard to say, Commander. Data figures we have several hours at least, but it could be longer. I'm sorry, but the power increases don't seem to follow a regular pattern."

Riker grunted. "Will the equipment survive another critical surge?" He waited for a moment, presumably as Geordi conferred with his colleagues.

"Negative, sir," came the engineer's measured reply. "If the station has a surge of the same magnitude as before, Data predicts severe damage to the remaining equipment, as well as to the structure of the station. I wish I had some better news, Commander. . . ."

That's just fine, the first officer thought. Without the alien equipment, even if they succeeded in finding the captain, they could forget about retrieving him from the past. Even though time travel was theoretically possible with a starship, the peril to the ship and crew was great, and the dangers posed by altering history were off the scale.

"Have you made any progress at all with the alien technology?" Riker asked finally.

"Very little, Commander. We have the subspace sensors and one monitor operating, but as we suspected, the memory seems to have been purged by the power surge. And so far, we haven't been able to isolate or operate any of the manual controls."

Riker could hear the frustration in Geordi's voice; he knew precisely how the chief engineer was feeling. So far, they had been thwarted at almost every turn since the moment they arrived at the damned alien station!

"Do your best, Geordi. And continue to report in at regular intervals. If you even suspect that the power surges are becoming a hazard, I want you to get the away team safely off the station. No heroics—I can't afford to lose any of you."

Riker almost added "as well as the captain," but he refused to give in to the doubts that were rising to the surface. If he didn't keep up hope, the crew would undoubtedly lose faith as well. And without hope, they couldn't continue to do the impossible.

"Understood. La Forge out."

"Entering system, Commander," Worf announced from behind him.

During the conversation with Geordi, Riker had pitched his voice low, so the bridge crew wouldn't hear. But his security chief, he knew, had heard everything. Still, Worf's voice was as sure as it was when the search began. Giving up simply was not in the Klingon's makeup.

Riker gave the order and the ship came out of warp. They made the orbital scans in thirty-nine minutes—a full seven minutes under the estimate. Well, at least, something had been going right on this mission. The crew and ship were continuing to perform minor miracles several times per shift.

"Time until next system?" he asked Worf.

"Five hours," came the Klingon's reply.

In that case, Riker decided, it was time for him to get some rest. Ro was currently on a rest period of her own, but Worf would be able to handle things easily enough during the warp journey to the next star.

Riker turned to his security chief. "Lieutenant, you have the conn. I'll be in my quarters."

Worf nodded, and the exec headed for the turbolift. He was almost there when Ro came bounding out of the lift doors. Riker could tell from the tension in her eyes that she hadn't been doing any resting during her rest cycle.

"Commander, could I have a word with you?" she asked.

Riker walked past her, entered the turbolift, and turned around. "If you don't mind accompanying me."

Ro immediately joined him in the lift.

"Deck seven," Riker said to the computer. Then he turned his attention back to the Bajoran. He had been expecting this visit. In fact, he'd expected it sooner. For a moment, he decided to forestall the inevitable. "You were under orders to rest, Ensign."

She frowned. "I was following a new line of inquiry that I saw as vital to our mission. It superseded my need for rest." There wasn't even a hint of apology in her voice.

Ro watched her commander, obviously waiting for a response or, Riker supposed, a challenge. But the ensign waited only a moment, apparently taking her superior's silence as a signal to continue.

"Sir, I have found a way to allow the *Enterprise* to complete the search in the time remaining to us."

"Ensign, I understand—" Riker cut his own words off. He had been expecting Ro to challenge the wisdom of continuing an effort as apparently hopeless as the search for the captain. He had been prepared to flat-out order her to carry out her instructions and not engage him in useless squabbling. Instead, he found himself momentarily thrown by her declaration.

"What do you mean?" Riker said.

Ro licked her lips. "I have contacted a consortium of Bajoran merchant ships in the area, who have agreed to discuss the possibility of joining the search. There are six ships available, and if we deploy them carefully, we can cover all of the systems in the search area before our deadline."

Was it possible? Riker thought. Were there merchant ships in the area? And if so, why hadn't Starfleet

Command been able to secure their help? "Ensign, what is the name of this consortium?"

Here, Ro faltered for a moment. "They are from the Bon Amar trading group—"

"Pirates," Riker spat out.

"Sir, they are—"

"They are *pirates,* Ensign." Now he was genuinely annoyed. The ship was conducting a massive search against astronomical odds and an important summit that was falling apart by the minute—and Ro was talking to pirates.

The Bon Amar were wanted in several sectors by local and Federation authorities. If Riker so much as *saw* a Bon Amar vessel, he would be obligated to arrest the crew and confiscate the ship on sight.

"The Bon Amar have been treated unfairly since—" Ro began.

"They are of no use to us on this mission," Riker said.

"They are willing to help!" the ensign insisted.

Riker allowed his voice to rise in volume a notch above hers. "That's *not* the kind of help we need."

Ro turned to the computer panel. "Computer, stop turbolift," she snapped. Turning back to Riker, she said, "Sir, it is the *only* kind of help we are going to get. While it is true the Bon Amar have had to resort to nontraditional trading practices—"

"They've plundered legitimate trading routes," he reminded her.

Ro shook her head. "They did what they had to do to help finance the Bajoran resistance. Most of their appropriations were from Cardassian or Cardassian-friendly vessels. It's true that they're not licensed to operate in Federation trade lanes, but the only reason they weren't exonerated and fully recognized by the Federation is that they didn't quit after the Cardassians left Bajor.

"They're still trying to recover a fraction of the damages done by the Cardassians to my people. And because they're still active, they have been a political embarrassment for the Federation, who would rather disavow them than risk upsetting the Cardassians."

Riker scowled. "I leave politics to the politicians, Ensign. When it comes to the Bon Amar or any recognized criminals, my duty and the duty of this ship is clear. Your contact with wanted criminals raises a lot of questions . . . which I will choose to overlook if that contact is not repeated."

But Ro wouldn't quit. "Sir, whatever feelings you may have about the Bon Amar, they're willing to help us for a fair price. And frankly, I don't think we can afford to turn down any assistance, no matter the source."

Riker drew his breath to respond, but the Bajoran obviously would not be satisfied until she had said her piece.

"With all due respect, Commander, I have watched you break every rule in the book on this mission to continue a search that any sane person would recognize as impossible. During that time, I and this crew have done everything in our power to support you. And now, when success may be in reach, you say that duty prevents you from finishing what you have started."

Riker had had enough. "Computer, start turbolift." He faced Ro. "Ensign, you're out of line. It's not up to you to decide what is and what is not acceptable in the course of fulfilling our mission. I took an oath when I joined Starfleet to uphold the laws of the Federation —and in case you've forgotten, you took the same one. That oath is not flexible or changeable when it becomes inconvenient. Captain Picard respected it, and I will not break it even to find him. I suggest you review it—and then take a long, hard look at your future here."

The turbolift doors opened and the first officer strode out. He turned back to Ro, making it clear from his face that he would accept no further argument on the subject of the Bon Amar. "And Ensign, get some rest. That's an order."

With that, he headed for his quarters.

Inside, Riker could feel the tension across his shoulders and his brow, and he realized that he wouldn't be doing any sleeping on this shift.

Moments later, he found himself sitting at his computer console. "Computer, access files on a trade consortium called the Bon Amar."

By the time Lieutenant Harold left, Picard was already feeling the toll of the day. He knew he needed rest. Both his head and his shoulder were beginning to ache and he could feel exhaustion creeping into his frame. He would need to conserve his resources if he was going to make a successful escape. Perhaps if he snatched a few hours' sleep now, he would be able to visit the kitchen and slip away later tonight.

Just then, his intercom buzzed. The captain fought an impulse to say "Picard here." Instead, he answered, "Dixon Hill." There was no response except for the whistle of the intercom repeating itself.

Of course, he thought, chiding himself for forgetting his time period—the intercom wouldn't be voice activated. He found the intercom on the desk and hit the button.

"Yes?" he answered.

"Dixon, it's Julia," came the reply. "I just wanted to ask you if you would care to dine with me tonight. The commodore is having his weekly dinner and I wrangled you an invitation."

"Julia, I'm afraid that—"

"The commodore sets an excellent table. In fact, it's common knowledge that ships go out of their way to use the supply facilities here just to take advantage of his hospitality." The doctor hesitated for a moment, then continued. "I'm afraid that we haven't done a very good job of making you feel welcome. Please give us a chance to change that."

Julia sounded sincerely concerned about his feelings, and Picard couldn't afford to turn down the commodore's invitation for fear of raising suspicions even further. "I would be delighted," he said finally.

"Excellent," she responded brightly. "I will stop by at seven-thirty. Good-bye, Dixon."

Moments later, Harold appeared at the door, with a suit of civilian clothes. Undoubtedly, the commodore's weekly dinner was too formal for Picard's generic coveralls.

Seven-thirty. That gave the captain nearly two

hours to sleep. Without wasting another second, he lay down, intending to make use of the time.

Julia arrived promptly at seven-thirty. When he answered the door, Picard didn't recognize the doctor for a moment. Instead of her plain civilian tunic and trousers, she wore a simple but striking green dress. It matched her eyes.

Her short, dark hair was worn up, making her look quite elegant. Picard was suddenly grateful to her for sending Lieutenant Harold over with more formal clothing for him.

"Julia, you look wonderful," he told her.

She smiled. "And you look very handsome, Mr. Hill."

Returning the smile, Picard nodded. "I thank you for the clothes. They are an excellent fit."

"I'm pleased. Shall we go?"

Outside, the captain saw that the sun was beginning to go down over the low, distant mountains, giving the sky a crimson cast. The sun itself was ringed with halos of subtly different shades between red and orange.

"It's a beautiful world, isn't it, Dixon?" Julia sighed. "When we first arrived, I watched the sun go down every evening for six months. I still try to make sure I'm outside this time of day whenever I can be."

"It is spectacular," Picard said honestly.

Julia maintained a slow pace, no doubt so that they could both enjoy the natural display. The captain found her eagerness to share things with a stranger quite refreshing.

The doctor looked at him. "Dixon, if you don't mind my saying so, you don't look much like a merchant captain."

"Why do you say that?" Picard responded, keeping his voice neutral.

"Well, for one thing, you're too dignified. Most of the merchant spacemen I have known have been, well . . . somewhat saltier."

The captain nodded. Commercial shipping did tend to attract a gruffer and more earthy variety of officer than Starfleet.

He shrugged. "I always wanted to go to space. My father owned a vineyard, and strongly encouraged my brother and me to take over the operation. My brother did, but there was really nothing there for me. I always wanted space travel."

"Why not Starfleet?" Julia asked.

He smiled. "I failed my Academy admission exams," he answered.

"I find that hard to believe."

"It is true, nonetheless, I'm sorry to say." It was, in fact, half true. The captain had failed in his first attempt to enter Starfleet Academy. But that failure had merely strengthened his resolve. After redoubling his efforts the following year, he was admitted.

"But that didn't stop you from going into space," the doctor observed. "It's rare that people stay so true to their ideals." Julia considered him for a moment. "Still, that's not all there is to you, is it?"

The question made Picard uneasy. "What do you mean?" he asked evenly.

"You have secrets, though I'm not sure what they

are yet." Julia's face kept the same slightly amused expression.

"But you don't think I'm a danger, as the commodore does?" the captain probed.

"No," she said. "I don't. Call it physician's instinct, but I think you're a good man. Just something of a puzzle. Fortunately, it will be some time before you can get away from us, and I'll have an opportunity to figure you out. That's one of the things we have in abundance here in the middle of nowhere— time."

Picard let her comment go without a response. He pondered how little time Julia and the others truly had left to them, and he could think of nothing to say to her. A moment later, they came to the commodore's building. It was one of the three freestanding structures in the center of the compound.

"After you," Julia said, gesturing inside.

Picard stepped through the automatic doors into a small hallway. Julia led him to another set of doors and then they were inside a well-appointed dining room. Travers, who was at the head of the table, stood as they entered. The five people with him immediately followed suit.

The commodore cleared his throat. "Captain Dixon Hill, I believe you already know Lieutenant Harold."

Using the smile he reserved for delicate diplomatic functions, Picard inclined his head in the direction of the young lieutenant. Harold smiled uneasily, and the captain guessed that he was taking his first turn at Travers's table as well. The captain also surmised that Harold was there primarily to keep an eye on him.

The commodore gestured. "May I also present my first officer and security chief, Hans Schmitter . . . my chief engineer, Michael Hronsky—whom you have also already met—my science officer, Rhonda Healy, and my communications officer, Benjamin Washington."

Travers waited until his people had each greeted Picard with a nod. Then he indicated the two seats closest to him, both of which were empty. "Please be seated," said the commodore.

Picard took his seat next to Lieutenant Harold while Julia took the one next to Security Chief Schmitter.

A few moments later, servers brought the soup out—an excellent cold gazpacho that the captain could manage easily with one hand. Travers broke the uncomfortable silence, directing his attention to Picard.

"So, Mr. Hill, where did you operate your merchant ship?" the commodore asked, keeping his tone casual.

Doing some quick calculations, the captain estimated the boundaries of legitimate shipping in this area during this period of time. "We confined our operation to sector one-four-five, as far out as the Chrysalis system, mostly rare minerals."

Travers wiped his mouth with a napkin. "Really. And you had trouble with Orions out there? What could they have possibly been doing that far out?"

"I really cannot say," Picard replied. "We were surprised to see them, and they never explained themselves to me. They merely took our cargo of Benzorite . . . and left." The captain could see Julia bristling, but did his best to match the commodore's casual tone.

"That begs the question of what they would be doing out here, after taking your Benzorite in the Chysalis system." Travers waited for an answer.

"Again," said the captain, "they gave no details."

The commodore smiled. "Forgive me, Mr. Hill. But we get visitors only rarely, and none have ever come to us as mysteriously as you did."

He let the comment hang in the air as the servers brought out the main course, a fish dish that Picard recognized as salmon in a cognac cream sauce. Next, the servers poured white wine from glass bottles.

Odd, thought Picard. Travers's apparently refined tastes seemed at odds with his coarse exterior. No doubt, given time, the commodore would be an interesting man to know.

Again, Travers eyed him. "Do you know much about Earth's second world war, Mr. Hill?"

"I remember a bit of what I learned in school," the captain replied.

The commodore put down his utensils to address Picard. "The story goes that the American forces were often in the position of having to determine rather quickly whether or not other soldiers were German infiltrators. It's said that the Americans would ask the solider in question what wine to drink with fish. If the person answered correctly, they knew he could not have been American." Travers leaned forward slightly. "Dr. Santos tells me you are from France. Do you know much about wine, Mr. Hill?"

"I did pick up a bit at home," Picard replied. "Where I am from, it was difficult not to."

"What do you think of this wine?" the commodore asked pointedly.

The captain was very aware of the silence that had descended on the room. Keeping his face neutral, he reached for his glass and took a sip. After making his determination, he nodded his head diplomatically.

"Considering your relative isolation, good wine is sure to be scarce," Picard remarked.

"What do you mean?" Travers probed.

"Well, unless I miss my guess, this is Chateau Briar, vintage twenty-one ninety-one. As a rule, a good year. However, one-fourth of the Briar crop was damaged by frost that year. As a result, a commensurate portion of that vintage was rendered somewhat bland. I suspect that your dealer was not entirely scrupulous."

The commodore's face betrayed the first genuine emotion of the evening for him: surprise. The others around the table kept their expressions carefully neutral—except for Julia, who was grinning behind her napkin.

"I apologize," Picard said to Travers. "I didn't mean to insult your choice. But . . ."

"I did ask," the commodore supplied. He was smiling, but it seemed to the captain that the good humor did not extend to his eyes. "You are something of an enigma, Mr. Hill. You really don't seem much like a merchant commander."

Picard glanced at Julia. "I have heard that before. Nevertheless, that is what I am, or was, until recently."

"For one thing, you're remarkably healthy. Did Dr. Santos mention that to you?"

"No," the captain replied, immediately on his guard.

Travers pressed on. "Besides that mysterious artificial heart, which my people are still trying to figure out, you are free of any signs of ill health whatsoever."

Picard considered his wine. "More a credit to my doctors than to myself, I am sure."

The commodore grunted. "Then your doctors must be really extraordinary, Mr. Hill. Our tests show absolutely no sign of past injury—no visible scar tissue, no healed fractures, not even the surgical scars one would expect from a cardiac replacement operation. Moreover, your lungs and blood are completely free of even the most minute traces of the pollutants and gases that starfaring crews are regularly exposed to."

An unexpected turn, thought the captain. He had known cardiac replacement would be trouble, but had hoped that his story of alien manufacture would satisfy Travers at least temporarily. Still, it was difficult to explain the differences in his body wrought by a century of medical advances. Techniques for healing wounds and repairing bones were much more sophisticated in his day than in the commodore's.

Stealing a glance at Julia, Picard could see by the set of her mouth that she was becoming annoyed, presumably at Travers. Certainly, she had the same questions, but was planning to wait and ask Picard about his medical history when they were alone. The commodore's public questions were both a breach of privacy and in very bad taste for dinner conversation.

But Travers was obviously unconcerned. He had leveled his gaze at his visitor and was not going to back off. "And do you know why it is," the commodore continued, "that you are immune to the common cold?"

Picard found anger rising in his throat, and had to fight down the impulse to respond more strongly to Travers's accusing tone. Reminding himself that the commodore was merely doing his best to protect his people, the captain kept silent. He didn't have to like Travers's methods of inquiry, but he did have to respect the man's position.

Meeting the commodore's gaze squarely, Picard replied, "No, I was not aware of that immunity. And as for the other peculiarities you noted, all I can say is that I have in the past sought treatment from alien physicians, who apparently did a better job than I realized."

The dining room never recovered its light atmosphere. The remainder of dinner and dessert passed quickly. When it was over, Travers thanked them all for coming. Then he directed his attention to Picard again.

"Mr. Hill, would you mind staying behind for a few moments? There's something I'd like to discuss privately with you."

Julia immediately spoke up. "Can it wait, Commodore? Mr. Hill must be exhausted. I'm sure he would like to go back to his quarters to rest."

Travers eyed her pointedly. "No, Doctor, I don't think it *can* wait. Mr. Hill?"

"Of course," the captain answered.

Picard and Travers stood as the others were ushered out. When they were alone, the commodore turned to his guest.

"Who are you really, Mr. Hill?"

"I don't understand," Picard replied evenly.

"I believe you do. Julia considers you charming and something of a puzzle. I agree with the puzzle part, but I think you're dangerous. *Very* dangerous."

"I'm sorry to disappoint you, Commodore, but I am a simple—"

"Damn that!" Travers shouted. "I don't know who or what you are, but you're not a merchant captain. You're playing some kind of a game with me, and that means you're jeopardizing the lives of everyone in this colony. You don't belong here, mister. I can *feel* it."

The commodore composed himself for a moment and then continued. "When I was at the academy, we studied star charts of this and the surrounding sectors. You know what they said? 'Here there be dragons.' Now, it was someone's idea of a joke to use old mapmaker nomenclature, but there are still rumors about this part of space. Legends about dragons, shapeshifters, and every other kind of monster you can imagine.

"The officer in me recognizes that most of that talk

is just old myths, the kind that have circulated since a ship meant only a vessel that floated. But I've been in Starfleet for thirty-eight years, and I've seen enough to realize that most stories born in space have some basis in fact. And sometimes those facts are unpleasant."

Travers brought his face close to Picard's. "Now, it's my job to initiate peaceful contact with alien races whenever possible, and I take that job seriously. However, it is also my responsibility to protect the five hundred and twelve people under my command. You may not understand what that's like, but understand this: If you're lying to me, I'll find out about it. If you're here peacefully, fine. But if you pose any danger to my people, you'll wish you had never even heard of Cestus Three.

"In the meantime, I think you're hiding behind a good doctor, who for some reason trusts you. I invite you to come out of hiding, Mr. Hill—and tell me the truth. That is, if you have the courage."

The commodore considered Picard for a moment in the silence that followed. In that moment, the captain wanted to tell Travers at least a portion of the truth. But as before, he kept his silence.

"I didn't think so," observed the commodore. "You're dismissed."

Outside, Picard found Julia waiting. "I'm sorry, Dixon. If I had any idea that he would behave so—"

"It's all right," he told her. "Believe it or not, I understand the commodore very well."

They headed for the residence area. "I'm not sure that this assignment was good for him," she remarked. "Even though he presides over dozens of families, as a commander, a family wasn't feasible for him. I think he needed one. It would have made him a better man."

Picard nodded. "It is one of the things many of us give up for a life in space."

"I know what you mean," Julia said, becoming thoughtful. "I don't regret my choices, but a career on the frontier of anything doesn't leave room for much else." Considering the captain, she allowed the silence to carry for a moment.

"It's funny. I don't remember making a decision to skip family life. I just became wrapped up in my work and kept postponing and postponing until the decision seemed to have been made for me."

Picard let disbelief show in his face. "I'm sorry, Julia, but I can't believe that there has never been someone special for you."

The doctor smiled wryly. "Oh, there have been a number of someones, and some of them have been special, but none of them stands out. I used to wonder if the person I was waiting for even existed." Julia punctuated her words with a short laugh. "Then again, if he's an alien, this is the perfect place to run into him. How about you? Was there ever a time . . . ?"

He shook his head. "No, it never seemed quite possible. For one thing, I was never in one place long enough."

Julia stopped beneath a lightpost and turned to face him. "You know, Dixon, I think I was right about you."

He met her gaze directly. "How so?"

She shrugged. "My first impression was that you looked like a good man."

Picard looked into her eyes, so open and vulnerable. "I think my first impression of you was correct as well."

"And what was that?"

"I thought you were lovely," he said.

Julia smiled again. "As I recall, you were suffering from a moderate concussion that was affecting your vision."

"Well, then," he went on, "my more sober state of mind has borne out that first impression."

Julia's smile faded and she leaned into him, so close he could feel the warmth of her face. Then the kiss came, firm and tender. Picard responded briefly, and they broke apart at the same time.

For a moment, her face remained open, then closed behind a wall of self-consciousness. "I'm sorry. That wasn't very professional of me. You are, after all, still my patient." She took a step back, composing herself. "I will stop by tomorrow to see how you are. You know the way back, don't you?"

Nodding, Picard watched as she walked away. Grateful for her retreat, he continued to his quarters. Julia was just the sort of complication he was striving to avoid. He couldn't have emotional ties to people who would so shortly . . .

Not when those ties could alter a history that he had no right to change.

"Mr. Hill," came a voice from behind him.

The captain turned to see Lieutenant Harold striding to catch up with him. "Sorry, sir, but I'm supposed to see that you, ah—"

"It's quite all right, Lieutenant. You're under orders," Picard assured him.

With his escort, the captain made his way back to his quarters. Though he wasn't certain, he guessed that Harold would be stationed outside the door at least until he was replaced by another person. Now that Travers had made his suspicions clear, Picard doubted that he would be shy about letting his guest know how closely he was being watched. The situation complicated the captain's plans significantly.

And Julia was an additional complication. He would have to keep his judgment absolutely clear. In the end, he would do what he had to do.

Yet the idea of sneaking out of the outpost like a thief in the night left Picard cold. Up until then, his unease with his plan had simply been a dark undercurrent to his thoughts. But now that he began to think in practical and immediate terms of his escape, it hit him: he would be running out on these people.

Julia and the rest of the colonists were not mere historical figures—at least not yet. They were living beings, Starfleet personnel—whom Picard had taken an oath to protect. And that oath did not specify the time periods in which those people lived.

Once again, he saw Julia's face . . . her pleasure at sharing things with a stranger she should have been suspicious of, but trusted instead. Then he thought of Travers's words.

The captain had never been called a coward before

—certainly not by a fellow officer. And despite the years that separated their service, the man *was* a fellow officer.

What's more, Picard still couldn't muster an ounce of indignation—because he couldn't be entirely sure that Travers wasn't right.

Chapter Six

PICARD SAT on the edge of his bed and sighed. Since his arrival on Cestus III, he had received regular visits from Dr. Santos—but not today. Apparently, he decided, she was too embarrassed by the events of the night before.

Truth to tell, the captain was embarrassed as well. He could not blame his behavior on the evening's beverage; he'd had more to drink every night with dinner as a child. No, it was not the wine that had intoxicated him to the point of forgetting—if only for a moment—who and where he was.

It was Julia who had done that. Picard had a difficult time even thinking of her other than by her first name now. After all, she was already more than a doctor—she was a friend to him. And he knew she could have become even more than that, if he'd let her.

But like her, he was a professional. Not just a man

155

lost in space and time, but an officer—with an officer's responsibilities. And like it or not, he had to put those responsibilities first.

Which is why he'd dedicated this morning to pondering his situation—and the fact that unless he could alert his first officer to his whereabouts, he would never see his own era again. Unfortunately, though he'd gone over it and over it, he still could not see a solution.

Yet there had to be a way to contact Will. There *had* to be. It was only a matter of finding it.

The captain kept coming back to his communicator, useless as it was. If only there were a way of preserving its signal long enough for it to be detected a hundred years from now. Then Riker could recover it and know not only where he was, but—by virtue of the ship's nucleonic dating techniques—*when* he was.

However, even in the twenty-fourth century, no one had developed a power source with that kind of staying power. There simply wasn't a need for it. And if it wasn't around in the twenty-fourth century, it certainly wouldn't be around in the twenty-third.

Forget the communicator, he told himself. *Think of something else. A signal that will be recognized by neither the colonists nor the Gorn, when they arrive— but will be seen and understood by your Number One a century hence.*

Something detectable by long-range sensors. Something which could not be mistaken for a natural formation or phenomenon. Something that could only have originated with—

His thoughts were cut short by a whistling at his door. "Come," Picard responded, appreciative that his visitor hadn't just barged in, as he or she could have. After all, he *was* still under surveillance here.

As the doors hissed open, they revealed the identity of his caller. The captain found himself smiling before he could prevent it. But then, *she* was smiling, too.

"Julia," he said, acknowledging her. So she had decided to come by after all, embarrassment or no embarrassment. And despite the ramifications, he found that he was very glad to see her.

"In the flesh," she replied. "And I've got some very exciting news."

Picard wondered a little warily what that might be. "Yes?" he prompted.

The doctor's eyes narrowed. "No. Come to think of it, I won't tell you." She held out her hand to him. "I'll show you."

Accepting her hand, he allowed her to guide him outside—and in the direction of the sensor control facility.

The Bon Amar.

Riker rolled the name around in his head. Six spaceworthy ships, he thought, running his fingers through his hair. An opportunity to cut down their search time drastically, maybe even within the parameters established by Admiral Kowalski. . . .

Abruptly, a high-pitched beep intruded on his cogitations. Turning to the door, he said, "Come in."

He wasn't sure whom he'd expected, but it wasn't Deanna Troi. He was surprised—and pleasantly so.

"Am I interrupting anything?" she asked.

Riker smiled wearily. "Absolutely not." Leaning back in his chair, away from his computer console, he indicated an empty chair across the room.

The Betazoid shook her head. "No, thanks. I won't be staying long. There is too much I still need to take care of today."

It reminded the first officer that even during a crisis, life went on. Troi would have her usual round of consultations and evaluations to perform, regardless of whether the captain was here or not—or what kind of political turmoil the Gorn homeworld was in.

"So," he said, "what brings you here in the middle of your busy day, Counselor? Not that you need an excuse, mind you."

"*You* bring me here," she replied. She glanced at the computer terminal. "You know, you're supposed to be using this time to sleep, not to tinker."

Riker shrugged, feeling some cramping in his shoulders where they met his neck. Reaching across his body, he kneaded the muscle on the left side with his right hand. It was as hard as a rock.

"Can't help it," he told her. "I was exploring my options." He glanced again at the computer screen. "Such as they are."

Coming around to a position directly behind him, Troi peered past him at the screen. "Bon Amar?" she asked. "The Bajoran *pirates?*"

"The pirates," he confirmed. "Deanna, would you mind . . . ?"

Before he could even finish the question, he felt her remove his hand from his shoulder muscle. In the next breath, her fingers probed along either side of his neck with just the right amount of firmness.

Of course, she was an empath. She could feel what he was feeling, even as he was feeling it, and make whatever minute adjustments were necessary. In the time it would take someone else just to figure out where the ache was, Troi would have already made it go away.

"The Bon Amar," she reminded him, making small, circular forays into the muscular trouble spots. "Am I to understand that they represent one of your options?"

Riker stared at the screen and sighed. "They could," he told her, "if I allow them to. Apparently, Ro knows how to contact them. She offered me their services in locating Captain Picard."

The Betazoid played the cords at the base of his neck like piano keys, loosening them up a bit more. "And will you take her up on her offer?"

He shook his head. "I don't think so. I keep trying to imagine what the captain would do in my place. And I can't see him enlisting outlaws in his cause—no matter how right or important that cause might be."

"The ends wouldn't justify the means?" Troi suggested.

Riker nodded. "Something like that."

Now that he was somewhat relaxed, she dug a little deeper. "And what about Geordi? What sort of progress is he making?"

The first officer frowned. He could see Troi's face reflected in the computer screen, superimposed over the data on the Bon Amar. She was frowning, too.

"Not enough," he confided. "And there's a problem now with the station. Some sort of power surges, which could destroy the equipment at any moment. And if the equipment goes . . ." He allowed his voice to trail off meaningfully.

The Betazoid nodded. "I see."

Her fingers delved as deep as the epicenters of his discomfort. Riker winced at the pain she aroused with her explorations, grateful for her assistance.

"And," she went on, "the situation on Gorn doesn't seem to be getting any better. Two days is not a lot of time when you are searching so large an area."

"No," he agreed, "it's not." He could feel his nostrils flare with frustration. "Deanna . . . between you and me . . . I don't think we're going to make it."

Troi paused in her massage for just a fraction of a second—but Riker was aware of it. "You don't think we're going to find the captain? But just the other day . . ."

"I know," he told her. "I was confident. Hopeful. Despite the odds, I wasn't going to give up. But that was the other day. Today, I've got a bad feeling. A *very* bad feeling."

In the next moment, he felt simultaneous, tiny bursts of agony—one on either side of his neck. Then the pain was gone. Just like that.

Reaching up, he grasped one of Troi's hands. It felt good in his. Slim and soft as it was, he took strength from it. And she left it there just long enough before reclaiming it.

"Of course," she said, "you could *change* the odds.

You could exercise the option that Ensign Ro has put in front of you."

He turned in his chair to look up at her. "They're outlaws," he reminded her.

Troi's dark eyes fixed on him. "Yes. But they could also be the captain's salvation."

"Then if you were me," Riker asked, "you'd bend the rules? You'd ask the Bon Amar for help?"

The Betazoid smiled wistfully. "I'm not you, Will."

And yet, he had a feeling which way she'd go.

The first officer grunted. "Thanks, Counselor. For your help—all of it."

Troi shrugged, gently patting Riker on the shoulder. "It's my job," she said, "to lend support to my commanding officer in times of duress."

He returned her smile. "And you're damned good at it."

Then she was on her way to the door, and those other responsibilities that awaited her. Riker waved to her as she departed, leaned forward in his chair, and eyed the computer screen.

The Bon Amar . . .

"Last time, I got the impression Commander Hronsky wasn't so eager to see me down there," noted Picard.

They were descending the metal stairs that led to the colony's sensor control facility. Julia looked back at him and winked.

"I don't think he'll notice," she said. "He's too busy accepting congratulations from everyone. Besides, he's always been a lot more close-to-the-vest than he has to be. I mean, you're not exactly a Romulan spy."

No, the captain agreed silently. He was something a good deal more dangerous, though he certainly wasn't about to say so.

"Congratulations?" he echoed. "For what?"

"That would be telling," she noted. "And I promised not to do that."

Fortunately, he wouldn't be kept in the dark for long. With Julia taking the lead, they entered the control center—only to find the place even more crowded than the last time Picard had been there.

In the middle of it all, Hronsky was holding up his hands for silence. "Calm down now," he was saying, though his expression said that he wanted anything *but* calm. "We don't know anything about them yet. We just know they're *there.*"

Them? Abruptly, the captain felt a trickle of ice water slide down his back. Could it be that Hronsky had . . . ?

"Then the rumors were true," observed a man with thinning hair and a red beard.

"Apparently," replied the chief engineer.

"Are they spacefaring?" a woman asked.

"As I said," Hronsky told her, "we don't know a thing. What we've hit on could be an entire civilization or an outpost world of something much larger. There's just no way to tell at this point."

But Picard knew. After all, he'd been through this part of space often enough to be an expert on it—and there was only one sentient race close enough for the sensors to have detected. Only one race close enough to resent the Federation's presence on Cestus III.

The Gorn.

The captain marveled at the bizarre irony. The colonists had had some advance knowledge of their attackers after all. Not the kind of knowledge that would have helped them, certainly, but knowledge nonetheless.

Yet history never recorded this. Which was to say, Matthew Harold never mentioned it, since he was history's only source in the matter. Had he simply neglected to mention it? Or had he been so badly traumatized that it escaped his mind?

"So," said Julia. "What do you think, Dixon?"

Picard returned her gaze. "It's . . . very exciting," he responded. "Very exciting indeed."

"How in blazes did you get a fix on something that far away?" The captain recognized the voice as belonging to Travers, though he couldn't see the man for the crowd between them.

The chief engineer shrugged. "It wasn't as hard as you might think. I just stepped up the magnetic injection ratio in the power source. Not much, just a dozen points, the way they did it on those starships recently. Once I had all that extra juice, it was child's play to extend the sensor range."

Picard was still mulling over Hronsky's discovery, so deep in thought as he considered the ramifications that he failed to hear the engineer's words on a conscious level. However, he must have heard them on some other level, because an alarm went off in his brain.

Hronsky had done *what?* Stepped up the magnetic injection ratio a dozen points? But when the captain had seen the ratio last, it was already at two hundred —the maximum recommended number for this kind of reactor.

At an increase of twelve points, the pressure would become too great. The dilithium crystal would shatter, causing a runaway reaction that would eventually breach the reactor's magnetic vessel and cause the whole thing to explode—taking the colony and a sizable chunk of Cestus III along with it.

"No," the captain said out loud. "It's too much."

Julia's forehead wrinkled ever so slightly. "I beg your pardon?"

"It's too much," he repeated. And before he realized it, he was making his way through the throng toward Hronsky—not knowing what he would say, but knowing that he had to say something.

Before he quite got there, however, he felt a hand close on his arm. Tracing it to a face, he saw that it was the commodore who'd gotten hold of him.

"Hill," Travers said flatly, as if the very word left a bad taste in his mouth. "What are you doing here? This area is supposed to be secure." Peering over the heads of the assembled colonists, he must have spotted Julia's among them, because his next comment was "Oh. I see."

"Let me go," insisted Picard. "I must speak with Commander Hronsky."

The commodore's brow furrowed. "And why is that?" he asked.

The captain frowned. "Because if he's not careful, he's going to blow up the whole colony."

Travers regarded him, not certain whether to get angry or to laugh. "Blow up the colony," he repeated. "And I suppose you've got some property on Risa you want to sell me."

Shrugging off the commodore's grip, Picard continued his passage toward the chief engineer—and beyond him, the control console for the sensor array. Hronsky held up his hand.

"That's far enough, Mr. Hill. Don't make me call for security."

All eyes were on the captain now as he pointed to the power gauge on the console. "Two-twelve is too high. Your dilithium crystal won't be able to take that kind of pressure."

The engineer looked at him askance, his arms folded across his chest. "And how would you know? This isn't the same kind of engine they use on commercial vessels."

Indeed, how *would* he know—if he were truly Dixon Hill, captain of a merchant ship called the *Stargazer,* and not the man in charge of the twenty-fourth-century *Enterprise?*

"I've known a few Starfleet officers in my day," said Picard. "And none of them would think of taking their injection ratios higher than two hundred."

Hronsky harrumphed. "Then, obviously, you haven't been introduced to Captain Lasker of the *Iroquois.* Or Captain Tranh of the *Peerless.* They've been running their injection ratios at two-fifteen for weeks now, with no sign of a problem." He shook his head derisively. "As if I need to answer to you, Mr. Hill."

The captain let the remark slip off his back. There was no room for emotions here. He had to get his point across before this celebration turned into disaster.

To be sure, Hronsky was right about both ships. But some twenty-five days after it initiated the experiment, the *Iroquois* suffered a runaway reaction that tore it in half. And the *Peerless* would have suffered the same fate—or at least, that's what an investigation showed—if it hadn't pulled back on its injection ratio when its sister ship was destroyed.

"Those vessels have bigger core chambers," Picard pointed out, rightly enough. "In their cases, it will take longer for the pressure to build up. But here . . ." He indicated the power gauge again. "The chamber is small. We've got to lower the ratio now, while there's still time."

Travers shouldered his way in front of the captain. "You sound quite sure of yourself, Mr. Hill. But Starfleet Command is quite sure of the contrary, or they wouldn't have authorized the experiments on the *Peerless* and the *Iroquois.*"

Picard's lips compressed in a thin, tight line as he tried his damnedest to hold back his frustration. He couldn't stop what Hronsky was doing without giving away who he was. And he couldn't give away who he was without risking a mutilation of this timeline.

"Starfleet Command is wrong," he told the commodore—rather weakly, he knew. "The *Iroquois* won't last the month. And the *Peerless* will discontinue the experiment." The captain cursed inwardly. "Listen . . . just humor me. Turn the pressure down for a few days. Run some more tests. And then, if—"

"If nothing," said Travers. "I don't recall asking you for advice on how to run this colony, sir. In fact, of all and sundry assembled here, you are the *last* person I would ask for advice."

He looked to Julia, who had come up behind Picard. "Sorry," she told the commodore. "I didn't expect there to be any problem with bringing him here."

The captain turned to her. "Julia . . . I am not trying to mislead anyone. I know of what I speak. If nothing is done, this colony will be annihilated."

She looked at him, wanting to believe—wanting not to think he was crazy, or worse, a deceiver of some kind. But he hadn't produced any evidence to convince her or anyone else. Nor was he likely to.

And in the long run, did it matter? The Gorn would be here soon enough. Either way, these people were going to die. Either way, they—

"Commodore?"

They all turned around to see First Officer Schmitter standing in the doorway. The man was looking straight at Picard—not a good sign, in the captain's estimate.

Travers returned his security officer's gaze. "Yes, Hans? What is it?"

Still scrutinizing the man he'd known as Dixon Hill, Schmitter cleared his throat. "I've just received a response to the inquiry we placed with Starfleet

Command, sir. They say there is no one named Dixon Hill currently operating a commercial vessel—nor, for that matter, has there *ever* been."

The commodore smiled grimly. "I see," he noted. "And the ship our Mr. Hill claimed to command?"

Schmitter allowed himself a small, private smile. Hell, Picard might have found this amusing too, if their circumstances had been reversed.

"A *Stargazer* was destroyed almost a year ago," replied the security officer. "On the other side of Federation space. According to Starfleet records, the *Stargazer*'s travels never took it within a hundred light-years of Cestus Three."

Picard swallowed. Apparently, the jig was up.

Julia Santos was shaking her head, refusing to believe that her newfound friend had lied about these things. But her bias in his favor was hardly a secret these days—and even she couldn't argue with cold, hard Starfleet facts.

Travers cleared his throat—almost happily, the captain thought. "Well, Mr. Hill—or whatever your name is. Care to comment on this less-than-startling revelation?"

Picard remained silent. What could he say now that they'd believe? At this point, not much.

The commodore looked at him askance. "Cat's got your tongue, I see. No surprise there either, I suppose. Of course, that still leaves us with a mystery on our hands, namely—"

"Wait a minute," interjected Hronsky. As he peered at Picard from beneath his shaggy, dark brows, he unconsciously laid a paternal hand on the top of his control console. "What if this man is a spy for . . ." He tilted his head to indicate the console's monitor, where the telltale sensor image was still in evidence. ". . . for *them?*"

That stopped everyone dead in their tracks—Travers included. He looked at the stranger in their midst with a whole new level of mistrust.

"That would explain why he was so eager to throw a monkey wrench into the project," Hronsky went on. "He didn't want us to catch on to the fact that there was a civilization out there."

Schmitter nodded. "Makes sense, in a way. Of course, he's human—but that doesn't really mean anything. He could have hired himself out to an alien race . . . maybe not even the one that the sensors picked up."

Travers turned to his security chief. "You mean the Klingons?"

"Or the Romulans," Schmitter suggested. "Could be they wanted that civilization all to themselves. And they needed someone on the inside to keep us from getting wind of it."

"That's ridiculous," Santos argued. She turned to the captain, her eyes clouded with just a hint of suspicion. "It *is* ridiculous, isn't it?"

Picard nodded. "Yes. I am not a spy—not for the Klingons or the Romulans or anyone else."

The commodore grunted. "Then who *are* you?"

The captain frowned. "Believe me," he said. "You don't want to know."

Travers looked from one of his officers to the next, taking them all in. Only Santos showed any faith at all that the stranger wasn't up to no good—and even she didn't seem so sure of it. Finally, the commodore turned back to Picard himself.

"I'm not entirely sure that I buy this spy story," he decided. "For one thing, you could have gone to more trouble to secure a believable identity." He shook his head. "But whoever you are, I don't trust you one little bit." Without looking at his security officer, he said, "Hans?"

Schmitter straightened. "The brig, sir?"

"The brig," Travers confirmed. "At least until we can get a starship out here to take him into custody. After that, he's Starfleet's problem."

"I've got another one," Barclay announced proudly.

Geordi turned away from his own work below a denuded control console to look at the lieutenant, who was standing in front of a similar console on the other side of the room. Barclay's fingers were running over the pads and keys on his control board while he eyed the monitor above it.

Data and O'Connor had popped their heads out as well. O'Connor looked hopeful; the android was as emotionless as ever, at least on the outside.

"Good going, Reg," said the chief engineer. "Any idea what it is?"

La Forge tried his best to keep the strain out of his voice. After all, Barclay was high-strung enough as it was. The last thing he needed was a stepped-up sense of urgency.

"Don't know," said the thin man, his eyes flickering across the screen. His lips pressed together as he concentrated. "Not for sure, anyway. But . . ." Suddenly, he cast a glance in Geordi's direction. "I wonder if this could be . . . their retrieval beam!"

The chief engineer cursed softly. So far, working like demons, they had coaxed a number of systems into operation—even if they hadn't the slightest idea how they worked.

First, there had been the sensor-access monitor, which was virtually useless as a search tool without its associated memory banks. Then they'd gotten something similar to an annular confinement beam up and running. Next, they had restored what appeared to be a transporter lock. And most recently, they'd added a time-space adjustment device, which allowed for the passage of planets through space.

After all, any given world could move tens of millions of kilometers in as little as half a solar year. If the transporter couldn't adjust for this, it might only send people and things to a world's current location, as opposed to the position it occupied at a designated point in the past. The result? It would be beaming its transportees into the void, which would hardly be to their liking.

In any case, with all these systems purring contentedly, they could now lock on to a subject—provided they knew where it was—and by virtue of the monitor, actually see what they had locked on to. Then, with the help of the time-space adjuster and the confinement beam analog, they could establish a path through space and time for the subject's atoms to travel along.

Now Barclay thought he had gotten the retrieval

system going. If he was right, they had everything they needed to bring the captain back. Except for two little items, of course. One was the ability to reassemble Captain Picard's atoms once they were drawn back into the station. The other was a set of coordinates describing where and when he was.

But first things first. If they really had a working retrieval system, it would be simple enough to prove it. And if not, at least they would know where they stood.

"Reg," Geordi ventured, "can you get your system working in tandem with the others?"

Barclay's brow creased as he attempted to comply. A moment later, he recoiled a couple of inches. Then he looked to his superior and shrugged.

"Apparently," he explained, in his characteristic start-and-stop way, "the system's beaten me to it. I mean, it's working in tandem with the other routines already. I guess that's how it was designed."

Geordi felt grateful for the small favor. At least *something* was going right. "All right, then," he said. "In that case, let's put it through its paces."

Careful not to hit his head as he had before, the chief engineer swung himself up to a standing position and crossed the room. Stopping just behind Barclay, he watched the man lock on to a subject pictured on the sensor system's monitor. Immediately, the images flickering across the screen stopped.

What it showed them now was some kind of ancient building, more than half in ruin. To Geordi, it looked like the remnants of the Achorri civilization that he'd seen with his family at the age of ten. Or was it eleven?

In any case, it gave them a convenient object to use in their test. The chief engineer pointed past Barclay to the central structure in the ruins—something that might have been a statue of a venerated ancestor, if the race in question had four arms and six legs. On the other hand, it could also have been a piece of furniture; it was hard to tell.

"Let's try for that thing," Geordi instructed.

Barclay nodded. Operating the controls accordingly, he activated the system. There was a hum, more felt than heard, which lasted only a few seconds. Then all was silent again. His pulse racing, La Forge turned to Data, who was closest to the monitor that kept track of the internal sensor network.

They had worked together for so long, and at so many intricate tasks, the engineer didn't even have to ask. Data knew exactly what he wanted.

"The object in question has been retrieved," the android reported, his eyes fixed on his screen. "What is more, it is on this level." He looked up and gestured toward the corridor outside. "Just down this hall, behind the third door on the left."

Geordi grunted. That solved *that* question. Up until now, they'd had no idea where anything beamed aboard the station would actually appear. Now they had located the beam-on point, at least in this particular node.

"I'm going to check it out," the chief engineer announced. He put a hand on Barclay's shoulder. "You too, Reg. You're the one that got the mechanism going. You deserve to see the fruits of your labor."

A brief smile of gratitude flickering across his face, Barclay followed him out of the control room and down the corridor. The third door on their left had a pad next to it, but Geordi didn't expect it to work for them. He was all set to pry off the panel next to it when the door simply slid aside at his approach.

Apparently, its program was still intact—unlike many of the station's programs, which had been wiped clean during the surge that sent the captain reeling through time and space. Stepping through the portal, the chief engineer peered inside.

The room was dark, and a lot bigger than it had looked from the outside, with graceful arches in the places where the walls met the ceiling. The only illumination within was a circle of very dim, red light at floor level—and even that was fading fast. As Geordi took a closer look, he saw that the ruddy glow had come from a series of energy coils recessed into the deck.

"Look," said Barclay. "There's something here." Kneeling just outside the circle of energy coils, he played his tricorder over the area described by them.

The chief engineer knelt beside him and used his tricorder as well. Sure enough, there *was* something there, something that wasn't part of the transporter arrangement. Geordi would have recognized it sooner, except the material had basically the same texture and energy absorption factors as the surface below it.

But Barclay was right. Concentrating, he saw that there was a solid film coating the center of the aliens' transporter platform. And it hadn't been there before, he bet.

"Could this be . . . ?" The thin man's voice trailed off ominously.

The chief engineer frowned under his VISOR. "I think it is, Reg. Whatever it was we transported here, this is the shape it arrived in." He sat back on his heels, still regarding the film. "So much for working without a reassembling device. But at least it got here. We're a step ahead of where we were before."

Barclay nodded and turned to his superior. "So I guess you could say this was a . . . success?" He glanced pointedly at the stuff within the circle of coils as he awaited an answer.

"I guess," Geordi agreed. Standing up, he took out his phaser. "But we've still got a long way to go." Adjusting the setting, he aimed the phaser at the platform. Then he activated it.

After all, if—no, *when* they ever got a fix on the captain, they didn't want to have to have to transport him with foreign material on the transporter pad.

The stuff burned off in a matter of seconds. When he was finished, La Forge put the phaser away. "Come on," he said, gesturing for Barclay to follow. "Let's—"

Suddenly, the energy coils lit up. Only for a second, but enough to make them wary. And before they could comment on it, it happened a second time. Out in the corridor, the light levels dipped—then, just like that, gave way to a darkness punctuated only by the lights they'd brought with them.

"Uh-oh," said the chief engineer. "I hope that's not

what I think it is." But even as he uttered the words, he knew his hope wouldn't amount to a hill of beans.

More than likely, there was a fair-sized power surge coming. And if that was the case, this room full of energy-transport coils was the *last* place he wanted to be.

"Come on," he urged Barclay, grabbing him by the sleeve. "We've got to get out of here."

The other man didn't have to be told twice. As Geordi lunged through the doorway, Barclay was right on his heels. No doubt, he remembered what happened when Varley was caught half in and half out of a chamber.

They had barely made the turn toward the control room when they saw a series of light pulses run the length of the bulkheads and back again. If there had been any doubt of what was going on before, there wasn't any now.

Geordi's teeth ground together as he ran down the hallway. Not now, he told himself. We were just starting to get to the point where we could bring the captain back. We can't have come this far only to have to close up shop ahead of time.

The chief engineer beat his companion back to the control room. Fortunately, the lights were still on in there. Planting his hand against the far side of the entrance to stop his forward progress, he wrestled himself inside. O'Connor was busy monitoring his tricorder while Data worked furiously at one of the consoles. The android barely looked up to acknowledge his friend's entrance.

"How bad is it?" Geordi asked.

O'Connor shook her head. "It's hard to tell, but it

seems to be escalating. And if the trend continues, it could be as bad as the surge that transported Captain Picard."

The chief engineer bit his lip. They would never make enough progress in the next few minutes to bring the captain back from wherever he'd gone. As much as he hated the idea, what choice did he have . . . but to evacuate?

"Commander," said Data, as calmly as if all of eternity were at his beck and call, "I am pursuing an idea that just occurred to me. Though there seems to be no way to prevent the energy surges, perhaps I can coax the station into *releasing* some of the pent-up energy."

Geordi thought about it for a moment. Release the energy? Sure . . . but how? He asked the question out loud. Nor was the android slow in giving him an answer.

"I am attempting," he said, "to boost the input levels on the aliens' confinement beam by recycling power through the emitter array."

Barclay, who had been standing off to the side, shook his head. "But we're not transporting anything else aboard right now. What's the point of sending out a beam if—"

And then he stopped himself, no doubt realizing what Data had in mind. By then, Geordi had seen the android's strategy as well. The confinement beam expended energy—a fair amount of it, too, considering it had to travel through time as well as space. And if they could get energy to leave the station almost as quickly as it was building up, the confinement beam might turn out to be a pretty good safety valve.

At least, that was the *theory*. In practice, there was no guarantee at all that it would work—other than the knowledge that Data had some confidence in it.

"Reg," said the chief engineer, "make sure all our forcefields are still in operation. If Commander Data's plan doesn't work, I want to know that we've still got an escape route."

"Aye, sir," replied Barclay, heading out into the corridor to carry out his orders. His voice trembled just a little, Geordi noted. But after that, his attention was fixed on the android, whose fingers were flying over his console so quickly now that no biological imaging system could have kept up with them.

"Power surges still mounting in intensity," reported O'Connor. "Also, they're coming no more than fifteen seconds apart. Estimate systems overload in four and a half minutes."

It would take at least a minute to leave the control room, return to the hatch, and get back into their shuttle. And another thirty seconds or so to remove themselves from the vicinity of the station, so that if something exploded, they would be well out of range.

So Data really had three minutes, maximum. And he must have known it, because his synthetic fingers seemed to weave and stitch their way over the controls even a little faster than before.

There was a sound of footfalls clattering along the corridor, and Barclay popped back into the control room. "All's clear," he informed them. "Everything's working the . . . um, the way it's supposed to." Before he finished, he was staring at the android, too.

"Data?" prompted Geordi. "How are we doing?"

His friend answered without taking his eyes off his work. "The beam is operating at maximum output. I cannot increase it any further; I can only make certain that the output does not tend to diminish."

"Three and a half minutes," noted O'Connor. Which really meant *two*.

The chief engineer had never felt so helpless in his entire life. The captain's life was hanging in the balance, and all he could do was watch. Each second seemed to drag on forever.

"Three minutes," announced O'Connor. And then: "Two and a half." Which meant one and a half, and finally one. One minute before they had to abandon the place—and Captain Picard along with it.

"Hang on," said O'Connor. Her brow creased as she stared at her tricorder. "The surges have stopped accelerating."

Geordi realized that his hands had curled into fists. He forced them to relax. "Stopped?" he repeated.

"Aye, sir," replied O'Connor. "We're still experiencing the surges, but they're not getting any worse. In fact," she went on, her eyes reflecting her readout, "they're starting to cycle down."

The chief engineer let out a sigh. They weren't out of the woods yet, of course. But he would embrace any excuse for optimism he could find.

And he found another excuse in the corridor outside, as the corridor lighting dimmed and went out. The station was returning to normal, or at least as normal as it got here. Data's idea seemed to be working just fine. It had just taken a while, is all.

"The surges are all but gone now," the android told

179

them. For the first time since the crisis had begun, he looked up at Geordi. "Power levels are stabilizing. Now would be a good time to resume our work, I think."

La Forge nodded. But first, he'd have to call Commander Riker and tell him that the situation was getting worse. If they were going to retrieve the captain, it would have to be *soon*.

Chapter Seven

THE COLONY'S BRIG had an inhospitable feeling about it—as if it hadn't been used for . . . what? Months? Years? Or, for that matter, *ever*?

As Picard paced the narrow limits of his cell, with its three solid walls and a transparent energy barrier across its front, he mused that *ever* was probably the correct answer. The plastic containers piled immediately outside the brig's entrance were a clue, telling him that his place of confinement had been used as a storage area until shortly before his arrival.

The captain eyed the tall, dark-haired security officer who stood guard in the larger room outside. He doubted that the man would fall for a feigned attack of food poisoning or the like. Even in the twenty-third century, the Academy had warned their security cadets about such ploys.

Leaning against one of the walls of his cell, Picard

181

sighed. He would not have thought it possible for his situation to get any more complicated. And yet, as if some fiendishly sadistic deity were looking after him, it had.

If time unraveled the way history had taught him it would, Lieutenant Harold was slated to survive the massacre by the Gorn. That was just about the only fact he could cling to with any certainty.

However, a matter-antimatter explosion would leave no survivors. That was an irrefutable scientific fact. Therefore, if time was to follow the course he knew, there would be—*could* be—no explosion.

And yet, he had seen evidence of the power source's instability. It was real, not imagined. If left alone, it would have devastating consequences.

The captain scowled. So there were two possibilities. Either history would be changed—or someone would prevent the explosion. And if someone did prevent it, who would that someone be?

Try as he might, he could come up with only one answer.

It was an almost poetic notion, wasn't it? To be thrown back in time by an apparent accident—only to find oneself the instrument by which history maintains its course. Poetic indeed.

Or—and there was always an *or* when dealing with the sanctity of the timestream—was it possible that his intervention would somehow have the opposite effect? Would he throw history off course, despite his best efforts, in some way he hadn't considered—and thereby eliminate the timeline in which he and the Federation made peace with the Gorn?

There was no way to know for sure. All Picard had to go on was his instincts—and his instincts told him that he had to prevent the matter-antimatter source from going haywire. As ironic as it sounded, he had to save the outpost and its people—so that the Gorn could destroy them a short time later.

The captain took in his surroundings and sighed again. But you can't do anything, he told himself, as long as you're stuck here in the brig. So the first step is to get *out* of here.

The thought had barely formed in his mind when the doors to the larger room opened and Julia Santos walked in. Immediately, her eyes flicked in Picard's direction—but only for a moment. Then she was giving the guard her full attention.

"I'm sorry, ma'am," the man was saying. "He's not supposed to have any visitors."

"I'm not just a visitor," Julia replied. "I'm a doctor. And despite whatever else may have happened, he is still my patient."

The security officer frowned. Casting a glance in Picard's direction, he seemed to momentarily assess the prisoner's potential for violence. In the end, he nodded.

"All right," he said. "But make it as quick as possible, okay?"

Agreeing that she would do that, Julia approached the energy barrier. This time, when her eyes met the captain's, they did not let go.

"How are you feeling?" she asked.

Picard shrugged. "I don't like being incarcerated. Other than that, not badly."

The doctor turned to look back over her shoulder. "I need to go inside," she told the security officer.

The man made a sound of exasperation, but Julia stood firm. Obviously acquainted with her stubbornness, and knowing where any argument would eventually end, the redshirt covered the distance to the brig in four long strides.

Taking out his phaser, he made sure that it was set on stun. Then he touched the pressure-sensitive wall pad that governed the barrier. A moment later, it was gone, allowing the physician to step over the threshold.

As soon as she was inside, however, the security officer reactivated the energy field. When Julia looked at him, he shrugged. But this time, she didn't protest. After all, the man was only doing his job—just as she was.

There was a bench built into the wall in the back of the cell. The captain indicated it with a gesture that smacked of more gentile surroundings.

Normally, the doctor would have been amused by the incongruity. However, her expression didn't change as she accepted his offer and took a seat. Sitting down next to her, Picard watched her eyes as she ran her tricorder over him.

He would have to keep his voice low. He didn't want what he had to say to be overheard by his guard.

"Julia . . ." he began.

She shook her head. "No," she corrected. "Dr. Santos. Julia was the one who trusted you, remember? Me, I'm just your doctor." With forced intensity, she studied her tricorder readings.

The captain nodded. "All right. I deserved that. But despite what I've done and said, I need your help."

The doctor chuckled dryly. "Of course you do."

"I mean it," Picard insisted. "I wasn't lying about that matter-antimatter core. It's going to experience a runaway reaction. And when it does, it will take the whole colony with it."

Julia's expression changed ever so slightly, as if she was at least thinking about believing in him again. Then she turned away.

"Look, Mr. Hill, or whatever you're *really* called. I don't have time for your shenanigans anymore, so let's just drop it."

"They're not shenanigans," he told her. "I can prevent the core from exploding. But to do that, I need your help. I need to get out of here."

When the doctor allowed her eyes to meet his again, they were full of undisguised, red-rimmed hurt. The captain winced at the sight of them.

"I trusted you," she said, her voice flat and accusing. "And I got burned. Now you want me to trust you again? To . . . to commit *mutiny* for you?" She grunted. "You must be out of your head."

Picard cursed inwardly. This was his one chance. He couldn't afford to let it get away—even if it meant risking everything on one roll of the dice.

He licked his lips. "What if I told you I could *prove* I know what I'm talking about?"

That got her attention. "Prove it?" she echoed warily.

"Yes. What then?"

Julia looked at him askance. "I'm listening. Just for the entertainment value, mind you."

The captain knew what kind of chance he was taking. But he was guided by the eerie knowledge that she wouldn't live to spread the story he was telling her; it was just a question of which disaster would claim her first.

"My name," he told her, "is Jean-Luc Picard. I command a Federation starship called the *Enterprise.*" He paused, letting what he'd said so far begin to sink in. Then he hit her with the punchline. "However, if you were to look up the captain of that vessel, you would find that his name is James T. Kirk. That is because *my Enterprise* exists in the twenty-fourth century."

Julia blinked—once, twice. Then an expression of disappointment came over her. "I thought you'd do better than that," she responded. "I mean, *really.*"

Of course, Picard had known this wouldn't be easy. "Think, Julia. I have a bionic heart, engineered to imitate my cell structure. Have you ever heard of any race, Federation member or otherwise, capable of manufacturing such a device?"

The doctor recognized the question as rhetorical. "Go on," she instructed.

"As the commodore pointed out, I have no scar tissue to indicate that the procedure ever took place. In fact, I have no scar tissue at all. And I'm immune to the common cold. Why? Because in my era, medical science has made great strides in cell replication and immunology."

Julia sighed. He had made it difficult for her to remain completely skeptical, but he still had a long way to go.

"Now you know why I didn't want to divulge my identity," the captain persisted. "Because I didn't want to upset the flow of sequential time by my presence here—which, I assure you, is completely accidental. And now you also know how I can be so sure about the defect in your power source. In this time, matter-antimatter technology hasn't come far enough to detect such problems. But in mine, even a cadet knows how to look for them."

The doctor's green eyes narrowed. "I'll give you credit. It almost sounds convincing. But if you were truly concerned about messing up the flow of sequential time, you wouldn't be telling me all this—would you? You'd be keeping your mouth shut, no matter what."

Picard shrugged. "Not if I knew that this outpost isn't *supposed* to be destroyed by a matter-antimatter accident. Not if I suspected that my presence here was necessary to the *prevention* of that accident."

Julia was wavering, but the captain still hadn't won her over. He could see it in the rather stubborn set of her jaw.

"Surely," he said, "you've heard rumors of time travel . . . of a planet, perhaps, where something called The Guardian of Forever provides access to all the ages of the universe?"

At the mention of that name, her expression softened. "Yes," she replied, after a moment. "I have heard rumors of people traveling through time.

But . . ." She paused. "Until now, I thought they were just fantasies."

Picard's heart pounded a little harder. "Then you believe me?"

The doctor swallowed. "Don't put words in my mouth. All I said was that I'd heard *rumors."*

The captain decided to switch tacks. "Not so long ago," he reminded her, "your physician's instincts told you I was a good man. What do they tell you now, Julia? That I'm an exquisitely apt liar, trying to obtain access to your power source for my own selfish ends? Or that I am who and what I say I am—and that if we don't act soon, you and all your colleagues will meet with catastrophe?"

Julia stared at him—and swore softly. "There's something strange about you, all right. I said that from the beginning. But . . . a man from the future? I don't know. I just don't know."

"Because the stakes are too high if you're wrong?" Picard suggested.

She nodded. "Yes. Because the stakes are too high."

The captain laid his hand on her tricorder—and in the process, brushed against the doctor's fingers. Her skin was soft and warm to his touch, reminding him of their embrace the night of the commodore's dinner. But he couldn't let himself be distracted now, no matter how much he would have liked to be.

"You want to be sure about me," he said. "Then program your tricorder to act as a lie detector. I'm certain that you know how—medical students have been doing it since the damned things were invented."

Julia hesitated. "You've got a bionic heart," she told him. "How do I know that this will work?"

Picard smiled. "Because my heart is the *only* thing that's artificial about me. And, ultimately, because you have to trust *something*, or we will never get to the bottom of this."

That seemed to satisfy her. Focusing her attention on her tricorder for the moment, she set it to measure his pulse rate and several other physiological indicators. Then she looked up again.

"What is your name?" she asked.

"My name," he told her, "is Jean-Luc Picard."

"And your business here?" The doctor glanced down at the tricorder's tiny, electronic readout.

"I came here accidentally," the captain repeated. "Ultimately, my goal is to return to my own time, if that is possible. But whether it is or not, I would like to prevent your power source from exploding—and wiping out this entire colony."

Julia's brow puckered. When she looked up at him, it was with an entirely new perspective. "It says you're telling the truth," she reported.

"As well it should," Picard remarked. "Now, will you help me?"

The doctor was obviously torn—between her wounded pride and skepticism on the one hand and the tricorder's evidence on the other. And from what the captain could see, it was a standoff.

Suddenly, he heard the approach of the guard, his heels rapping sharply on the hard-plastic floor. He looked as if he'd made about all the concessions he was going to. After all, how long did it take to make a pass over someone with a tricorder?

His opportunity was slipping away. But what could he do? If he tried anything, the guard would be treating him to the wrong end of a phaser.

"Julia," the captain pressed, "we dare not wait any longer. If I'm to keep this colony from being—"

"Shut up, already," she told him. She glared at him. "Just shut up, will you?" Abruptly, her gaze softened. "And when you see your chance, take it."

Picard almost smiled. *Almost.* But since that would have given them away, he maintained as dour and downcast an expression as possible. The guard didn't seem to notice that anything was wrong as he stopped in front of the energy barrier.

"I know," said the doctor. "Time's up." She stood, casting one last, remonstrating glance at Picard. "If that bothers you anymore, tell this officer. Don't keep it to yourself that way."

The captain nodded. "Whatever you say," he told her.

The guard drew his weapon as he moved to the switch that would turn off the energy field. His eyes glued to the prisoner, he didn't take any notice whatsoever of Julia. After all, she was one of the most trusted people in the colony. Who in his right mind would suspect her of colluding with an alien spy?

A moment later, the barrier fizzled out of existence. "Come on, Doctor," said the dark-haired man. "Before our friend here gets any funny ideas."

By way of reply, Julia brushed the hand that held the phaser with her tricorder. A blue aura seemed to envelope the guard's hand for a fraction of a second—

but that was enough to make him yelp and drop his weapon.

Wasting no time, the captain leapt up and put all his weight behind a blow to the man's jaw. He caught him as solidly as he'd hoped; there was a sound like a branch breaking and the security officer's knees buckled.

Before he could recover, Picard grabbed his phaser. Unfortunately, the man still had some fight left in him, because he tried to swipe it back. Rather than take any chances, the captain fired—and sent his captor sprawling against the wall in back of him.

Only then did Picard turn to his benefactor. "Neat trick," he observed, pointing his phaser at her tricorder.

She advanced and knelt beside the guard, making sure he hadn't been hurt worse than the captain intended. "I picked it up in medical school," she said. "Though I never thought I'd ever need to really use it." A pause. "Looks like George here will be fine, except for a whopping big headache."

With his free hand, he took hold of hers. "Let's go," he urged. "We've got a matter-antimatter core to shut down."

Julia hesitated—but only for the amount of time it took to draw a breath. Then she let the captain pull her after him as he emerged into the bright light outside.

If anything, thought Riker, Admiral Kowalski looked more hollow-cheeked than the last time he'd communicated with the *Enterprise*. Obviously, the political situation on Gorn hadn't improved any.

"I take it," said Kowalski, "You've had no luck finding Captain Picard?"

The first officer felt the emptiness of the captain's ready room all around him. "No luck," he echoed. "We've investigated seventy-six star systems without turning up the slightest sign of him." He took an almost perverse pleasure in the extent of his frustration. "But that doesn't mean—"

"It means," the admiral interjected, "that you've got a day and a half left. And believe me, my colleagues think I'm crazy to even give you that much, considering the upheavals taking place among the Gorn." He leaned forward. "I know how much you think of Captain Picard, Commander. But your duty is clear. Thirty-six hours from now, I expect you to be entering orbit around the Gorn homeworld. That's understood, isn't it?"

Riker nodded. "It's understood, Admiral. I'll be there."

And he would. The captain had worked hard to establish relations with the Gorn. He wouldn't want to see them jeopardized now—even at the expense of his own life.

"Good," concluded the admiral. "I just wanted to make sure. Kowalski out."

Sighing, the first officer sat back in his chair. One day wouldn't be anywhere near enough unless they got lucky. And the way things were going, he didn't *feel* very lucky.

Damn. He couldn't let it end this way. He couldn't.

Suddenly, he pounded Captain Picard's desk, watching its polished surface shiver under the force of his blow. It felt good—but it didn't change anything. They were still leagues from their goal, and Starfleet and circumstances had hobbled them until they could barely walk.

Then he remembered. There was a chance, if he was willing to seize it. But he couldn't wait any longer. Hell, it might already be too late.

"Ensign Ro," he said, looking up at the intercom grid.

The reply came almost instantaneously. "Aye, sir?"

"Join me in my . . . in the *captain's* ready room. I think there's something we have to discuss."

Ro didn't bother to acknowledge his order. But a moment later, he heard a beep at the door.

"Come in, Ensign."

The doors had barely slid aside before the Bajoran was past them, approaching him with an eagerness that told him she knew exactly what he wanted. Under the circumstances, Riker decided, he would get right to the point.

"Not too long ago," he said, "you offered me the services of the Bon Amar. If the offer's still on the table, I'd like to take you up on it."

He searched her face for a hint of the triumph she must have been feeling. He couldn't find any. Ro was a professional, he'd give her that.

"I'll contact them immediately," she answered.

Riker nodded. "Thank you, Ensign. In the meantime, I'll have Lieutenant Worf map out the routes I'd like your friends to search. And—"

"Begging your pardon, sir," Ro interrupted, "but I think they'll prefer to map out their own routes. That's just their way."

He could live with that. He said so. The ensign turned to go, then stopped herself and looked back at him.

"You know," she said, "you surprised me. I thought you'd hold out until the bitter end."

Riker allowed himself a smile. "So did I," he admitted.

Ro looked at him frankly. "What changed your mind?"

He shrugged. "I don't know, exactly. I guess desperation has a way of clarifying your priorities."

She smiled back. "Right." And a moment later, the ready-room doors were closing behind her.

Squinting in the rays of the hot midday sun, Picard kept his phaser hidden in the crook of his arm as he and Julia made their way across the colony's plaza to the sensor facility. Fortunately, there were few of the colonists around, and those who were didn't seem to take any inordinate interest in them.

At the entrance to the facility, they stopped, waiting for the security system to announce their presence. The captain looked around uneasily, then turned as the doors started to slide aside.

Of all people, it had to be Hronsky himself who stood there, his eyes popping open suddenly as he realized whom he was facing. Before he could sound the alarm, Picard drew his weapon and pressed the trigger.

The chief engineer staggered under the impact of the blast, hit the wall behind him, and slid to the ground. With one last sweeping glance, to make sure this hadn't been noticed by anyone in the plaza, the captain took Julia by the arm and led her inside.

"Damn," she whispered, kneeling for a second by the unconscious Hronsky. "Did you have to stun him, *too?*"

"Yes," Picard replied—also in a whisper. "There was no time to do anything else."

Scanning the interior of the structure, he saw that it was sparsely populated now—in contrast to the day before, when the chief engineer had announced his discovery. And all those present were too occupied with their monitors to notice what had happened to their superior.

The controls that related to the power source were in the center of the room. No one was watching them at the moment. Perhaps that had been Hronsky's job. Or perhaps he had decided not to post anyone over them, as a show of disdain for the prisoner's warning.

In any case, the captain and Julia were able to get halfway to the controls before anyone even glanced in their direction. But once one of the engineers noticed them, the others all raised their heads—almost as if there were a telepathic link between them.

"What do you want?" blurted one of them—the red-bearded man that Picard had seen here before. He was looking not at Picard's face, but at his leveled phaser.

"Not to harm you," the captain assured him.

"He's here to sabotage the power source," concluded a woman with long, blonde hair tied up in a braid.

There was no point in explaining, Picard decided. He had tried that once already and failed miserably. So instead, he merely took the few extra steps he needed to reach the control console.

Julia stayed with him. She must have felt terrible, the way her fellow colonists were staring at her. Like a traitor. But she was acting in their best interests, even if they would never believe it.

A stocky man with graying temples seemed on the verge of making a move. The captain froze him with a glance.

"Don't even think about it," he said.

The man scowled. "Why are you doing this?" he asked. "Who are you, anyway?"

Picard ignored them, lowering his gaze to the level of the power-source monitors. He didn't like what he saw there. Pressure in the containment vessel was up markedly. Punching a few raised pads on the console, he saw that the trend was accelerating. Another couple of hours of this and it would have been too late to stop the process.

But it wasn't too late now. At least, not according to the captain's calculations. There was still time to keep these people alive, at least for a while.

He was just about to reduce the magnetic injector ratio to two hundred when he heard the doors to the place slide open and felt a hot breath from the air outside. Whirling, Picard saw a single figure silhouetted in the brightlight.

"Damn," spat Travers, starting toward the limp

body of his chief engineer. "What in the name of heaven is going on here?"

The captain realized that, with his body in the way, he'd been blocking the commodore's view of his phaser. Instantly, he remedied that.

Travers's eyes opened wide as they fixed on the weapon. Then, slowly, he looked up to meet Picard's. For a moment, the man just stood there, trying to decipher the situation—to find an option worth pursuing.

If he were a character in a Dixon Hill novel, he might have tried to "make a break for it." As it was, the commodore seemed to know when was out of luck. Of course, he wasn't going to step inside until the captain asked him to. There was still a chance that someone might spot him and realize that the sensor control section had been taken over.

"Please," said Picard. "Come in."

Frowning, Travers complied. The doors swept closed behind him as he got down on his haunches to look at Hronsky. Satisfied that the engineer was still alive, he looked up at his antagonist.

"I'm curious," he said, "about how you expect to get away with this."

Very simple, thought the captain. *I don't. Not unless I can figure out a way to signal my first officer, and quickly.*

But what he said was "Never mind that, now. Move over here, with the rest of your people." He gestured with his phaser, to make it clear as to what he wanted Travers to do.

En route, however, the commodore appeared to notice that the doctor wasn't standing with everyone else. She was right in front of the power control console. Travers put two and two together.

"No," he said, his eyes screwing up in his face. "Not you, Julia. Not you, too."

"I believe him," she told the commodore, refusing to lower her gaze. "Though I don't expect anyone else to."

"That's good," Travers replied, not bothering to keep his scorn out of his voice. "Because no one else here is that gullible, as far as I can tell."

Julia didn't say any more. She knew that she would be called to a court-martial for helping a mystery man sabotage the sensors' power source. And her only defense would be the readings in her tricorder.

If Picard were the judge advocate assigned to the case, he was sure he'd have a difficult time finding her innocent. So would anyone else. But apparently, the doctor had already accepted that prospect.

"If it is any consolation," said the captain, "I do not plan to disable your power source. Only to make it impossible for you to tamper with the injection ratio —in the short term, at any rate."

Glancing back and forth between the console and the colonists, he remembered to keep his phaser aimed at the latter with one hand, while he worked at the former with the other. Before long, he had discovered the subprogram that governed the action of the magnetic injectors. Adjusting it, he instituted an elaborate password system to stand guard over the alteration. Then he stood back.

Travers was glowering at him. "We'll meet again, Mr. Hill. You can count on that. And when we do, you'll have occasion to regret this incident."

"Perhaps," Picard conceded. "However, *you* will not."

The question in the captain's mind now was where to go from here. With the power-source crisis firmly fixed in the front of his mind, he hadn't had time to make any longer-range plans. Now he had no choice.

The problem, of course, was that he hadn't yet figured out a way to contact Riker. And until he did, it would be impossible for him to formulate a real plan of action. On the other hand, he couldn't stay here— or anywhere in the colony, for that matter. That left just one option: taking to the hills.

Before he could withdraw, however, he saw the man with the red beard glance over to the corner of the room. Following the glance, Picard saw the intercom unit on the wall—and remembered that there might be engineers elsewhere in the facility. Engineers who would rush to his prisoners' aid upon hearing a call for help.

Seeing that the captain had caught on to his intention, the bearded man either took the initiative or panicked. Either way, the result was the same. He darted in the direction of the intercom, moving more quickly than anyone his size had a right to.

Picard had no choice but to try to stun him. Tracking the man with his phaser, he pressed the trigger. In almost the same instant, the phased energy beam lanced across the room and struck its victim square in the shoulder.

As the captain expected, it knocked the bearded engineer off his feet. But he had also expected it to deprive him of consciousness—and that it did *not* do.

Though the man was woozy, he was still in control of his senses.

Bad news, Picard remarked silently. *Very* bad news. Apparently, the phaser had all but expended its power reserves. *Leave it to me,* he thought, *to be afflicted with a guard who forgets to recharge his weapon.*

Nor was he the only one who'd grasped the situation, he noted. A couple of the colonists, including Travers, were looking at him with slitted eyes, wondering if he was as vulnerable as they thought.

"That phaser's out of energy," the commodore growled. "Now's our chance. Get him—before he can escape!"

As the engineers started to move forward, the captain hurled his weapon into their midst. Then, casting a last, grateful glance at Julia, he spun about and took off for the exit.

As he reached the doors, they started to part. Picard braced himself for the wash of hot air—and felt something close around his ankle, causing him to fall forward. As he caught himself with his hands, he looked back and saw that Chief Engineer Hronsky had begun to emerge from his phaser-induced siesta.

Shifting his weight forward onto his hands, the captain lashed back at Hronsky with his free foot. It caught the man in his jaw, snapping his head back. For the second time in the last several minutes, the engineer slumped senseless.

Then Picard was diving out through the open doors, squinting against the sudden glare of the desert sun and trying to remember the general direction of the place where he had been found. Not that there was any advantage in returning there, but it seemed as good a destination as any.

Riker sat in the middle seat of the *Enterprise*'s command center and stared at the blue-green world pictured in the viewscreen. According to its last survey, it boasted no less than three presentient species, each one the master of a different continent, each one more or less on an evolutionary par with the other two.

Things would get interesting there in the next several million years. But that was someone else's concern. All the first officer cared about right now was whether or not a single sentient being had been transported there accidentally by an alien space-and-time machine.

Rubbing his eyes, Riker could hear the quick, sure tapping of Worf's fingers as they moved over his controls. Without looking, the human knew that his tactical officer was studying his monitors, trying to expedite the operation of the ship's sensors as they completed their planetary scan.

The Klingon, at least, had used his rest period to get some legitimate shut-eye. The first officer envied him that. For Riker, sleep simply hadn't been in the cards. It had eluded him like a wily fugitive in a maze of shadowy corridors—each of which led back to the bridge and the search for Captain Picard. As a result, he'd returned to the center seat half an hour ahead of schedule, telling himself that there was no point in prolonging the agony.

After all, this was where he wanted to be, where he needed to be, and where he *would* be—for another thirty-three hours or so, until his orders forced him to call off the search. At this point, horrible as that prospect might be, the first officer could envision no other conclusion.

Sure, he still held out a slim hope that somehow, some way, they would find what they were looking for. But his Alaskan upbringing had forcibly made a realist out of Riker, and he knew, in his heart of hearts, that they were just playing out the string.

"Commander?"

The first officer turned at the sound of Worf's voice. He couldn't help but search the Klingon's face for a sign of good news. But Worf's expression told him that it was just more of the same.

"The scan is negative," he concluded softly, knowing the Klingon would be as disappointed as he was.

Worf nodded. "That is correct."

Riker returned his attention to the viewscreen, where the class-M planet with its three presentient species still hung in the void. There were seventeen other worlds in this star system, but none of them were even remotely equipped to support human life.

The first officer sighed. "Proceed to the next system," he said.

Worf ran a quick calculation. "That would be Beta Artemnoron. Estimated time of arrival twelve hours and thirty-six minutes."

Riker felt his heart sink inside him. That was more than a third of the time they had left. If they failed to locate the captain there as well, they would have no choice but to recover Geordi's away team and make a beeline for Gorn. And even then, they'd be cutting it close.

"Beta Artemnoron," he told his helmsman. "Best speed."

"Aye, sir," came the reply, as Ensign Rager—whose shift had just begun—brought the *Enterprise* about. A moment later, they were making their way out of the system at full impulse, waiting for clearance to go to warp.

As Riker watched, he found himself wondering what would have happened if he had taken Ro up on her offer a little sooner. Say, a day earlier. Or two. That might have made the difference. But he had let his pigheadedness get in the way of his finding the captain, and he would have to live with that the rest of his life.

Speaking of Ro . . . she deserved some thanks for her efforts, both as acting exec and as proponent of the Bon Amar plan. The ensign had done all he had expected of her and a good deal more. As soon as she reported to the bridge, he would ask her into the captain's ready room and let her know what all her help had meant to him.

For now, however, he had a more pressing responsibility. He had to contact the moderate faction on Gorn and let them know that Jean-Luc Picard would not be available for the negotiations. Riker would take the captain's place at the . . .

Riker stopped himself. *No one* could take Captain Picard's place—not in this or anything else. He would merely fill in as best he could.

Of course, he had never even met a Gorn, much less matched wits with one—except in the holodeck recreation of Captain Kirk's historical first encounter. And he had a feeling that that would be slim preparation for what was ahead.

In short, the outlook wasn't very bright.

Chapter Eight

PICARD LOOKED BACK over his shoulder. The distant buildings full of colonists were hidden behind a bone-white shoulder of rock. That was good. After all, if he couldn't see them, they couldn't see him either.

Of course, that situation wouldn't prevail for long. Though the captain hadn't seen any signs of pursuit earlier, as he made his way posthaste across the flats between the outpost and the low-lying mountains, that didn't mean there wouldn't be any. Travers was not the sort of man to just let him go, after what he had done.

Negotiating the blunt ridges and folds that composed the foothills of the range, he tried not to think about the heat. He had already soaked through most of his clothing, and sweat still ran in rivulets down the sides of his face. Pretty soon, he would need something to drink, though he hadn't the slightest idea where he would find it.

It was not exactly the way he had hoped to leave the colony. Apparently, the old saw was correct: beggars could not be choosers. And for all intents and purposes, he had been a beggar these last few days, depending on the kindness of others.

No more. Now he was on his own—in more ways than one. He still hadn't concocted a method of contacting Will Riker. Nor, given the pace he'd have to keep up in order to stay out of the commodore's clutches, was he likely to again have the luxury of pondering the problem at his leisure.

Maybe you're approaching this the wrong way, he mused. *Up until now, you've been looking at the problem from your end. Put yourself in Will's position instead. If it were you looking for the captain now, not vice versa, what type of signal would you be watching for?*

Once more, his thoughts returned to his communicator. Disgusted with himself, he attempted to tear them away again, but they kept veering in that direction. *This is ridiculous,* he told himself. *Will would know that the damned thing couldn't maintain its signal into the next century. He would reject that line of inquiry and try a . . .*

No. *Wait.* Picard stopped himself short. There *was* a way to signal his officers with his communicator. Not the way it was normally done, but effectively nonetheless.

All along, he had been thinking of his comm badge as only an *active* signaling device, and therefore having no value here. But it could also be a *passive* signaling device—because terillium, one of the metals that enabled it to operate over long distances, was an alloy that would not be developed for another fifty years!

Will would know that. And even if it didn't occur to him right away, someone else would point it out. Then all he would have to do is conduct a long-range sensor scan for terillium—knowing that when he found *it*, he would find Picard, because no undeveloped planet would possess it naturally.

That would lead him to Cestus III. By nucleonic dating, he would determine how old the alloy was. And then would know approximately how far back in time the captain had been tossed. Of course, it wouldn't provide a precise fix, but Picard hoped that Geordi could take it from there.

Why hadn't he thought of this before? It was so . . . so *obvious.* Or anyway, it should have been. Perhaps if he had not been disoriented to such a degree, he would have come up with the solution days—

Suddenly, the captain's mouth went as dry as the dirt beneath his feet. His jubilation turned into a cold and cloying fear. True, the terillium in his communicator would serve as a red flag to Riker—but only if it wasn't *destroyed* in the interim.

Picard looked about him, at the gentle slopes that rolled higher and higher as they left the colony behind, eventually piling one on top of the other like playful lion cubs until they became full-fledged mountains. These were the hills that Captain Kirk would bombard shortly after his arrival. And before he would finish chasing the Gorn back to their ships, the entire area would be an explosion-pocked mess.

Rocks would be pulverized into dust, dust would be

ground into finer dust. And what were the odds, in the midst of that complete and sweeping devastation, of a single terillium element remaining intact? Or at least, intact enough to be discerned by a starship's sensor array one hundred years later?

What's more, the communicator might not even last until Kirk arrived. After all, the reason Kirk had trained his phasers on this area in the first place was because this was where the Gorn were entrenched. It didn't stretch the imagination much to picture one of them stumbling on something round and shiny, picking it up, and taking it with him when he fled.

The captain's teeth ground together purposefully. He had to locate his comm badge—that much was clear. He had to find it and relocate it somewhere else. Somewhere it would be safe from both the Gorn and James Kirk's plasma grenades.

And he had to do it quickly, before Commodore Travers and his security people caught up with him. Everything rested on his success in this. If he valued the future—both his own and that of the Federation —he dared not fail.

"Captain?"

Tal Ephis, one of the founding members of the Bon Amar "trade consortium," turned to look at his first officer—who also happened to be his wife. She was the only one on board who called him by that honorific, and even she meant it as a joke.

Still, he liked the sound of it. It made him feel, at least for a moment, that he was something more than the master of a third-rate transport vessel, which had taken its share of lumps to see the Cardassians pried loose from Bajor. It made him feel like a *true* captain, which is what he had dreamed of becoming at age five or six.

Of course, that was before reality had set in. Before the Cardassians took away his father and mother, and slaughtered them slowly in some prison camp too horrible to think about. Before he saw that he'd be lucky just to *survive,* much less help others to do so.

Not that his life as a pirate had been so bad. Hell, at least he'd been in space. He'd gotten to see the stars. And serve with the finest men and women anywhere. All in all, he'd come a lot closer to realizing his dream than most Bajorans.

The pity was, when the dust cleared, the Bon Amar had remained outlaws. Maybe most of the rebels had accomplished what they'd set out to do, or thought they had—but the "trade consortium" 's work wasn't finished yet. Nor would it be, until the Cardassians had paid at least a part of what they owed the Bajorans. ·

"Yes, Ilam?" he responded. "Don't tell me you've found what we're looking for."

He was just joking back at her. But her expression told him that she might very well have found the thing after all. Rousing himself from his command chair, Tal crossed the ship's cramped bridge and came to look over his wife's shoulder.

According to her monitor, their sensors had picked up something interesting. Unfortunately, they weren't Starfleet sensors. They were given to the occasional glitch, and one could only pray that it didn't come at a crucial time. So now, as Tal peered at the computer screen, he wasn't as confident as he would have liked.

"What do you think?" asked Ilam, looking up at him.

He shrugged and rubbed his chin. It was getting stubbly. He needed a shave. "I don't know," he replied at last. "That *could* be it. Of course, it's probably just something similar." Yes, he *definitely* needed a shave. "Still, I guess it's worth checking out."

His wife nodded. "I'll get a group together. Pakris and Hatil, probably. That is, if they're both awake. And Mison. She hasn't been off the ship since who remembers when."

"Neither have I," muttered Tal, coming to stare again at the monitor. "But that's all right. I have other prerogatives." He glanced at Ilam and smiled. "I get to sleep with the prettiest first officer in the fleet."

"Flatterer," said his wife, but she was smiling, too. "I'll try not to be gone too long."

Then she was making her way toward the lift at the rear of the bridge. Tal didn't watch her go. Instead, he found himself staring again at the tiny red blip on the screen.

What if it really *was* the thing they were looking for? What then? The Starfleet officer they were helping didn't have the power to sanction their use of the shipping lanes. When this was over, no matter how it ended, they would still be outlaws.

But it would tickle him blue and purple to accomplish something that high-and-mighty Starfleet couldn't. To put them in the debt of a lowly Bon Amar pirate and his hunk-of-junk ship. He chuckled. It would be a hoot, all right.

Not that it was going to happen. But he could dream, couldn't he?

For a world capable of supporting life, Cestus III seemed to have precious little in the way of wind. Picard was grateful for that fact.

In a harsher environment, the landslide where he was found might have been obliterated. The same for the soft, sandy ground around it, which was still marked with the colonists' footprints and the shape of his own body.

As it was, he'd been able to find the place with little trouble. It was just where Julia had said it would be. And with any luck, his communicator would be nearby.

Keeping low so as not to be spotted, the captain used his fingers to sift through the dirt and detritus at the bottom of the slide. It had to be here somewhere, didn't it? If it had been found on his person, Travers would certainly have mentioned it. After all, he'd mentioned everything else that seemed odd about Picard.

Given enough time, the captain told himself, he was certain he would turn up the device. But he didn't *have* much time. Travers was no doubt leading a search for him by now—a search that wouldn't last long at all, once the colonists picked up his trail with their tricorders.

Odds were the communicator hadn't been buried very deeply; it had probably slipped just under the surface when it fell. With that in mind, he hastened to cover as much area as possible, feeling the sand grind into his knees as he moved from place to place.

Abruptly, the knuckles of his left hand struck something hard. Most likely, a rock—but if so, it was an unusually smooth one. Groping for it, his fingers closed around a wonderfully familiar shape.

Dredging it up, Picard confirmed his most fervent hope. Holding the device up to the sun, he brushed it off. It was his *communicator,* looking every bit as functional as when he'd last used it on the alien station.

He felt like a treasure-hunter who had just un- earthed a chest full of gold dubloons. Better, in fact—for his very life had depended on this discov- ery. And even more than his life, given the responsi- bility he'd been charged with on the Gorn homeworld.

Suddenly, the captain heard voices. Ducking in- stinctively, he took a quick look all around him. So far, there was no one to be seen—which meant that his pursuers probably couldn't see him either. But that would change momentarily, as they used their tricorders to track him down.

He had to move—and quickly. But which way? Picard tried to ignore the sound of his pounding pulse, to listen through it. There were the voices again, about as faint as before. And unless he was imagining it, they were coming from the direction of the armory—more or less the same approach he had followed in seeking out his communicator.

It was hardly a coincidence. The hills were easier to negotiate if one entered them by that route, the slopes longer and gentler and less rocky. It made for a quick pace—one that had worked to the captain's advantage earlier, but was helping Travers's search team now.

Again the voices, noticeably closer—and definitely following his track, whether they knew it or not. Turning the other way, Picard assessed the terrain: a shallow, meandering valley, ending in a pronounced cleft. The footing wouldn't be too bad, as far as he could tell; loose dirt and rocks seemed to be at a minimum.

But there wasn't much in the way of cover. If he sprinted out from behind the debris of the landslide, and the commodore's party was anywhere nearby, he would be difficult to miss. No—make that *impossible*.

Still, there wasn't much of an alternative. Gritting his teeth, the captain took off for the distant cleft, not daring to look back over his shoulder. For a fraction of a second, he could almost feel a phased energy beam bearing down on him, reaching out to strike him square in the back.

However, the only phaser beam was in his mind. Two-thirds of the way to his destination, his breath rasping sharply in his throat as he pushed himself to the limit, Picard realized that he was home free.

Once he had a hillside for cover, he could circle back around the colony and find a place to hide his communicator—a place where the Gorn wouldn't stumble on it. After that, his job would be over. It would then be just a matter of Will Riker's scanning the right—

Pummph!

The captain dove sideways, reacting to the tiny geyser of dirt and pebbles that erupted just ahead of him and to his left. As he scrambled to his feet, he spared a quick glance over his shoulder at the origin of the explosion.

And saw Schmitter, Travers's security chief, flanked by two red-shirted officers. Noting how he'd missed Picard with his first attempt, Schmitter leveled his phaser again and fired.

Darting to his left, the captain narrowly avoided that blast as well. It tore a chunk out of the slope up ahead of him, but left Picard himself unscathed. Running for all he was worth, knowing that the comm badge in his hand could damage the timeline as easily as anything else, he again set his sights on the cleft—and hoped that Schmitter's next shot wouldn't be any more accurate than the last two.

His hope was answered. All at once, three ruby-red beams sliced through the hot, dry air—but none of them came closer than a couple of inches. Then he was through the cleft, squinting in the face of full sunlight, looking for the next leg of his getaway.

Unfortunately, he hadn't given Travers enough credit. No sooner had the captain emerged from the valley than he spotted two more redshirts in the distance—and these were flanking the commodore himself.

Worse, Picard had just entered an even deeper valley, between two rather steep and featureless inclines. There was no room to maneuver, no place to hide, and no outlet. The captain's only option was to try to make it up one of the slopes before either Schmitter's team or Travers's took him down with a well-placed phaser beam.

In fact, that wasn't much of an option at all. But given the alternatives, he seized on it, starting up the escarpment on his left. Up ahead, the commodore's security people did the same, in an attempt to head him off. Picard considered the angles and decided they'd catch him before he got anywhere near the top.

He'd failed, he told himself, feeling the sting of that realization. He'd failed completely and utterly. It was too late to hide his communicator from his pursuers, which meant he'd placed the timeline in jeopardy. What's more, there was now a good chance the device would be destroyed in the colonists' defense against the Gorn, making it unlikely that Riker would find it a hundred years later.

The result? No return to the twenty-fourth century. No Picard to talk peace with the Gorn. Nothing to prevent a war that would devastate both sides of the conflict—assuming that those two sides would even exist in the future that would be created.

All this flashed through the captain's mind in the merest part of a moment. It didn't cause him to break stride, however. If Travers wanted to stop him, he would have to knock him out. It wasn't in Picard's nature to surrender while there was even a glimmer of hope.

Then something happened. The captain wasn't sure what it was, but the commodore suddenly stopped dead in his tracks, only partway up the slope. His security officers stopped with him.

A quick peek over his shoulder told Picard that Schmitter had stopped, too. It was as if something else had caught their attention, something more important than a lone fugitive. They looked panicked, almost terrified. What could be scaring them so much? What . . .

Damn. The captain felt the blood drain from his face as he realized what must have distracted his pursuers.

The Gorn were here.

In his mind's eye, Picard could picture what must have happened. The colony's sensor array had picked up the approach of an unfamiliar vessel, but discounted it as just another alien ship making use of its facilities.

At least, at first. Then, as the vessel had gotten closer, it had powered up its weapons banks—something no peaceful alien would do. And the officer in charge of the sensor array had instantly contacted Commodore Travers for instructions.

After all, the sensor reading could have been a mistake; the equipment might have malfunctioned. And even if the reading was accurate, it didn't necessarily mean there would be hostilities.

Once again, Picard could see Harold's face as it had appeared on the *Enterprise*'s mission tape, wan and hollow-eyed. As if he had seen the recording only yesterday, he could hear the man's horrified account.

"They knocked out our phaser batteries with their first salvo. We weren't expecting them; why should we? We didn't have anything anyone would want."

He could still prevent the massacre. He could warn Travers about the Gorn, persuade him to fire on the alien vessel. Of course, the commodore probably wouldn't listen to him.

And in any case, the question was moot. The

captain had made his decision, which was really no decision at all.

History had to take its course.

"Damn you, Hill!" Travers yelled. The commodore shot Picard a hot, angry look—one that he could read all the way across the valley. He wanted to catch the mysterious Mister Hill so badly he could taste it. But he had a more pressing matter at hand.

As the captain watched, amazed, almost giddy at his good fortune, the commodore's security team went back the way it came. Looking back over his shoulder, Picard saw that Schmitter was doing the same, returning to the cleft through which he'd come.

Travers could have given his sensor officer instructions from here. He could have returned to the colony himself, and left Schmitter to continue the chase. But, practicing caution, he didn't do either of those things.

It wouldn't help the commodore preserve his colony. However, it had given the captain a second chance to preserve the timeline.

Ensign Ro Laren had thought to find her commanding officer in the center seat on the bridge. However, when she burst out of the aft turbolift, she saw that the captain's chair was empty.

Turning to Worf, she asked: "Where is he? Where's Commander Riker?"

The Klingon's brows came together slightly: no doubt he was a little taken aback by her demeanor. Acting executive officer or not, he wasn't used to Ro addressing him that way.

As a result, his only answer was a tilting of his massive, bony-browed head—in the direction of the captain's ready room. But that was all the ensign needed to know.

Rushing past the circuitry access boards and the food dispenser, she stopped in front of the ready room door. Inside, Riker would be alerted to her presence by a series of chimes. A second or two went by, as she waited for the doors to slide apart.

Finally, they did just that—revealing the first officer, who peered at her from behind the captain's desk with eyes as tired and red-rimmed as her own. Obviously, he hadn't slept much during *his* rest period either.

"Ensign," said Riker. "I'd planned to speak with you after I—"

"They found him," she blurted out, physically unable to contain herself.

The first officer blinked. "I beg your pardon?" he replied. Obviously, she had thrown him for a loop.

"The captain," she got out, forcing herself to speak slowly and calmly. "The Bon Amar found him—or at least, the terillium he was carrying in his communicator when he vanished." She clenched her fists, flushed with their success. "We know where he *is.*"

Riker stood, his eyes narrowing as the significance of her words sank in. Had it really happened? When Geordi had first suggested how they could track down the captain, Riker had hailed the idea as brilliant. But after day after day of failure, he'd begun to wonder if it all wasn't just a wild-goose chase. Now . . .

"You're certain? he asked.

Ro nodded. "I can give you the coordinates."

Slowly, a smile spread over the first officer's features. Not his customary, devil-may-care grin, but an expression of sublime joy that the ensign had never expected to see there.

"Well, then," said Riker, his voice growing stronger with each uttered word, "let's give Commander La Forge the good news. You didn't, by any chance, catch the *name* of the planet?"

Ro nodded again. "It's called Cestus Three."

Riker's eyes widened. His eyes became large and round. "Cestus Three . . ." he muttered.

"You've been there?" asked the ensign.

Riker swallowed. "Only in a manner of speaking," he replied cryptically. Tapping his comm badge, as if he were off-ship, he said: "Mr. Worf, get me Commander La Forge. Ensign Rager, plot a new course. We're going to return to the alien station."

"Aye, Commander," came Rager's response. "Course plotted."

"Engage," commanded the first officer.

There was something about the way he said it that reminded Ro of Captain Picard. If the prophets were with them, maybe she'd hear that order from the lips of the captain himself before long.

"Cestus Three?" repeated Geordi. *"The* Cestus Three?"

"That's right," confirmed Riker, his voice charged with an excitement that the engineer could feel right through his comm badge. "The world in the Academy simulation. The one where we first ran into the Gorn."

Data was already seated at the monitor, feeding the

information into the console below it. As soon as he was finished, the local computer nexus went to work calculating the distance to the world in question.

It only took a moment to obtain a readout on the bottom of the screen. Armed with this figure as well as the power curve recorded during the captain's transport, Data was able to distill out of the equation a temporal element—in other words, how far Picard had traveled into the past.

When the android was done, he just sat there for a second or so, his brow wrinkled ever so slightly. Then he looked up at Geordi.

"What is it?" the engineer asked, disturbed by his friend's expression. "How far back did this thing send him?"

"One hundred and three years, one month, and six days into the past," answered Data. But he didn't elaborate any further.

Geordi frowned at the android. "Is there something significant about that date?" Sometimes, dealing with Data was like pulling teeth.

"There is indeed," came the reply. "It is only a few days before the Gorn invasion of that world, which killed every colonist but one."

"Lord," breathed Riker. La Forge had almost forgotten that the first officer was still listening in. "If the captain was really there when the Gorn arrive . . ."

He didn't have to finish the sentence. They all had a pretty good idea of how it would end—with the death of Jean-Luc Picard. Or maybe, worse, his mangling of the timeline, as hard as he would no doubt fight to prevent it.

And talk about your *ironies*. To be transported back in time to the incident that opened the way for relations between the Gorn and the Federation— while en route to a meeting that would attempt to preserve those relations. If the situation were not so desperate, Geordi would have managed a smile.

Just then, Barclay and O'Connor entered the room. They'd been working on hooking up the reassembly controls, which required some work out in the corridor. No sooner had they walked in than they realized something was wrong.

"Good news and bad news," Geordi told them, saving them the trouble of asking. "The good news is we've located the captain. The bad news is where we found him."

Barclay nodded, his brow rippling as he considered the information. O'Connor, who was a good deal less intense than her colleague, just nodded.

Geordi turned to Data. "Think you can do it?" he asked.

The android's lips formed a straight line. "I can try," he responded. Then, without any further ado, he bent over the console and applied himself to his task.

Picard knew that he should have left the place as soon as he was able. But he couldn't do it. Something held him back.

Certainly, it wasn't the need to hide his comm badge—not anymore. He had safely buried the device nearly an hour ago, out here in the shadow of the almost metallic-looking crags that rose up erratically behind the doomed outpost.

When Captain Kirk landed in another day or so, he would find the Gorn encamped on the other side of the colony, past the armory and the administration center and the now-disabled generator. Kirk would launch plasma grenades at the enemy, keeping them at bay until he could figure out what had happened here.

Some Gorn would be killed in the encounter. Some of their weapons would be damaged or destroyed. But not Picard's communicator. That would remain intact, so that Commander Riker could find it a hundred years from now.

No, it wasn't the communicator that kept the captain here, riveted in place. It was the sight of the colonists, scurrying from one part of the installation to another, escorted by grim-faced security personnel.

By now, of course, Travers had to have ordered the shields up. Picard couldn't see them, but he was certain that if he hurled a rock at one of the buildings, it would have been deflected short of its target.

The commodore would be trying to communicate with the aliens, to find out the reason for their apparent belligerence—and to see if there were some way to dissuade them from it. But the Gorn wouldn't respond; their own historical records showed that. They would simply wait until they had assessed and targeted all the colony's defenses, then go to work.

As the captain watched, spellbound, a young man carried a little girl in his arms as a young woman kept pace with him. With a start, he recognized them as the family he and Julia had seen on one of their walks. Even at a distance, Picard could discern the worried expressions of the adults—their fear for their lives and that of their daughter.

They were right to be worried. The colony's shields were no match for the Gorn's weapons systems. Before this day was over, all three of them would be dead. The captain felt his throat constrict at the thought of it.

In all, more than five hundred colonists would fall victim to the Gorn invasion before the slaughter was complete. Once, he had seen them as statistics, to be pitied—but only in the abstract. Now, he saw the pallor of their faces in his mind's eye, saw the way they looked back at the heavens in their haste—and he felt their dread as surely as if it were his own.

It was impossible not to. One could not be human and ignore what was happening here. One could not be made of flesh and not cry out inwardly at the injustice. These people were innocents, as Lieutenant Harold would later testify. They had committed no offense. They had only come here, to the fringe of known space, to further the Federation's stores of knowledge.

Would they still have come if they had known that this was to be their fate? To be exterminated by an unknown enemy? To lose their lives without ever understanding why?

Again, Picard replayed Harold's account in his mind, seeing the man plead for compassion from his enemy even after it was too late. *"We tried to surrender. We had women and children, we told them that. But they wouldn't listen."*

The captain let his forehead fall onto his forearm, which in turn rested on an outcropping of hard rock. He tried to swallow back the guilt. But he couldn't. It roiled in his belly like a living creature, scratching and clawing to get out.

That was why he couldn't leave this place, wasn't it? Because he could have prevented what was happening here. Because it had been within his power to warn the colonists in time, and he had chosen not to.

Picard forced himself to look up again, to fix his gaze on the people whose doom he had sealed. It was the least he could do. If he couldn't stop it, he would at least bear witness to it. Certainly, he owed the colonists that much.

Even as he came to that decision, the first green disruptor beams began to rain down from the otherwise flawless blue sky. Those who were still in the plaza screamed and ran for the shelter of the nearest building.

A good many of them didn't make it. They were skewered by the slender bolts of green fire and eaten from within. As the captain watched, his eyes stinging with horror, his guts twisting, the slaughter came on in earnest. Beams of destruction walked the expanse of the plaza, claiming life after life, turning living beings into charred, smoking husks.

Then the disruptor bolts plunged into the buildings themselves, one of them striking a phaser battery. As soon as the beam touched down, the battery erupted in a conflagration of warring energies. A moment later, the other phaser battery went up as well.

The next objective was the sensor analysis section, not far from one of the ruined phaser facilities. As a bolt plummeted to earth, it drove deep into the heart of the building. For a long, eerie moment, the place crawled with what looked like a swarm of tiny, green insects. Then, as if it had never existed in the first place, that portion of the colony's semicircle was gone—exposing its soft, living insides to the next devastating barrage.

That was the pattern the assault would follow, now that the bulk of the colony's population was nestling itself deep in the bowels of the installation. It was all in the Gorn histories. They would take the place apart piece by piece. Perhaps half the semicircle would be destroyed in the next few minutes—and with its shields useless, the rest would soon follow.

The procedure would be cold, methodical. Like a praying mantis dismantling a beetle for the succulent meat inside its shell. There would be no animosity, just savage and unswerving purpose. No cruelty, just cultural imperative.

But lives would be sacrificed on the altar of that imperative. The tender lives of children, of fathers and mothers, of men and women who had brought their grace and dignity to this place.

So intent was he on the havoc in the installation, he almost failed to notice the glint of sunlight on red-gold scales. Rolling sideways just in time, the captain avoided the stab of green light that shattered the rock he'd been resting on.

In a fraction of a second, he took in the extent of his peril. Three Gorn stood before him, all of the smaller, red- or brown-streaked variety, each one armed with a hand disruptor. As far as he could tell, they were alone.

But they wouldn't be for long. He remembered

now . . . the hands-on stage of invasion, the bloodiest part of all.

Not that any strategy dictated it. Certainly, the Gorn could have destroyed the colony from their position in orbit, without ever risking one of their own in the process. But they were warriors first and strategists second—and their tradition demanded that a commander meet his enemy face-to-face.

That was why they were beaming down—to apply the coup de grâce in person. And as far as these three were concerned, Picard was just another human to be cleansed from Gorn territory.

There was no chance of their letting him live. Nor could he get away without disarming them, at a minimum. Unfortunately, he would have to accomplish that without being armed himself.

As the foremost Gorn aimed his weapon for another shot, the captain did the last thing his adversary would expect: he charged straight at him, ducking low to avoid the imminent disruptor beam. Even as the weapon discharged, Picard slammed into the Gorn's knees.

The impact rattled the human's teeth, but it accomplished what it was supposed to. The Gorn lost his balance, staggered to catch himself—and in the process dropped his disruptor. Before either of the other invaders could react, Picard's fingers had latched on to the device.

There was a moment when the captain's eyes met the Gorn's, both of them struggling to resist an almost hypnotic inertia. Then he raised the disruptor and fired. One of his adversaries was sent hurtling backward by the force of the blast, interfering with the other one's aim.

As green energies ran helter-skelter over the first Gorn's serpentine hide, tearing him apart from within as well as without, his companion recovered. Picard and the invader fired at the same time.

One of them missed. The other didn't.

Picking himself up off the ground, the captain winced as he saw the Gorn shiver and smoke under the influence of the disruption effect. The air turned ripe with the acrid stench of burning lizard flesh.

Now there was only one enemy left to deal with. As Picard turned to him, the two of them acknowledged with a mutual glance that the human possessed a distinct advantage, considering he was the only one holding a weapon.

But before the captain could decide what to do about it, the situation changed again—radically. Some fifty yards off, another team of Gorn began to materialize. Obeying an instinct, Picard whirled—and saw a third team taking shape behind him.

Seeing that he was distracted, the last of the human's original adversaries made a break for it. Nor did Picard attempt to stop him. He was too busy trying to figure out what to do next.

Certainly, he couldn't remain here. Not with the place growing thick with Gorn. The prudent thing to do would be to retreat deeper into the midst of these crags, where he might escape the invaders' notice.

For a fleeting moment, he thought of the fate that awaited the colonists now—the way they would be dragged from their shelters and individually subjected to the Gorn's handheld disruptor beams. It made him flush with anger and revulsion.

But it was too late for it to turn out any other way. There was no saving these people, not at this late juncture. There was no going back on his decision to let them die.

Just then, a group of perhaps fifty armed colonists broke from a point in the semicircle, headed for the administration building. The group consisted of men and women, in roughly equal numbers—and it seemed to Picard that Julia was among them, though he couldn't be certain.

They were going to try to make a stand there. They had no chance of success against the invader's superior numbers, against his superior weaponry, but they were going to make the attempt nonetheless.

The Gorn were materializing all over now. If the captain was going to escape, he had to do it quickly, before the newcomers realized that there was a human among them. Otherwise, all his efforts to survive would come to nothing.

Let the colonists put up their last-ditch defense, he told himself. *It's what the timestream demands of them. It has nothing to do with you.*

Still, he found himself unable to run for it. He hesitated, against all common sense. And turned again toward the colony. And felt his teeth grate as a titanic struggle took place inside him.

He could not leave them, could he? And not as a result of his guilt alone, but because he had become a part of this colony—a victim of this insupportable tragedy as surely as anyone else.

Even though he had spent his entire stay here fighting history, he had been a component of it from the beginning. He saw that now, with startling clarity. And seeing it, he had but one choice.

With all the speed he could muster, he took off in the direction of the administration building.

Chapter Nine

AS BARCLAY WATCHED, Commander Data worked the controls that would fix the captain's position in time and space. Knowing where to look was a big help, but the job at hand required the utmost precision—and the android hadn't had much in the way of practice. In fact, when it came to a live transport with this alien equipment, he'd had no practice at all.

Still, with his inhumanly quick reflexes and his ability to compute necessary adjustments on the fly, he was by far their best shot. As long as the various systems remained functional, there was a good chance they would see Captain Picard again in one piece.

Barclay sincerely believed that—until he saw the lights flicker and heard the low hum that had accompanied the last two power surges. All at once, the three humans in the room exchanged glances. If Data noticed, he gave no outward sign of it.

"Damn," said La Forge. He looked about, obviously using his VISOR to track things that Barclay couldn't hope to notice. "It's starting again."

"I am at a crucial stage in the retrieval procedure," said the android. He still hadn't looked up. "If I attempt to siphon off the excess energy as I did before, I will have to begin the process all over again."

The chief engineer continued to track phantoms across the walls and ceiling. At least, they seemed like phantoms to Barclay. But the fact that he couldn't see them didn't mean he couldn't be hurt by them. No, sir.

Varley had been hurt by them. He had been hurt a *lot*.

And they were so close to getting Captain Picard back. If only there were a way to activate the confinement beam, boost its output as Data had, and nip the power-acceleration pattern in the bud—without interrupting the android's work . . .

Then again, maybe there *was*.

"Wait," blurted Barclay. "I've got . . . I've got an idea."

La Forge turned to him. "We could use one about now. Let's hear it, Reg."

The thin man licked his lips. "All the nodes on the station are connected by major power circuits, right? It's just the controls and the transporter mechanisms that seem to be decentralized."

The chief engineer looked at him. "So?"

Barclay shrugged. "So we don't have to use the confinement beam in this node to let energy out of the system. We can use a confinement beam in a different node. All we've got to do is find another control room and activate that system the way we hooked it up here."

La Forge frowned as he thought about it. "It's risky, Reg. We've made this area safe by putting our own locks on the doors. But anywhere else on this station . . ." His voice trailed off ominously.

The thin man swallowed. "I know," he said. "Still, I'd like to try it."

The chief engineer's attention was caught by another will-o'-the-wisp of electromagnetic energy. "All right," he decided. "But I'm going with you."

Barclay nodded.

A moment later, he was jogging down the curving hallway with Commander La Forge beside him, hoping that nothing terrible would happen before they could put their plan into effect.

Julia Santos had never used a phaser in her life. There had been an optional course in its use at the Academy, but she had decided not to take part in it.

After all, she was a doctor. Her business was saving lives, not ending them. Until *now,* she thought, hefting the weapon that Travers had slipped into her hand before they took off across the open plaza.

As the last of the colonists piled into the still-intact administration center, Julia peered out the window and looked around. Her heart sank like a stone in a deep, dark pool.

She had been prepared for the sight of the lizardlike invaders, ugly as they were to her human sensibilities. Hell, the whole reason they decided to hole up here was because they had glimpsed the bastards on their short-range monitors, and knew that they were now approaching on foot.

But she was unprepared for the numbers in which they swept toward the colony, like a tide of green and gold, glittering in the sun. There must be a couple of hundred of them already, and there were more beaming down all the time.

It was hopeless. Utterly hopeless. Their phasers might as well have been slingshots, for all the good they would do them.

And Dixon . . . or rather, Jean-Luc. Had he known about this? Had it been preordained, a fixture in his future timeline? Or had this come as a surprise to him as well? But why would he save the colony from destruction only to see it ravaged by some—?

"My god," spat the commodore, pressing forward to get a better look through the window. "It's *him!*"

Julia followed Travers's pointing finger to the leftmost extremity of the colony's semicircle, where one of the phaser batteries had been before the invaders blasted it out of existence. Sure enough, there was someone there, running toward them. And he wasn't lizardlike at all.

Without warning, the commodore thrust forward the muzzle of his phaser rifle, punching a webbed hole through the shatterproof window glass. Julia flung an arm up out of instinct. But she recovered quickly enough to grab hold of Travers's arm.

"What are you doing?" she demanded of him.

The commodore glowered at her, his face florid with hatred. "I'm paying him back," he snarled. "For betraying his own kind." His nostrils flared. "For throwing in with *them.*"

The doctor shook her head. "No. Can't you see? If he was one of them, he'd be *with* them—not running from them. He's no more their friend than we are."

But Travers wasn't buying it. "Now I'm to believe *you,* am I? A traitor, just like him?"

Julia could see that it hurt him to say that. Of course, he didn't really believe it, or he wouldn't have let her pick up a phaser and join him here in the administration center. The commodore's lips trembled, but it was too late to take back what he'd said.

"You know I'm not a traitor," she replied evenly. She jerked her head, to indicate the man from the future. "And neither is *he.*" At least as far as she could tell.

As if to underline her conclusion, a couple of fiery green beams sliced across the plaza, cutting into the dirt at Jean-Luc's feet. He went down in a cloud of dust, making her heavy heart sink even deeper.

Then she realized that he had only lunged forward and rolled, in an attempt to make himself a more difficult target. A split second later, he was back on his feet again, pelting forward with all the speed he could muster.

"We've got to help him!" cried Julia. "They'll kill him!"

Without thinking, she made her way to the door they'd locked behind them. Maybe she wouldn't be able to hit anyone, her marksmanship being what it was—but even a few scattered shots might buy her friend the time he needed.

"Where the devil do you think you're going?" bellowed Travers.

But she was already halfway out the door, seeking out the lizard-beings who were trying to end Jean-Luc's life. Nor were they hard to find. There were two of them, charging at him as fast as they could, which wasn't fast at all.

Gauging their relative progress, the doctor decided that they would beat the human to the administration center—unless she acted first. Raising her phaser to eye level, she aimed and prepared to press the trigger.

As it happened, she never got the chance. Someone else's phaser beam lanced across the plaza and took down one of the lumbering invaders. Julia turned just in time to see the commodore fire a second time—and with unerring accuracy, plant a beam in the chest of the second lizard-being.

For a moment, their eyes met—and the doctor realized what Travers had done. He had apologized for his outburst in the only way he could. This time, his eloquence left nothing to be desired.

Still, Dixon wasn't out of danger yet. Several more of the invaders were closing in on him from the other side. Discharging his weapon on the run, he cut down one of them in a slash of emerald energy, but the others scored the ground around him with their fire.

Gritting her teeth, Julia got off a shot. Through sheer luck, she hit the foremost of the lizard-beings, hurling him backward—and slowing down the ones in back of him. It was only then that her mystery man seemed to have a real chance.

Following up with another quick blast, Jean-Luc put his head down and turned on the afterburners. The ground sizzled and erupted in front of him and behind him, but he somehow managed to remain unscathed. And then, with a last-ditch effort, he dove for the doctor.

Not expecting to have to support his full weight, Julia fell backward—and thereby eluded the explosion of green destruction that slammed into the wall just behind her. As she regained her bearings, she realized that Jean-Luc had saved her life.

Hustling her back into the building, he thrust the door closed behind him and barked, "Everyone get down!"

It was a voice used to being obeyed. Not surprisingly, everyone got down. Nor were they sorry they did, as a barrage of green energy stabbed through the facility, dissolving glass and metal alike—a barrage that would have killed several of the colonists if they had remained on their feet.

Taking hold of her face urgently but gently, Jean-Luc looked at her. "Are you all right?" he rasped, still out of breath from his sprint across the plaza.

The doctor nodded. "I'm fine," she said, managing a grim smile. "Now."

He smiled back for a moment, then turned to Travers. The commodore's craggy features had softened a bit.

"I thought I had you figured out, Hill. The way I saw it, you sabotaged our long-range sensors to keep us from finding out about these lizard people. Then you took off into the desert to await their arrival."

236

"Then I show up here," said Dixon, "and play hob with your theory. My apologies."

Travers frowned. "So? Are you going to tell me the truth about yourself or not?"

The visitor from the future looked wistful. "Not," he answered. "But I will say this: I'm no traitor. I never had anything but good intentions toward you or your colony."

The commodore sighed. "I had a feeling you were going to avoid the issue." He turned to Julia. "How about you? Care to shed some light on our mystery guest?"

The doctor considered it for a moment. After all, it was possible that they would all die in this place. But what if they didn't? What if someone here survived to screw up the timestream?

She shook her head. "No. You won't get anything out of me, either. In fact—"

Before she could finish her comment, another barrage cut through the air above them, sending a rain of debris down on their heads. Coughing, Julia dusted herself off and leaned close to her friend, as Travers inched nearer to the place where the window used to be. It gave the two of them a moment of relative privacy.

"Jean-Luc," she whispered. "Will you tell me something?"

His eyes found hers. "If I can," he responded.

The doctor licked her lips. "You went to the trouble of saving the colony from a devastating accident—even risked your life in the process. And now, you've come back to make a stand here with us—again, at great risk."

Her friend seemed to see where she was headed with this. "Why would I have done any of that if the colony was destined to be wiped out? If at least some of your people were not meant to survive?"

He gazed at her with infinite kindness, with infinite sorrow and regret. And his hazel eyes told her all she needed to know.

Julia swallowed. So they really *were* doomed. They were all going to *die;* history had already decided that. But then . . .

"Why did you come back?" she asked. "If it wasn't going to accomplish anything . . . what was the point?"

Jean-Luc shrugged. "Perhaps it was because of something someone once told me—that there's no such thing as a meaningless sacrifice. That any positive act, no matter how hopeless or insignificant, is ultimately worthwhile."

The doctor looked at him. "Me? I said that?"

He nodded. "It appears I have memorized it. I suppose it struck a chord." There was a pause, as he turned away from her. "Julia, I have done things in the last few days that I am not proud of. I have lied to people who trusted me. I have spent all my time planning ways to abandon you and your fellow colonists to your fate.

"And for what? So I could *live*. Oh, there are good reasons for me to do so—reasons that I cannot go into now. But what I planned to do can be done by others almost as well. I see now that I am not as essential to the future as I wished to believe. And without that justification, what was left?"

Julia did her best to understand. "Is it so bad to want to survive?" she wondered.

Jean-Luc shook his head. "No, of course not. However, there are worse things than dying." He stroked her cheek with the back of his hand. "There is shame, for instance. And there is the loss of someone dear to you, when you haven't even put up a fight to try to keep her—as futile as that fight may be."

The doctor could feel tears welling up in her eyes, and she willed them back. She wasn't going to cry, she resolved. She had been strong all her life. She wasn't going to falter right at the end.

"They're coming," said Travers. He looked back at Julia and her friend. "This might be a good time to lend a hand, Mr. Hill."

"That's not my name," Jean-Luc confessed to the commodore.

Travers shrugged. "It's the name I'll always remember you by," he said, keeping a straight face under his iron-gray brows.

Under different circumstances, Julia might have laughed at the gallows humor. As it was, she merely grasped her phaser more tightly and crawled forward next to her strange companion.

It seemed like a long time before they reached the neighboring node, guided through the darkness by their handheld light sources. In the meantime, the power surges hadn't gotten any worse. The lights went on dimly for two or three seconds at a time, or flickered brightly for an eyeblink and then died, but there was no sign of those flashes that ran the length of the walls like a herd of wild horses.

All in all, it seemed to Barclay, they had been lucky. He wondered how much longer their luck would hold out.

"There," said Commander La Forge, pointing. "That looks like the way to a control center."

Following his superior's gesture, Barclay saw the mouth of an access tunnel, just like the one that led to the control room they'd left behind. He nodded. "Let's give it a try, sir."

The chief engineer hunched over first and led the way. As Barclay followed, he couldn't help but hurry through the little entranceway, reminded again of what had happened to Varley. He felt a lot better once he was actually inside the tunnel—despite the shadows that danced insanely all about them, projected on the walls by their light sources.

Even before Barclay reached the far end, where Commander La Forge was waiting for him, he could see that the equipment up ahead was pretty identical to that which they had been working on. It was a good sign—a good sign indeed.

"Come on," said the commander, helping Barclay to his feet as he emerged. He kept his light trained on the opposite wall. "Unless I miss my guess, that console over there is the one we're after."

Barclay turned to look in the same direction. "Aye, sir," he decided, approaching the control bank in question with a critical eye. "That should be it, all right."

He touched one of the pads, expecting the thing to remain dormant—as lifeless as its counterpart back in the other control room, the first time he had checked it out. To his surprise, it came to life right away, its monitor displaying a quick scroll of alien characters.

Then it died.

Then it started up again.

"Something's loose," judged La Forge. "But the connection is there."

"Seems that way," agreed the thin man, starting to shimmy the cover off the console. If there was one thing he had learned in this place, it was that such casings came off rather easily. Nor was this one an exception.

The insides of the console looked familiar, too. And Barclay could see where the loose connection was. It would be a little tricky to secure it without exposing himself to an open circuit, but far from impossible.

"What a stroke of luck," observed the chief engineer, obviously assessing the situation the same way Barclay had. He looked up. "I've got to admit, I was a little pessimistic about this, but—"

Suddenly, the lights in the room went on, so brilliantly that the thin man was almost blinded by them. And then, just as he started to get used to the idea, they began to flicker erratically—complemented by a new deep-throated quality in the accompanying hum.

"Damn," said La Forge. "I should have known it was too good to be true."

Barclay could feel his heart beating faster. Oh, no, he told himself. Not yet, please not yet. We still have work to do.

But even as he thought it, he placed his light on the

top of the open console, where it could play on the guts of the machine, and got to work stabilizing the loose circuit. Being afraid was something he couldn't help. But there was no way he was going to let his fear get in his way again.

The commander came around to the side, where he could see what was going on, but he didn't say anything. He didn't offer to help, either, fully aware of the fact that this was a one-man job. He just watched, to make sure it went right.

Abruptly, the lights went off—only to give way to a spitfire sizzle of energy that ran all around them, from floor to wall to ceiling and back down again. The hum grew louder, grating on their ears.

Barclay could feel beads of ice water collecting in the small of his back. This was just the way it had happened that other time, when the captain disappeared. And if he didn't work quickly, something bad was going to happen again.

"Careful, Reg," said La Forge. "Don't worry about anything else. Just get it right."

Barclay nodded, recognizing the wisdom in his superior's advice. But the hum was getting increasingly difficult to ignore. And the flash of power that surrounded them seemed to be cycling faster and faster.

At last, he did what he had set out to do—the circuit was secure. Without waiting to double-check his work, he replaced the metal console sheath and began tapping the pads that would bring the thing on-line. For the space of a heartbeat, nothing happened.

Then there was a subtle, soft whirring sound, and Barclay knew that he had been on the money. The controls came to life. Up above them, the image on the monitor transformed into a schematic that he had seen before.

"We've got liftoff," he said, using an old Starfleet witticism. His voice sounded painfully flat and humorless, even to him.

"So we do," La Forge confirmed. "Move over and I'll give you a hand."

It was necessary for the two of them to work side by side now, Barclay knew. Last time, it had been Data who'd activated the alien confinement beam and released the station's energy buildup into space. But they were without the android's quickness, so they had to make do with what they had.

What's more, there was no O'Connor present to tell them how far the surges had gone or how much time they had left—though if it looked as if they were approaching the point of no return, she'd make them aware of that. Until then, she knew better than to distract them.

The commander swore softly as he worked to maximize the output of the confinement beam. "It's not enough," he insisted. And then, turning to Barclay: "Data boosted the gain by recycling power through the emitter array. Ours isn't working, so we can't do that."

The hum was as bad as ever, and the lights in the bulkheads were racing around them just as quickly. The thin man bit his lip as he forced himself to think.

"What about . . . what about engaging the backup module? We can run them both at once."

La Forge shook his head. "Too risky. We might trip the shutoff. Then we'd have to bypass it, and there's not enough time for that."

Barclay sighed. The commander was right. He scolded himself inwardly for even suggesting it.

Barely taking his hand off the controls, La Forge punched his comm badge. "O'Connor—how are we doing?"

The answer came so quickly, she must have been expecting the question. "It could be worse, sir. You seem to have achieved a kind of equilibrium. The surges aren't accelerating anymore, but they're still at a pretty high level. If something goes the wrong way, even just a little bit . . ."

She didn't finish. But then, she didn't have to.

"What about Commander Data?" asked La Forge, still keeping a close eye on the controls. "Has he made any progress finding the captain?"

"I'm afraid not, sir. We're having trouble establishing a—" For a moment, the chief engineer's communicator went silent. Then, with an unconcealed excitement: "We've got him, Commander. We've got a lock on Captain Picard."

It was the best thing Barclay could have hoped to hear. Apparently, La Forge thought so as well, because one of his hands closed into a fist—a symbol of triumph.

"Bring him back," the chief engineer told O'Connor. "We'll meet you at the airlock."

"Aye, sir," she replied. And then the comm link went dead.

La Forge's hand closed on Barclay's shoulder. "Let's get out of here, Reg."

The thin man looked at him. "But, sir . . . shouldn't we keep trying to maximize the siphon effect?"

"We've done all we can," the chief engineer explained. "With any luck, the current output will keep things stable a couple of minutes longer. And after that, we'll be gone."

Barclay hesitated. He couldn't help it. He felt as if the job was incomplete.

La Forge must have noticed that something was bothering him. "Listen, Reg, once Commander Data brings back the captain, he can discharge some energy, too. Now, we've got to get going, before—"

Without warning, the control panel in front of them erupted in a geyser of blinding white energy. The commander, who had been touching it with one of his hands, seemed to leap backward with a cry of pain and shock. Then he hit the bulkhead, slipped to the deck, and was still.

Barclay just stood there, aghast, as the console sputtered and sparked. He forced himself to accept that something had happened—and that he needed to do something about it. Kneeling, he took a look at his superior.

La Forge was breathing, but not deeply. And he still had a pulse. Maybe he hadn't been hurt so badly after all. If Barclay could get him out of here, get him back to the airlock, he would probably be all right.

But why had the panel flared up that way? Could it be he hadn't secured the circuit properly after all? Could it have been . . . was it *his* fault that the commander was lying here, in danger of his life?

Barclay set his jaw, placed his hands under La Forge's armpits, and swiveled him around toward the entranceway to the tunnel. Unfortunately, the commander was heavier than he looked. And at this rate, it would take a long time to return to the airlock—maybe *too* long.

But he would do whatever was necessary. Commander La Forge had trusted him against his better judgment, hadn't he? One way or another, Barclay would show him that he was worthy of that trust.

Leaving their light sources behind, since there didn't seem to be any shortage of illumination, the thin man dragged the commander across the room. Stopping at the entrance to the tunnel, Barclay sat down and inserted himself backward. Then he tugged on La Forge. Again, he shoved himself backward. And again, he pulled his burden after him.

It was slow going, and Barclay's back and shoulder muscles hadn't worked so hard in a long time—or maybe *ever*. But he didn't let that stop him. Inch by inch, meter by meter, he negotiated the length of the tunnel. Eventually, he could see the end of it with a glance over his shoulder. And not long after that, he reached it.

He was just about to dig his heels in and push himself out into the corridor when he thought he heard the omnipresent humming start to grow louder. And not just louder—more ominous, somehow. A sixth sense told Barclay that he was in danger. *Terrible* danger.

Just in time, he bent himself forward as far as he could go—and felt the hatch close behind him, so close it scraped the skin beneath the bottom of his uniform top. With nothing else to impede it, the metal piece slammed into the deck below it with a resounding clang.

A chill climbed Barclay's spine and didn't let go. It seemed to spread throughout his whole body, turning his blood to ice, making him shiver uncontrollably.

Another second, and the hatch would have closed on *him*. In his mind's eye, he replayed the horror of what had happened to Varley. He saw the guillotinelike descent of cold, dark metal, heard the crunch of bone and cartilage, saw the pool of blood that spread along the smooth, shiny deck.

It started a gibbering in his throat. He tried to swallow it back, but he couldn't. He had to let it out, to set it free or choke on it. Despite his shame and humiliation, he screamed—just like that other time. He screamed long and loud, and barely noticed when the hatch slid open again—as if enticing him to try to make it through.

But then, just when Barclay thought he'd lie in that tunnel and scream forever, his eyes focused on the helpless form of Commander La Forge. He'd made a promise to himself to return the commander to the airlock. And damn it, he would *do* it—hatch or no hatch, Varley or no Varley.

Taking a deep breath, then another, he hooked his

hands under La Forge's arms with renewed purpose and thrust himself backward. The hatch gave no indication of coming down again. But outside in the corridor, the racing lights created a strobe effect, and the hum was definitely grinding deeper.

Swallowing hard, Barclay forced himself to pull the commander after him. Then he slid backward again, all the while keeping his eyes on the slot that the hatch had retreated into. It was almost directly above him now.

If the thing came down, he might have enough time to avoid it—or he might not. Closing his eyes against the thought, he yanked La Forge along.

Another slide backward, and part of him had to be past the hatch, in the curving hallway outside it. Just to make sure, Barclay opened his eyes—and saw the hard, dark edge of the hatch looming right in front of him. As his heart slammed hard against his ribs, he had a sudden desire to run—to leave the commander behind and save himself from its deadly, crushing weight.

But, biting deep into the inside of his mouth, he resisted it—and pulled. And thrust himself back again. And pulled once more. And before he knew it, he had nearly dragged the other man clear of the tunnel. *Nearly.*

That's when he heard the hum change again— assuming that awful, warning timbre that had saved his life before. Gritting his teeth, he dug his heels in and hauled for all he was worth.

Both he and Commander La Forge shot backward into the corridor. The hatch, as dark and deadly as ever, met the deck just inches below the commander's feet.

Barclay took a deep, tremulous breath and let it out. Unfortunately, there was no time for self-congratulations. He had to get La Forge to the airlock before the station self-destructed.

Chapter Ten

FOR THE FIRST TIME in several long minutes, there was silence. In its way, it was even harder to bear than the sounds of destruction that the Gorn had inflicted on them. Made uneasy by the respite, Picard lifted his head and peered out of the ruined shell of the administration building.

The invaders were still out there, of course, their scaly hides glittering in the sun. Not as many as before, thanks to the colonists' marksmanship. But they comprised a formidable assault force nonetheless.

It appeared to the captain that they were organizing for another push. A *final* push, by all indications. Then again, he had thought their *last* push would be the final one, and the humans had somehow managed to stave them off.

Glancing back over his shoulder, Picard counted

twelve people, besides himself. Twelve of the fifty or more who had emerged from their bunkers to give the Gorn a fight—and without question, they had accomplished that. But the cost . . .

The captain had seen each colonist fall, had marked each death with an acute attention to its details. He had done this not out of any morbid fascination with death, but rather to give each tragedy meaning, at least in his own mind. Perhaps he would not make it back to the future, but for now—until he himself perished in a furnace-blast of green fire—he would memorize the events of this dark and grisly day.

Why bother? Because, like the deaths themselves, it meant something. The gesture was worth making for its own sake, regardless of any connection with history or value systems or civilizations. In the end, Picard thought, perhaps that was all there was to the phenomenon they called "life": a series of gestures, all of them ultimately futile, all of them powerless to make a chink in the armor of the inevitable.

The captain sighed. If he could stop it all right here, freeze time so that he and his comrades would go on staring at the invaders across a wide, dirt plaza forever and ever, he would make it so. He would spend eternity with these people at his side, their hearts pumping with fear, their eyes blazing with defiance.

He frowned. If *only*. If he could have prevented this while there was still time. If he could have defied the Prime Directive and found a way to forestall this massacre . . . to save *her* . . . to save *Julia* . . .

"Yes, Jean-Luc?"

Picard smiled as she nudged a bit closer to him.

"Nothing," he told her. "I was just thinking. I didn't mean to do it out loud."

She chuckled dryly. "It figures. I find a man who thinks of me even when he's looking down Death's ugly maw—and we're both going to die before I can take advantage of it."

There was only the slightest catch in her voice. She was a brave woman. A *very* brave woman. And like her, he wished they could have met in a better time and place.

"Hill," growled Travers, from the recesses of what remained of their shelter.

The captain looked back and saw the commodore extending a phaser rifle in his direction. Without questioning, he took it.

Travers felt compelled to explain, however. "It was Schmitter's," he noted. "He won't be needing it anymore."

Following the commodore's glance, Picard saw the spot that Schmitter had occupied until sometime during the last wave of attack. There was nothing left of the man but a charred stain on the floor.

One thing about the invaders' disruptor blasts—they didn't leave any wounded. Once the disruptor effect had taken hold of living tissue, it didn't let go until the entire organism had been disintegrated.

The captain laid down his nearly spent hand phaser and laid the rifle in the crook of his arm. Too bad he couldn't actually use it, he mused—only finish off Gorn who were already caught in someone else's beam. It was bad enough that he had been forced to kill and disable some of the invaders in order to reach this point; to continue in that vein would only put the timestream in undue jeopardy.

After all, the colonists were doomed to die; history required it. But that same history had seen the invaders take precious few casualties. And who was Picard to say which of the Gorn on this field of battle would go on to become a major benefactor to his race? Or a major supporter of relations with the Federation?

Then there was no more time to think. The invaders were coming at them again, plodding ahead in their slow but unyielding fashion. And all around him, the surviving colonists began to fire at the lizard-skinned enemy.

"Jean-Luc?" whispered Julia.

He turned to her, drinking in the sight of her, knowing he would not have much longer to do so. "Yes?"

"Do me a favor," she said. "Don't die before I do, all right? I don't want to have to see you go."

The captain grunted. "I'll do my best," he responded. Then he raised his rifle and started firing along with the rest of them.

Two Gorn in the forefront of the charge were cut down by a barrage of angry, red beams. A third fell a moment later, causing some confusion in the ranks. However, the rest kept coming, undaunted.

All the while, they were returning the colonists' fire, obliterating what was left of the administration building's superstructure in a wash of green chaos. Like a river that has run into a huge rock in its path, the middle of the invasion force slowed down, while its extremities expanded in an attempt to encircle their objective.

Of course, they couldn't surround the place completely, or they would be hitting each other when they missed. But by forming a semicircle, the Gorn had made it necessary for the humans to defend a larger area than before. It was a tactic they should have used hours ago—and would have, no doubt, if they'd had any way to measure the colonists' tenacity.

Travers was shouting orders as he took aim again. "Hill, Santos, Yamaguchi . . . take the left flank. Persoff, Mittleman, Aiello . . . on the right. The rest of us will try to split them up the center."

Courageous words, thought Picard, coming from a man who was beaten and knew it. But then, the commodore was not the type to give up easily.

Another Gorn fell, and another. But the administration center was being torn away piece by piece, and soon there would be nothing left to provide cover for them.

The thought had barely occurred to him when a protective fragment of wall sizzled out of existence, exposing him to a well-placed shot. Through the still-smoking gap, he could see the oncoming swarm, each Gorn cruel of visage and relentless in his progress, envisioning the captain's death in his insectlike orbs.

A ball of emerald fire seemed to reach out for him. Hugging the floor as hard as he could, Picard heard a scream behind him. Glancing back, he saw the colonist named Yamaguchi writhe in the grip of the disruptor effect. Then, before the echoes of the scream had quite died, Yamaguchi was a wisp of vapor on the hot, still air.

Another cry, and Aiello was gone. Then a female

security officer whose name he didn't know. Ten of them left. Two more wails of horror and pain cut their number to eight.

"The bastards!" someone barked. "The stinking, murdering bastards!"

The captain traced the curse to its source: O'Dell, the red-bearded engineer who'd been part of Hronsky's long-range sensor team. The man's face was contorted, torn by fear and hate, revulsion and sorrow. Unable to bear up under the stress any longer, he had snapped.

"Darby!" cried Julia. "Get down!"

And before Picard could stop her, she had risen to pull down the bearded man. But she was too late. In the next moment, a tongue of disruptor energy lashed itself around O'Dell, infecting him with its virus of annihilation. As the doctor watched, openmouthed, it turned her fellow colonist into a twitching bag of flaming flesh and bones.

The captain reached for Julia's ankle and pulled, toppling her, removing her from harm's way. Dropping his rifle, he reached for her with his other hand as well, to pull her to him, to comfort her in her terror.

Then he saw the green energies swirling around her leg, and he instinctively pulled both his hands back. Julia fell to the floor, breathless in her agony, gripped tight by the knowledge of what was happening to her. As the disruptor field enveloped her, picking her apart like a flock of maniacal birds, she raised her eyes to Picard's.

"Jean-Luc," she blurted, reaching out for him. Defying his instincts, defying the nightmarish forces that devoured her, he reached back.

But where her hand had been, there was nothing left. And when he looked again into her eyes, there was only hellfire looking back at him. Then that too diminished, and Julia was gone.

In the wake of that sight, the captain couldn't move, couldn't think, couldn't even see for the tears that filled his eyes. The only sense that worked was his hearing, and that was consumed with the thunder of the Gorn horde.

"Hill!" rumbled a voice nearby.

Picard turned. Blinking away his tears, he saw Commodore Travers, a nasty gash in his temple oozing blood. The commodore took him by the shoulders and shook him.

"Come on," he rasped. "Damn it, man, it's down to you and me!"

The captain nodded and sought out his phaser rifle. Finding it, he raised it and sighted on the nearest grouping of Gorn. And seeing their serpentlike faces, the inhuman savagery dripping from their fangs and lighting their eyes, he almost pressed the trigger.

But in the end, he didn't. Because, first and last, he was Jean-Luc Picard, captain of the *Enterprise*. And no matter what cruelties he had witnessed this day, he could not mar the future.

It proved his undoing. Together, the Gorn trained their weapons on Picard and fired. The last thing he saw was the white-hot fury of their converging disruptor beams.

Picard had braced himself for the hideous sensation of being plucked apart by the Gorn's disruptor fire.

But as he knelt there, he was surprised to see that they had missed him somehow. And that wasn't all that surprised him.

He was no longer in the wreckage of the colony's administration building. He was somewhere else, someplace that looked vaguely familiar. And then he guessed where that was—and what had happened to him.

Judging by the look of the chamber he found himself in, he was back on the alien space station. And the flash he had seen, the white-hot flare that he had mistaken for the blaze of disruptor energies, was nothing more than the aura given off by the aliens' transporter process.

He had no sooner come to that conclusion than the door on the far side of the chamber slid up—and revealed Commander Data standing in the corridor outside. The android beckoned, making no mention of the captain's torn and dirtied garb.

"There is no time to explain, sir," he said, his voice tinged with just the slightest hint of urgency. "We must get to the shuttle."

The shuttle? Picard wondered. Why not the *Enterprise* itself? Then he realized: the *Enterprise* would have been needed to search for him.

"I'm coming," the captain promised. And he traversed the chamber in several quick, long strides.

Once out in the corridor, Picard could see why time was of the essence. Taking note of the light patterns that ran helter-skelter along the length of the bulkheads and back again, he realized that the station was caught in the throes of another mounting power surge.

And if he'd had any doubt, the thrumming in the deck confirmed it.

"This way," said the android, leading the captain down the corridor. As Picard looked about, it seemed to him that they were in the area between the control room and the airlock—headed in the direction of the latter.

He hoped that Data had corrected the problems that the captain had encountered earlier. Otherwise, shuttle or no shuttle, the same kind of transport might take place—or maybe even something worse.

In the few minutes it took them to reach the airlock, Picard could hear the telltale hum rise and fall several times. The light panels were flashing on and off so quickly, they seemed to blur. Surely, the station couldn't take much more of this.

Finally, as they negotiated the curvature of the corridor, O'Connor came into view. With an equipment kit hanging from her shoulder, she was waiting outside the airlock, her hand on its control plate. No—*beside* the plate, Picard realized—where she or someone else had installed a set of button controls. The captain recognized the thin line of circuitry and the generator below it as standard Starfleet equipment.

Excellent, he thought. We're in good shape, then. All we have to do is get into the shuttle and shove off.

Then Data spoke up. Addressing O'Connor, he asked, "Have you heard from Commander La Forge or Lieutenant Barclay?"

The woman didn't seem happy about the news she had to impart. "Commander La Forge received some sort of shock, sir. He's unconscious. Lieutenant Barclay is trying to bring him back here on his own. I would've gone after them, but—"

"But you were told to stay here," Data finished. "And you obeyed orders." Abruptly, he turned to Picard. "Shall I attempt to expedite their arrival, sir?"

The captain nodded. After all, Barclay and La Forge had risked their lives to bring him back here. He wouldn't abandon them unless and until it was absolutely necessary.

"By all means," he told the android. "Get going."

As Data took off down the corridor, Picard turned to O'Connor. "You did what you were supposed to do," he assured her. "You remained at your station."

She nodded, only half-consoled. "Aye, sir."

Then, to pass the time as much as anything else, he asked, "Have you allowed for the failure of the outer door as well?"

"We have, sir," she assured him. "There's another switch like this one, inside. Also, we set up forcefield projectors—so if the outer door somehow opens before we want it to, the field will keep the atmosphere intact."

Picard expelled a breath. "Good thinking."

O'Connor nearly smiled, despite her fear for her comrades. "Thank you, sir."

Outside, through the window in the airlock door, the captain could see the shuttle. It waited only to be boarded.

Inside the corridor, the humming and the flashing lights suddenly stopped—and then resumed again a second later with almost maniacal intensity. Picard swallowed and craned his neck to see a bit farther around the curve of the hallway.

Come on, he urged silently. *We cannot wait much longer.*

And then, as if in answer to his mental summons, he heard a distant tapping on the deck, which grew stronger the closer it came—a tapping like footfalls. At last, the three of them—Data, Geordi, and Barclay—rounded the bend. The android had hoisted the chief engineer over his shoulder and was pelting along at a torrid pace. Barclay, red-faced and panting, was doing his best to keep up.

At the same time, the captain heard a bellicose roar come to life in the bulkheads—the same kind of roar that had presaged a stationwide overload and his transport through time and space. Scowling, he tried to ignore the strobing light trails all around them.

"Open the inner door," he commanded.

Almost before he finished uttering the words, O'Connor had pressed the green button under her hand. Immediately, the door slid up, allowing them access to the airlock. The outer barrier, and the invisible forcefield just inside it, were all that separated them now from the vacuum.

As Data came to a stop in front of them, Picard got a better look at Geordi. He was relieved to see that the engineer was moving, if only barely. With luck, his injury would be something they could treat on the shuttle.

Removing a remote-control unit from the kit on her hip, O'Connor established a link with the craft's computer and prepared to open the door.

But before she could clear all the security protocols, the station seemed to jerk sideways beneath their feet, sending them sprawling into one of the bulkheads. Energy pulsed through the place with such intensity it made the deck shiver beneath the captain's cheek.

Forcing his every sense to focus on the task at hand, he dragged himself up off the floor—and noticed the remote-control device lying not a meter away. Being closer to it than O'Connor, he scooped the unit up and tapped in the rest of its instructions.

Fortunately, the thing hadn't been damaged when it struck the deck. The shuttle door hissed open.

"Get in!" cried Picard, barely able to hear himself over the dangerously increasing hum. And to underscore the need for urgency, he helped O'Connor up and guided her in the direction of the shuttle.

By then, Data was already slipping inside, with Geordi still slung over his shoulder. But Barclay wouldn't enter until the captain and his fellow engineer had preceded him.

A chivalrous action, Picard noted—though right now, practicality was a lot more important than chivalry. As soon as O'Connor was safely inside the craft, he shoved Barclay in after her.

However, as the captain himself prepared to follow, the airlock and the corridor outside it were bathed in a surge of stark, white brilliance. Blinded by it, Picard lost sight of the shuttle entrance—and then lost his balance to boot.

Just as he imagined he was about to go careening again through space and time, he felt something grab the front of his tunic and jerk him forward. There was a sound of something heavy locking into place, and the roar of the station was suddenly gone.

As his vision cleared, the captain realized he was on the shuttle, with Reg Barclay kneeling over him. The thin man looked apologetic.

"Sorry, sir," said Barclay. "But there wasn't time to be . . . well, a little gentler."

"Quite all right," Picard assured him. Sitting up, he caught a glimpse of Data in the pilot's seat. The android was manipulating the controls as only he could.

O'Connor, who was sitting next to Geordi amidships, glanced back at the captain. "We're getting out of here," she said.

Picard nodded. He could see through the shuttle's observation port that they were accelerating, putting distance between themselves and the station.

Getting to his feet, the captain made his way forward to determine how his chief engineer was doing. He was pleased to see Geordi's head rotate as he approached.

Picard bent over him and smiled. "How are you feeling, Mr. La Forge?"

Geordi shrugged. "I've felt better, sir." A pause. "But I have to admit, I've also felt worse." His head rolled again as he turned to face Barclay. "Your grandfather was wrong, Reg."

The thin man's brow creased. Obviously, he didn't understand. "Wrong, sir?"

The commander chuckled. "You're not rubber after all. Considering what you just pulled off, I'd say you're made of some of the toughest stuff around."

Barclay grinned. "I am?"

"You are," Geordi affirmed.

Picard looked from one of them to the other. "Rubber?" he repeated.

The commander grunted. "A private joke, sir."

The captain nodded. "I understand." Patting Geordi on the shoulder, he got up again and deposited himself in the seat beside Data. The android had locked one of his monitors onto a view of the station as they left it behind.

The place was convulsing with one violent flash after the other. Then, as Picard watched, a piece of the station started to come away. And another. And finally, the whole structure erupted in a blossom-cloud of blue-white light. What's more, the cloud hung there long after the station itself had been turned into debris.

Data turned to the captain. "It is a pity," he observed. "There was still a great deal we might have learned from it."

Picard frowned, intent on the spectacle. "No doubt," he replied, sincerely. Or was it, perhaps, better this way?

There were some things best left unknown, he mused. And some places best left unvisited. He sighed and, sitting back in his chair, closed his eyes.

Before long, they'd rendezvous with the *Enterprise*. Until then, he wanted only to sleep.

Lieutenant Harold had used the last of his strength to drag himself out of the bunker, which had been the colony's main residence complex until just about a day ago. The bunker was where the last of the colonists had huddled after the invaders destroyed the brave people in the administration center.

To the best of Harold's knowledge, he was the outpost's only survivor. And then, only barely. The skin on one side of his body was dark and cracked, the result of severe radiation burns. And something inside him had been damaged. Every few minutes, he coughed up blood and had to clench his teeth against the intolerable pain.

But at least he was alive. The others—the people with whom he had shared the bunker—were gone. Just like that, without a trace, except for the stink of disruptor energies that yet lingered in the still, hot air.

If he hadn't been buried under a collapsing interior wall during one of the heavier salvos, he probably would have been just as dead as the rest of them—just as untraceable. As it was, the concealing debris had probably saved his life. It had kept the lizard-beings from finding him and frying him like the others.

Harold shivered at the thought of the invaders. He had only caught a glimpse of them, but it had been enough. They were as cruel-looking, as cold-blooded, and as efficient as their fiery green beams. Like many of his comrades, he had screamed for them not to shoot. After all, there were women and children in the bunker.

But none of that made any difference to the lizard men. They had simply fired their weapons of destruction. And fired. And *fired.*

And where were they now? Had they left, their hellish job accomplished? Or were they still here somewhere? Gazing across the plaza, Harold saw no evidence of them, only waves of shimmering desert heat. But then, it was difficult to trust his senses, what with all he had been through.

Steeling himself, he tried to pull his body forward again, in the direction of the ruined administration building. Maybe the communication system was still intact, he told himself. Maybe he could call for help, warn other colonies about the horror that had overcome them.

But as he inched ahead, a wave of nausea overtook him, and he started to dry-retch uncontrollably. Finally, spent, he looked up—hoping that he had made some progress toward the administration center, knowing full well that he hadn't.

Gritting his teeth, he took another stab at it. This time, movement came a little easier. He wasn't sure if that was a good sign or not, but he continued crawling. And, eventually, reached the debris that was all that remained of the administration building.

Setting his back against a partially destroyed wall, he took a burning breath and let it out. There was no communication equipment here. There wasn't anything at all, except a few twisted hunks of metal and some severed cables.

Then something caught his eye. Something moving across the plaza. His heart thudded in his chest. The invaders?

No. Not them, he realized. It was a handful of men in Starfleet uniforms. A landing party—a couple of them in gold shirts like his own, another one in the red shirt of operations, three more in the blue of science and medicine. And they were coming his way, as if they had spotted him and wanted to help.

Unless . . . they were a mirage. They could have been, too. An illusion born of suffering and fever, of wanting and needing, aided and abetted by the blinding rays of the afternoon sun.

No. Illusions didn't talk. And he could hear these men talking, their words getting louder and louder, more and more distinct as they approached. Finally, they were right in front of him, and there was no doubt as to their authenticity. They were close enough now, and tangible enough, for him to see that one of them was a Vulcan.

Two of the men knelt beside him—a goldshirt with captain's bars on his sleeve and a doctor. The physician pulled up one of Harold's eyelids as he activated his tricorder.

"Shock," he announced. "Radiation burns, internal injuries for certain. He's in a bad way, Captain."

The other man frowned. "Keep him alive, Bones. I want to know what's been happening here."

Harold felt a pressure against his arm and heard a hiss. The doctor had given him something for the pain, he realized. He could feel himself getting woozy.

That's when the Vulcan spoke up. "Getting another life reading, Captain."

The goldshirt stood. "Survivors?"

"Not survivors," the science officer corrected. "Not warm-blooded. Living creatures. But not human."

Harold could have told them that. He had seen the lizard-beings. He knew that they were anything *but* human.

"Where?" asked the captain.

The Vulcan consulted his instrument. "Azimuth

ninety-three degrees, range one-five-zero-seven yards."

Nodding, the captain directed the red-shirted security officer to move forward, to take a look around. The man's name was Hurlihy, apparently. Doing as he was told, he seemed to catch a glimpse of something in the distance.

Harold tried to tell him to get down, to watch out for the lizard men's disruptors. But he couldn't get the words out, just a rasping sound that barely got even the doctor's attention.

"Calm down, son," said the medical man. "Conserve your strength."

"Captain," said Hurlihy, "I see something. . . ."

Suddenly, he was caught in a greenish aura. Turning the color of blood under the glow, the security officer grimaced and disappeared.

"My God," breathed the doctor.

Then the ground around them erupted with bomb blasts. The captain opened his communicator. "Kirk to *Enterprise*. Lock on transporters. Beam us up."

Harold couldn't hear the response, but there seemed to be a problem. And then he realized what it was: the invaders' ship. It would be up there in orbit somewhere, attacking the Federation vessel, forcing whoever was in charge to defend himself.

"Keep those screens up," commanded the one called Kirk. "Fire all phasers."

There was a moment of silence, during which even the invaders' bombs stopped falling. Then the captain spoke again, as if in response to some new information.

"Take all action necessary to protect the ship," insisted the captain. "We'll hold out here."

Harold heaved a sigh. It still wasn't over, was it? Maybe it would never be over. Maybe it would be like this from now on, now that the lizard-beings had shown up.

"Keep those screens up," shouted the goldshirt. "Worry about us when the ship is safe. Kirk out."

Abruptly, the bombs started falling again—started shaking the ground with their thunder. Geysers of fire and black smoke shot up all around them.

The captain shook his head. "If they lower those screens to beam us up," he told the Vulcan, "they'll be open to phaser attack."

The other man nodded. "We are hopelessly outnumbered here, Captain. With those disruptors versus our hand phasers . . ."

Kirk waved away the Vulcan's pessimism. "We're stuck with it, Mr. Spock. We'll have to make do with what we've got." Turning to look back at Harold, he gestured for the doctor and two others to pick him up. Then, together, they headed for the shelter of the still-intact residence structure—the place where the survivor had just come from.

Bombs shattered the air all around them. Despite the painkiller, Harold could feel the heat of their blasts on his tortured flesh. And being moved this way awakened new agonies inside him. But if the alternative was to be torn apart by the invaders' barrage, he would endure whatever he had to.

The captain turned to a couple of his officers. "Kelowitz, Lang . . . flank out. Lay down fire on the coordinates Mr. Spock gave you." And then, as they departed: "Even if you don't see them, keep your heads down."

Turning to the Vulcan, he noted: "We're helpless down here. And the *Enterprise* . . ."

The response was meant to reassure him. "Mr. Sulu is an experienced combat officer, Captain."

But the man called Kirk shook his head. "It's my ship, Mr. Spock. I should be there." He cursed their fate. "We can't even get at them."

"Nor can they at us, at the moment," replied the science officer. "Not unless they move their original position. That intervening high ground . . ." He gestured to the hills.

The captain nodded. "You remember the layout of this place? The arsenal . . . ?"

The Vulcan pointed. "About one hundred yards in that direction. But after an attack as thorough as this one . . ."

Kirk set his jaw. "I'll risk it," he said. Abruptly, he darted out into the plaza, drawing enemy fire on all sides. Harold couldn't see if he got hit or not.

"Is he . . . all right?" he asked the doctor, who was kneeling beside him. The man looked down at him.

"He's fine," he answered. "For now." A pause. "What happened here, son?"

The lieutenant thought about it. It all seemed like a vast, dark nightmare. He couldn't remember who had done what, or when. The only things he could picture in his mind right now were the green disruptor beams that had walked the ground in long, deadly strides, and the screams, and the pain. Everything else was a blur.

Vaguely, he recalled a man he'd been ordered to

look after. The man had meant something, hadn't he? He'd been important to someone. But Harold could no longer remember why. The man, and many of the other details of the massacre, were already receding on the other side of a shadowy veil—one he never wanted to pull away, no matter the cost.

"It's all right," the doctor assured him, seeing he'd get no ready answer. He smiled pleasantly. "We'll talk about it after we get you up to the ship." Reacting to a nearby blast, he peered out at the plaza through narrowed eyes.

The lieutenant winced as a bead of perspiration traced a path along the charred skin of his cheek. Yes, he told himself. Maybe then, he could tell some things. *Some.*

But others, he would keep behind the veil, where he wouldn't have to think about them. Not *ever.*

As Picard entered his ready room, he had the distinct feeling that something was different. Looking around, he checked off each furnishing in his mind, reassuring himself that all was as it had been several days ago, before his time-space accident.

Not that he would have been surprised if Commander Riker had made some small changes in his absence. After all, there was no harm in tailoring a place to one's own needs—even on a temporary basis. But nothing was out of order. The room was just as the captain had left it, down to the lionfish swimming in his small, round tank.

Then why the feeling of alteration? Even before Picard had completed the unspoken question, he believed he knew the answer.

It was *he* who was different. *He* who had changed since he'd last walked this deck and performed the duties of a starship captain here. A week earlier, he had been interested in the past, even intrigued by it. Now he was *involved* with it. He was *part* of it.

And though he had been snatched from the trap that snapped shut on the doomed colonists of Cestus III, he had not escaped it completely. He had left a portion of himself behind.

Abruptly, the chimes outside his door sounded, alerting him to the presence of someone on the other side of it. "Come," he replied, tugging down on the front of his tunic.

A moment later, his first officer was framed in the open doorway. The man smiled in that way that seemed to come so easily to him and walked in.

"How do you feel, sir?" asked Riker.

Picard shrugged. "I am glad to be back," he noted sincerely, allowing his fingers to brush the hard, polished desktop alongside him. "Very glad, in fact. And grateful to those who made it possible."

The first officer tilted his head slightly. "All in a day's work," he demurred. "If there's credit to be given, it belongs to the crew. And, of course, to Ensign Ro. If she hadn't convinced me to enlist the help of the Bon Amar—"

The captain felt his spine stiffen. "The Bon Amar?" he repeated. "What did they have to do with this?"

Riker swallowed. Apparently, he had ventured onto dangerous ground without thinking. "Uh . . . are you sure you want to know, sir?"

Picard felt a surge of disapproval—but it was instantly tempered by an appreciation for the outcome. "You asked the Bon Amar for assistance," he concluded. "And are they the ones who found me? Or rather, my communicator?"

The first officer nodded. "They were," he confirmed.

The captain frowned. "You know that was a breach of Starfleet policy?" he asked.

Riker nodded again. "I do. But at the time, it seemed like the only way to get you back. And as it turned out, it *was*. If not for the Bon Amar . . ."

Picard held up a hand. "It's all right, Will. No need to continue." He paused. "Under the circumstances, we'll call it a forgivable offense. . . ." A subtle smile played at the corners of his mouth. "An *eminently* forgivable offense . . . and leave it at that."

The first officer seemed relieved. "Agreed, sir."

Picard came around the desk and sat down. Riker just stood there, waiting patiently for the captain to acclimate himself.

"We're headed for Gorn?" asked Picard finally. Tentatively, he leaned back, getting the feel of his chair again.

"At best speed," his exec assured him. "With any luck, we'll be there in time to salvage the situation."

"Good." The captain sighed. "I suppose I should prepare myself," he said meaningfully.

"Of course," responded Riker. "I'll leave you to it."

But halfway to the door, he stopped and turned around again. Noting the first officer's hesitation, Picard looked up at him.

Riker shook his head, as if in envy. "I was just wondering," he said. "What it was like. To see history unfolding like that, right before your eyes."

The captain looked down at his hands. The same hands that had held Julia Santos as her life ebbed away, a hundred years ago.

"Not history, Number One. I cannot look at it that way. Not anymore."

It was not much of an answer, but it was the only one he was prepared to give. Nor did Riker press for him to elaborate.

All he said was "I understand, sir." As soon as he was gone, the doors whooshed closed behind him.

Once again, the captain was alone with his thoughts. And one thought was foremost: to reach the Gorn homeworld and forge a new treaty—one that would serve as a tribute to the dead of Cestus III. To *Julia*.

He would brook no obstacles. He would shape a lasting peace between the Gorn and the Federation. He would not—repeat, *not*—allow those good and courageous people to have died in vain.

Epilogue

PICARD FELT AWKWARD standing with his back to the transporter operator, but there was a reason for it. As he knew from experience, this was the way the Gorn positioned themselves for transport.

Of course, he could have had Lieutenant Kandel turn him around one hundred and eighty degrees when he materialized. It would hardly have been the most difficult maneuver she'd had to execute. But it was important for the captain not only to materialize like a Gorn, but to think like a Gorn.

"Ready, sir?" called Kandel.

He nodded, even though she could only see the back of his head. "Energize," he intoned.

In accordance with protocol, he turned to face his hosts. The next thing he knew, there was a reptilian face in front of him. Not at a polite distance, as he now expected, but mere inches from his own.

He should have been prepared for the flaring nostrils, the rows of cruel and deadly teeth, the orblike eyes. But he wasn't.

All he could see was a sea of broken colonists, torn and burned and disfigured by nightmare weapons—and in the foreground, Julia, her brows knit tight against the awful pain. He could smell her charred flesh, hear her pitiful moans, feel the weight of death pressing down upon her.

An anger rose up inside him, a geyser of hate and loathing that threatened to consume him utterly. And why not? Was this not the face of the enemy, the inhuman destroyer?

No, the captain told himself. You must not do this. It will make their deaths a hollow thing—and then you will have done something worse to them than the Gorn ever could. Hadn't Julia herself spoken of sacrifices? And what it cost, sometimes, to ensure the future?

It was difficult, *exceedingly* difficult, but he wrenched his emotions back onto firmer ground. Composed himself. And addressed the Gorn who stood before him.

"Bring me to Leader Keeyah," he demanded. It was the way a Gorn himself would have put it, if he expected to command any respect.

The large, almost insectlike eyes seemed to consider him for a moment. Then the muscular, green-scaled figure stepped aside and indicated the leader with a sweep of his arm. Keeyah was standing among a number of other leaders, judging by their statures and the cut of their garb.

"You are here," the Gorn said. "It is not a moment

too soon, Captain Picard. The opposition is on the verge of victory."

The captain grunted derisively—also in keeping with Gorn behavior. "Then we have our work cut out for us, do we not? Come, Leader Keeyah. Let us meet our adversaries like warriors. Let us put things right again."

The Gorn nodded his massive head. "Yes, Picard. We will put things right—no matter how many of them we need to knock down."

It was the closest that Keeyah would ever come to a joke. Turning, he led the human into the metal-framed council chamber beyond.